Trystin S. Bailey

Cosmos

Cosmos (Book 2 of the Reverie series)
Copyright © 2019 by Trystin Steven Bailey

To my editors, proofreaders, and opinionated friends.
Sorcerers, all.

Prologue

Claire Ashford, strands of her messy blonde hair matted against her face, carefully held the newborn in her arms. Her name was Esperanza, Anza for short, the Spanish word for "hope." It was Victor's idea. Their daughter had been born less than an hour ago.

Claire and her newborn lay on a bed of iridescent crystal, though it was soft as a cloud. The rest of the world was formless, white, and seemed to go on for eternity in all directions. This place was called Origin Point. A slice of emptiness between the three realms.

Victor was beside Claire, of course, with tears of joy streaming down his cheeks. Claire ached all over, but it didn't matter. Nothing mattered but the tiny, pink baby squirming, cooing, looking at her with big brown curious eyes, just like her father's.

It was a moment of pure contentment; one that all but faded when she remembered that the three of them were not alone. The things that had summoned them nearly seven months ago were watching.

Manifestations. That's what they called themselves. Six beings, two tied to each of the three realms.

Somni and Timor were the youngest of the manifestations; a brother and sister who ruled over Reverie, the land of dreams. Claire found them the least intimidating, despite Timor literally being a tentacled, red-eyed, monstrous manifestation of fear. Somni was the manifestation of desire. The bubbly, waifish creature with robin's egg blue skin was obviously Victor's favorite.

Claire, on the other hand, preferred Initia, manifestation of growth. She had hair like lush vines and dark brown skin. She had been pregnant when Claire and Victor first met her and remained that way now. Her lover, Mortem, was a manifestation of decline. He looked as if he had been carved out of a volcano, his veins running with magma and skin like ash. The pair exuded compassion and were co-rulers of Cosmos. Earth and the physical universe belonged to them.

Claire had almost nothing positive to say about Vita and Nihilo, the final pair. They were the eldest of the manifestations and ruled the oldest realm: Eternia, realm of spirits. They were proud, vain beings. Vita, manifestation of existence, appeared as a woman of great wealth, sculpted from diamond and other precious stones. Though she often spoke of saving the realms, Claire didn't trust her.

And then there was Nihilo, manifestation of nothingness. His voice was like thunder and he appeared as a black hole in the shape of a large man. He seemed incapable of doing good. Of saving anything. Vita and Nihilo hated one another.

When Claire and Victor arrived, the manifestations told them all sorts of stories. Tales of how the universe began. Initia and Mortem swelled with pride as they explained the Big Bang, the first signs of life on Earth, evolution, and...

"Humanity!" the rulers of Cosmos exclaimed. "We'd hardly gotten over the excitement of life and then here come these humans and they can think and create!" The lovers stopped, allowing ample time for their excitement to fade to sadness. "The humans also seemed to have a knack for destruction, in the name of the pursuit of power. Destruction, not to be confused with decline. Decline, you see, is natural; as crucial to life as growth." A frown stretched in unison across their faces. "They were throwing off the balance."

"To ensure that life continued on Earth," Vita said, "we decided to interfere, darlings." Claire hated how Vita said 'darling' so much. "As we were and are quite powerful, we thought it best to create role models for the humans; beings to lead a powerful example. Long story short, we created the gods."

"But we didn't think it through," Mortem remarked. "We can only directly impact the realms if we all use powers in unison, so while we created gods of life and hope and love, we inadvertently tainted them with lust for fear and death and decline."

"In short," Initia clutched her chest, clearly feeling the truth as an ache, "the gods were ultimately little more than super-powered humans who, like humans, were compelled to use their power in selfish and petty ways. But on a far grander scale."

Initia/Mortem groaned. "It was a disaster."

Vita shrugged, her face a veil of disinterest. "Fortunately, the brutes took care of themselves, for the most part. The Roman gods fought the Egyptian gods fought the Celtic gods and so on and so forth. Lots of bloodshed. Problem solved, darlings. Except that when the gods left, the humans thought themselves even more godlike for surviving them."

Claire tried her best not to roll her eyes. Gods? Walking the Earth? Even after all she'd been through her days in Reverie, that sounded ridiculous. One look at Victor and she could tell he believed the manifestations' every word.

The manifestations explained that, having failed humanity, they decided to look for another problem in need of solving.

Reverie.

"It was extremely disconcerting, darlings," Vita lamented. "An entire realm of creatures armed with the unlimited reach of human imagination? And the idea of something like that leaking into Cosmos or," she forced a gasp, "my exquisitely regimented Eternia…it pained me, simply pained me to think about."

"It is a beautiful, magical place," said Somni, one of Reverie's rulers, "but chaotic since it's made up of the fruits of humanity's unlimited potential for imagining the greatest and most horrifying things."

"So we had to be proactive," said Initia.

The manifestations once again decided to come together. This time to stop the chaos of Reverie from spilling into the other realms, something they thought inevitable. They built impassable walls between everyone's dreams, but Reverie was in such a rapid, chaotic state of growth, that the walls began to fade to smoke and mist.

So they had to come up with another plan. A subtler, more manageable plan than gods or impenetrable walls that somehow had become penetrable.

Initia and Mortem of Cosmos spoke in unison: "We wanted to create something to maintain balance in Reverie once the walls collapsed. Someone, actually. One person. We couldn't let things get out of hand this time."

"Right!" Somni giggled. "One person who had to be from the physical world. Cosmos. Humans helped give birth to Reverie so a human was the perfect choice."

"Correct," Mortem/Initia agreed. "We also decided on a very specific set of rules about who this person would be. More rules, less chance for catastrophe."

Somni explained that unborn children begin to dream at around five weeks. The agreed-upon rule stated that the first child to dream at the moment the final wall turned to mist would be transferred to Reverie, with their parents, to be born and raised as the Savior of Dream.

Vita clasped her hands together, pleased. "And there you have it."

"Wait." Claire furrowed her brow, a frown on her face. "So you're saying that all of this happening to us was completely random?"

"Oh, darling, we don't use the word 'random'. Fate. It's fate." Vita appeared content with her answer.

That was seven months ago.

Claire and Victor agreed to stay in Origin Point until the baby was born, thinking any place would be safer than

Reverie, since the manifestations had no intention, it seemed, of sending them back home to Earth. Victor, as always, easily accepted the whole Savior of Dream thing. But Claire, holding a child she never wanted, now wanted nothing more than for Esperanza to be far, far away from all this nonsense.

The manifestations allowed Claire, Victor, and Anza to stay in Origin Point for two more months. They visited now and then, all except for Nihilo, which they counted as a good thing. At the end of the two months, Vita summoned them to the long crystal bench where all six manifestations awaited them, just as they had nearly a year before.

Vita smiled a worrisome smile. "First of all, darlings, thank you. We sincerely hope we were able to accommodate your every need." Nihilo grumbled at this. Claire rolled her eyes. "The time has come for you to return to Reverie; to fulfill your destiny and bring balance to a realm overflowing with turmoil. As I once said, there—"

Vita halted her speech. They'd all felt it. A wave of fear coursed through them. Claire shivered. Anza squirmed in Victor's arms. Vita shot a hard glare toward Timor, black and tentacled manifestation of fear.

"Sweet, beautiful, guests," Somni began, toying with her hands like a guilty child. "As my brother so abruptly reminded us, we have terrible news to share with you." Claire instinctively reached for Anza. "In the year that you have been here a few things have changed. The walls between dreams are completely gone. And, well…" The manifestation of desire looked to the others. They bid her to continue. "Guillelmina opened the portal that allowed you to come to Origin Point. She was instructed to open it once again upon your return. Unfortunately, four months ago, Guillelmina was, well…"

"She passed away," said Mortem.

Vita added, "She served her purpose well. Her spirit has returned with honor to Eternia."

"What this means for the two of you," Somni

added, "is that the portal cannot be reopened as easily as we had hoped."

"Why are you just telling us this now?" Claire asked.

"Stress affects the baby," Initia said as she rubbed her own bulging stomach.

"We couldn't risk it!" Somni added.

"What does that mean for us?" Victor wondered aloud.

"Well, you see." Vita's lack of confidence in her chosen words was disarming. "What this means is not entirely clear."

"Guillelmina's portal also functioned as an anchor," Initia/Mortem said. "It allowed for you to return to the exact space where you left. But with her gone things have become a bit trickier."

"Fortunately," Somni pressed on, hopeful, "we were able to retrieve this guy." With the wave of a hand, Victor's furry, floppy-eared pet, named Pet, appeared. It was pixelated, like something out of an old video game. "He slipped into the portal just behind you. We kept him under our care, so that you wouldn't be distracted."

Initia/Mortem smiled. "This creature can return you to Reverie. Exactly where, we can't be sure. Normally such things would not have been possible from Origin Point, so——"

Vita interrupted. "Simply grab onto this animal, darlings, and wish yourselves back."

Nihilo, the vile manifestation of nothingness who had said little over the past months, crossed his arms and snickered.

Claire made the universal "time-out" gesture. "Wait. Are you saying that you don't know where——" Before Claire could finish her thought, Somni placed Pet between the young parents and Anza, their daughter.

The family of three disappeared in a flash of light.

—

PART I

1

A cold breeze, the kind that pierces you at your core, blew over the Alder Scott Cemetery, just outside of Addley's town square. What leaves remained on the trees rattled, some coming unhinged and floating to the earth. The sky was a solemn gray. Rain had passed and would come again. Atop a hill already overcrowded with aging tombstones, a small, strange collection of people gathered to say their final goodbyes to their teacher, their guide, their friend: Guillelmina.

The leader of the ceremony was a wiry old man practically drowning in an oversized robe fashioned out of crudely sewn squares of colorful fabrics. His voice crackled like the windblown leaves. "Guillelmina was a servant to a world much different from this one. And I know that her friends and family in that other place are gathered just as we are here, celebrating the joy and, more importantly, the grand realization of something far greater than ourselves. You are all here because of the gifts she has given you. I now call anyone who wishes to share something about Guilly to please, please come up and do so."

A plump woman in her forties dressed in a tasteful black pantsuit stepped forward, a dashing salt-and-pepper-haired man at her side. Broadening her stance, the woman wiped a tear from her eye and marched to the open patch of grass between the wiry old man and Guillelmina's grave. The man with the salt and pepper hair followed closely.

The woman cleared her throat. "This won't take long. I wasn't planning on saying anything." She bit her lip, seemingly holding back tears. The man clutched her shoulders. "My husband and I never really subscribed to any of this psychic stuff. We're not what you would call spiritual people. But when our Mindy—" She stopped to compose herself. "When our little girl disappeared, we feared the worst. And then Jason Baker," Mindy's mother pointed to a young man with black hair and piercing blue eyes, "her friend Jason suggested we see Guillelmina. Oh, we thought she was crazy at first, communing with this wacky world of dreams. But then she would relay these messages from our girl, things that no one could possibly know and…" She buried herself into her husband's chest, sobbing loudly.

"Thank you, Guillelmina," said Mindy's father as he guided his wife back to their seats.

Jason Baker himself took the floor. There was something magnetic about him, even in these somber times. He smiled. "Mr. and Mrs. Sparks. Just because Guillelmina is gone, that doesn't mean that your relationship with your daughter is gone. I promise you that." Mindy's mom nodded and blew Jason a kiss of gratitude. Jason addressed the rest of the attendees. "Like many people here, it took Guillelmina a bit of work to convince me that Reverie was real. But when she did…" He chuckled to himself. "I worked closely with Guillelmina in the last few months. Trained under her, actually. It turns out I've got a gift. I mean, I'm not like her, but I can go there now, every night when I sleep without fail…" Addressing the Sparks, he said, "I see Mindy every night. I do everything in my power to keep her safe. To let her know how loved she is by all of us here. And that—"

Someone sighed so loudly, so disruptively, that there was no doubt it was meant to bring Jason's speech, the whole event, to a halt. All eyes were on a woman in her late forties with graying blonde hair. She was loaded down with jewelry and wearing a black dress a little too provocative for the occasion. She took a gulp from a travel mug and stumbled backwards a few steps before righting herself. It was no mystery what sort of liquid the mug contained.

"Oh, la de da," grumbled Karen Ashford, her voice slurring. "Mindy, Mindy, poor Mindy. God, give it a rest. At least you know where your daughter is. Mine is – who knows? Pregnant and alone in some nothing place in some secret dimension with God knows what and some skinny

Hispanic boy? All the while your precious little Mindy's in a damned fairytale land—"

"You have no room to talk, Karen," snapped Mindy's mom. "If it wasn't for your daughter, Mindy would still be here!"

Karen spat her drink on the grass. "My daughter? My daughter?" She marched toward Mr. and Mrs. Sparks, waving her mug madly in the air. "My daughter is a sweet, innocent, beautiful girl, who needs her mommy very, very badly. The monster who took your daughter from you is just a sick, sad nightmare who wears my sweet, sweet baby's face, but is nothing like her!" Tears rolled down Karen's face. She tripped over her feet and toppled to the damp ground. "Nothing…nothing…like her…"

Standing decidedly apart from the majority of the people were two curious figures. One had olive skin and thick locks of black curly hair. He looked like a teenager on the verge of adulthood. The other was a woman with skin so dark it almost resembled the starless night sky. She was a foot taller than the other and perhaps a decade older, with a bald head. Both had full lips, high cheekbones, toned bodies, and were dressed to perfection: him, a raspberry suit; her, an African tribal gown of black and forest green. They also wore mirrored aviator glasses despite the weather.

"Well, this is certainly entertaining," said the young man with a wide, satisfied grin. "Are you glad you came yet?"

"I'm just glad that old bag is dead," the woman moaned. "I had to come and see it for myself."

"And raid her stuff," he added.

She raised an eyebrow. "First of all, she stole it from me. Secondly, none of these classless troglodytes will have any use for it."

"I dunno, Ollie." He glanced at Jason, who, along with some others, were helping Karen to the limo. "I think I see some promise."

Ollie rolled her eyes behind her glasses. "I've had

enough of this place for one lifetime. Are you coming along to retrieve my things, hm, what are you calling yourself these days?"

"Dion," the young man replied. "And no. I think I'd rather live amongst these 'classless troglodytes' for a little while."

"Suit yourself." Ollie disappeared into thin air, completely unnoticed by anyone except Dion. A few short seconds later the sun began to show through the dispersing clouds.

***

After the funeral, Jason and his friends grabbed a bite at Eddie-O's Diner, their usual spot. Eddie-O had been dead for decades. The current owner was a tall, round Indian man with a thick moustache named Basu, who expanded the classic American menu to include a few specialties from his native country.

"Pani puri, freshly made," announced Basu as he arrived carrying a tray dwarfed by his massive frame. He placed the plate of smoking, stuffed treats on a table already housing partially eaten burgers and baskets of onion rings and fries. "On the house, kids. Sorry for your loss." He offered them a sad smile and lumbered off to another group of customers.

"Well, that was depressing," said Max Grayson, his mouth full of burger. He had short-cropped red hair and zero tact. He was also a few bulbs short of a chandelier, but he had a heart of gold. He was, with Jamal Anderson to his left, a star player on Addley High's varsity basketball team, the Addley Ospreys.

Seated directly across from Max was Anne, looking out of place amongst the three suited, male athletes at the table in a plain black dress that was much too big. Her brown hair looked half-styled. Thick glasses with frosted pink and purple rims magnified her already big brown eyes. But if there were any feelings of insecurity within her, no one could see it. And there was certainly no judgment coming from the boys at the table. "Jason," she asked quietly, kindly, "how are you doing?"

"I'm okay," Jason said, eyes cast downward, a contrast to the way he'd held himself at the funeral. "I mean, I'm not, but I will be, you know? Guillelmina wasn't just a teacher to me. She helped me with other things, though, so I'm worried that I'll, like, go back to the way I…" Jason's eyes reddened and glazed over, painfully aware that the others were uncomfortable seeing him cry.

Anne placed a hand on Jason's back. "It's okay. It's okay."

Jamal reached a muscular arm across the table and gave Jason a friendly punch to the shoulder. "Yeah, bro, we're here for you. We got your back. For life."

Jason nodded, mouthed the words "thank you" and looked away from his friends and out the window. He appreciated their words, their support, but remained terrified of the part of himself that so few knew.

"Um, Anne." Jamal lowered his brow and ran his long fingers across the black mohawk on his head. He smiled, a flash of white against his brown skin. "How's Claire been?"

Jason noticed a shift in posture from everyone at the table at the mention of her name. Jamal had been Claire's boyfriend almost six months now.

"Not too well," said Anne. "She doesn't eat. She hardly comes out of her room. My mom is looking into maybe getting her some help."

"Oh." Jamal exhaled. "Do you think it would help if I dropped by?"

Anne shrugged. "It's worth a try."

"Okay." Jamal slammed his fist on the table. "I was so sure that she was going to show up today."

—

Anne lifted a fry from the basket, looked at it quizzically. "It's probably for the best that she didn't. You saw Karen."

"True," admitted Jamal.

Anne popped the fry into her mouth. "Vic didn't show up either. Did he even know?"

"Screw him," barked Jason. Then to Jamal he said, "I think it would have been good if Claire came, too."

"Guys?" Max swallowed his final bite and chased it with a pair of pani puri balls. "Not to be this dude, but I think we're all avoiding the rhino in the room."

"Elephant?" offered Jason.

"Uh, sure, whatever—a big freaking animal, right?" Max continued. "Anyway there's only one reason Claire is locked in her room and not here right now and we all know it: if it wasn't for her, Guillelmina would still be alive."

2

Claire, Victor, Pet, and baby Anza emerged from a blazing white portal above the ground and dropped into a puddle, more mud than water. Claire hopped to her feet, snatching Anza from Victor's grasp. She pulled a particularly large glob of mud from her hair and took in their new surroundings.

It was nighttime. They were in a narrow winding valley of mud and dead grass. Skeletal trees with little to no leaves dotted the land around them. To the right was an gentle incline. To the left, a dirt path that disappeared around a corner. The air was cold, biting, and smelled like a musty basement. Everything was damp.

Victor was just starting to climb to his feet. "Where are w—"

Claire raised a finger, silencing him. "Shh." Anza cooed. "You 'sh,' too. Do you hear that?"

"I don't hear anything," Victor said.

"Something's coming up the path. Come on. Hide." She grabbed Victor and the three took cover behind one of the trees that looked like something that would be more at home in front of a haunted house. Pet, seeming to hear it, too, scurried up the tree into the shadows above.

The sounds were soft at first, but grew quickly louder. A blend of feet dragging through the mud and sparse whispers. Victor nodded at Claire just before the strangest collection of creatures she had ever seen emerged on the path. There were around ten, covering a range of heights and weights, shapes and sizes and species. The only thing that connected them was a shared expression of melancholy and exhaustion.

The odd group shuffled up the path. The man in front, a muscular guy in full medieval armor with spiky red hair and a long spear, held high a torch to light their way. Another torch-holder near the back was too short to see.

"We should be there by daybreak," said the man in front. "It'll all be worth it soon."

In the middle of the group stood a dinosaur; a scaly velociraptor wearing a white collar and bowtie. Victor's face lit up in recognition.

"Victor, don't—" Claire whispered, but it was too late. He was already making his way to the group.

"Miles?" Victor squinted past a round woman with pink skin and what appeared to be a beach ball with legs and a mouth. The group was startled by his sudden appearance and weapons were drawn, pointed right at him. Claire remained hidden in the brush, clutching the baby to her chest.

"Victor?" The dinosaur had the high-pitched voice of a human boy. He edged his way past the sentient beach ball that was wielding a plastic shovel. "Guys, it's okay. I know him."

"What's going on?" Victor asked. "What are you all doing out here? Where's Lady Thrice? Reginald Von Roar?" Miles lowered his scaly head. A tear, reflecting torchlight, weaved its way down his face.

"Gone," he said. "The robots killed them."

"Oh God. I'm sorry." To the trees, he called, "Claire, come out! It's okay!"

Claire stepped from behind the tree and out into the open with Anza cradled in her arms. She maintained her distance. "What's going on?"

"This is Miles Hooktoe. My friend." Victor made a half-smile to the velociraptor. "I met him when you and I split up. After the island incident. Miles, we've been away for a long time. What's going on in here? Where are you going?"

The young velociraptor sighed. "The walls went down. You know, the foggy ones you came through? Well, they're gone. Before that, the robots came, destroying anyone or anything in their way if they didn't submit. The creatures that did submit were taken away. The ones that didn't were either killed or forced into hiding." Miles took a deep breath. "I wish the robots were the worst part. After the walls went down there was a flood. No one's sure where it came from. On the bright side, it took out all the robots, but ultimately it was more destructive than they were. Almost all of us lost friends and family." There were a few nods from the group. "As for where we're headed. It's a place called 'Black Rock.' Word is there's a town there that's taking in refugees and a queen who's making sure there's food and shelter for everyone. It's probably just a rumor, but it's all we have." He added, "You're welcome to join us. We don't have much, but we could at least all be together. Protection in numbers."

Victor looked to Claire. "We should join them."

"No."

"No? Claire, you heard Miles. Everything was destroyed. It's not safe."

"I said 'no.'" Claire stood, unflinching.

Victor trudged through the mud to her side. "Claire. Wh-what are you doing?"

"What am I doing?" Claire spoke in bursts. Each word was crisp and sharp. "I am protecting our baby." Before Victor could reply, she continued. "We were prisoners for a year, Victor. A year. Twelve months listening to those manifestations talking about how powerful they were. How they created the gods and dreamed up some almighty prophecy that hinges on a damn teen pregnancy? Then suddenly, suddenly it's time for us to be set free and they're all, 'We don't know what's going to happen next!', 'We're so confused!' Bullshit, Victor. They know exactly what's going on and they knew exactly where we were going to land. How else would we so conveniently end up in this place at this time when your old dream pal just happens to be passing by?"

"We have to keep moving!" called a red-headed man holding the spear.

Miles patiently awaited Victor's decision, but Claire was unwilling to budge.

"Claire?" Victor said.

She shook her head.

Victor turned to Miles. "We'll catch up with you later."

Miles nodded. "Just follow the path. They say if you stick to it, you can't miss Black Rock."

Victor thanked his friend and the refugees walked away, disappearing around the corner. "Claire," he began, "why are we doing this? Anza would have been safe—"

"Would she?" Claire snapped back. "Whatever the manifestations have planned for Anza can't be safe!"

"You know what else isn't safe, Claire?" Victor shouted. "Two defenseless teenagers, a Pet, and a baby wandering around alone at night in a world full of floods and robots and monsters. A world without Jack to protect us or Guillelmina to…to…" Victor sunk to his knees, the mud swishing around him. "Sorry. I'm sorry." He raised his hand to his face, wiping the tears from his eyes. "I'm scared, Claire."

"And you think I'm not?"

"You seemed so certain," he said, his voice shaky. "Like you wanted Anza to save the world. Like you believed in it."

"What else could I do? Who knows what they would have done to her?" Claire and Victor's attention moved to the baby. She was getting cranky.

Victor stood. Pet scurried down the tree and nuzzled Victor behind the knee. "What do we do now?"

"Well," said Claire. "After I feed her we'll use this thing to find our way home." She reached into her pocket and pulled out a small wooden box with a spinning red arrow on one side.

They returned to the cover of the woods so Claire could feed the baby. There were no leaves in the trees so the starlight shone through just enough to see. Aside from their footsteps and the occasional howl of the passing wind, the world was silent. And in that silence, Claire felt comfort. A comfort so complete that she was entirely unaware of the thing watching them from above; a dark monster that blended in with the night itself. Its eyes so bright that if you didn't look too hard you'd think they were stars.

3

Nine months ago Claire discovered her special dream power. She and her friend Anne were perusing luxury fashion online in their shared bedroom. "Anne," said Claire, "You have to have these!"

"Oh." Anne wasn't interested in fancy clothes or makeup or things like that, but she gave in to Claire's excitement. Sort of like how Claire would give in to Anne's excitement over discoveries around the mating habits of certain species of mantis.

"French Sole FS/NY Passport Flats. You're a size six, right? Right." Claire clicked to zoom in on the fancy footwear. "Oh my God, they're perfect."

Anne glanced at the shoes, seeing nothing special about them until noticing the price. "Two-hundred dollars?"

"Plus tax," said Claire like a lovestruck tween. "You need these."

Anne rolled her eyes. "I am positive that I don't."

"Ugh!" Claire wrapped her arms around Anne and talked to her in that 'I know better than you' voice. "Okay, then I need you to have these."

"I'm going to the kitchen. Getting some ice cream. Ignoring you." Anne walked off.

"Ice cream makes your belt scream!" Claire sung, more for her own amusement than anything else.

An hour or so later, Claire and Anne were plopped on an old gray couch, both of them eating ice cream and watching a documentary on animal abuse in circuses (Anne's idea) when the doorbell rang.

"Are you expecting someone?" asked Claire.

Anne shook her head.

"Maybe your boyfriend," Claire said with a sinister grin. "Oh. I forgot. Your boyfriend's in a coma." She got a couch cushion hurled at her face for that comment.

"Not funny, Claire. Not even a little bit."

"Sorry, sorry!" she said, half laughing as she went to the door and pressed the "Talk" button. "Who is it?"

"Uh…I…" The voice sounded confused. Scared even. "Delivery for, uh, Annabelle Grimmly?"

Claire released the button. "Please tell me you didn't order another one of those frog dissection models. Ick."

Anne shook her head.

Claire pressed the "Door" button. A knock followed shortly after. Claire opened the door, doing that sexy, flirty thing she always did when any boy was around. "Hey there, babe," she said to the scrawny, pimply guy who was most likely in his early twenties. He was sweaty and nervous, looking around like he thought an axe murderer would pop out at any second.

"Here you go, ma'am." He handed Claire the box.

"Thanks, babe. Have a good night. Make sure you think of m—"

He cut her off. "Uh, could you please tell me where I am?"

Claire slammed the door in his face. "Freak."

She handed the box to Anne and sat down beside her. "Open it! Open it! The suspense is killing me!"

Anne did open it. The package contained a pair of French Sole FS/NY Passport Flats. Size six.

The two girls sat in silence for a second. Claire broke it, loudly. "Oh, Anne, you little bitch! That's why you were pretending to be so disinterested when I showed them to you! You already ordered them. I knew my flawless fashion sense would rub off on you sooner or later!"

Anne was spectacularly confused. "I did not order those shoes."

"Ha. Good one."

"I'm serious!" Anne stood up, dangling the shoes on

the ends of her fingers. "When have I ever had two-hundred dollars? And, if I had two-hundred dollars, when would I ever not donate it to wildlife preservation efforts in the Amazon?"

"You make good points, Anne. Excellent, nerdy points."

Anne tossed the shoes back into the box and paced. "Do you think you did this? I mean, with your dreamy-skills? This isn't the first time you've inexplicably gotten what you wanted."

Claire crossed her legs and batted her lashes. "I just assumed it was because I'm pretty."

"Shut up. We're going to see Guillelmina tomorrow."

And they did. The eccentric old woman poured the girls each a cup of tea and they talked it out, finally getting to the bottom of Claire's gift: she could have anything she wanted, as long as she worded it as a personal need.

"I need that dress." Claire's final words before she was given a six-thousand dollar gown to wear to the spring dance.

"I need to win this." Claire's final words before Mindy's sudden disappearance and her rise to high school royalty, receiving the title of Spring Queen in Mindy's place.

"Oh my God." Anne wagged her finger in the air. "The delivery guy! He had no idea where he was. You must have summoned him from wherever he was delivering those shoes. And changed the name on the box to mine?"

While Guillelmina was warning Claire of the repercussions of such a power, Claire was envisioning herself in a mansion with butlers and a private masseuse and chef and yoga instructor, hosting parties for all of her friends. "This is amazing!" The mere thought of the things she could have nearly brought her to tears.

The next six months had been a whirlwind of consumerism and parade of confused delivery men (at

Anne's suggestion, Claire had a pile of Southwest Airlines gift certificates to send them back to wherever they'd come from). Claire summoned enough money to move into her own condo a few blocks away from Anne's. She also left Anne's mom with a hefty chunk of cash as a 'thank you' for taking her in when no one else would.

Just two weeks ago, Claire was hosting a small get-together with Anne, Max, Jamal, and Jason. She handed them each a gift bag with expensive perfumes, colognes, and an iPad. This had become common practice. While Max and Jamal basked in the extravagance, Jason and Anne weren't keen on it. In fact, they'd decided to turn this particular get-together into a surprise intervention.

"Claire," Anne began, "you have to stop this. There's no telling what all this warping of reality is doing. Teleporting mailmen could just be the tip of the iceberg. You might be destroying the fabric of time and space!"

Jason nodded. "Exactly. In fact, Guillelmina said that—"

"Blah! Blah! Blah! Guillelmina said! Guillelmina said!" Claire was a little drunk at this point. "Who gives a flying freak what Guillelmina said? We're all just young and beautiful and having fun, Jason! Anne!" She hiccupped. "You know what I need? Do you?" Everyone sort of froze at that moment. "I need Guillelmina to stay the hell out of my business."

When Anne and Jason reached Guillelmina's house, she was already dead. Her tiny body sprawled across the floor, a spilt cup of tea near her hand. And while no one could prove Claire did it, everyone assumed that was likely the case. Claire spiraled into depression carrying the weight of someone's death on her hands. She stopped needing much after that.

While the rest of the gang attended her funeral, Claire holed up in Anne's room, crying in the dark.

"It'll be okay," Spoke a whisper from inside her

mind. "It'll be okay." Again. The voice had spoken to her ever since she woke up in this strange world more than a year ago. She didn't know where it came from or why no one else could hear it. She kept its existence to herself.

"This will blow over, Claire. Remember you are loved."

"Shut up!" she shouted. "Shut up! Shut up!" Again and again she shouted until she was red in the face and her voice was hoarse. She curled up into a ball and hid under the covers, wishing she could just disappear.

Then came a knock on the door.

In walked Jamal, tall and muscular, his thick dreads tied back into a ponytail. He looked at the shape under the covers. He listened to the muffled whimpers coming from beneath them. Jamal Anderson said nothing. He only climbed into bed and lay beside her, placing a hand gently on her back, letting her know she wasn't alone.

4

"I think she's asleep," said Victor. Anza was cradled in his arms. "Do you think we should rest for the night?"
Claire walked at least ten feet in front of him. She hadn't said a word for the past hour. Ever since she whispered "Home" to the tiny wooden block and the arrow failed to point in any certain direction, she had nothing to say. She had simply handed Anza to Victor and walked on through the old forest.

"Claire." Victor's voice was stern this time. "We should rest."

She didn't slow.

Victor closed the gap between the two. "Look, I know you thought that compass would work. It was a good plan. I mean, they always worked for us in the past, right? But, it didn't this time. Maybe our time at Origin Point short-circuited it, or Jack turned it off. I dunno. But, whatever, it's fine. Pet can take us back to the path and—"

Claire turned sharply to Victor. Her face was red, nostrils flaring. Tears swelled in her eyes. In a deceptively calm tone, she said, "Let's rest here." And that was the end of it.

Victor lay down on the muddy ground with Anza on his stomach. He adjusted himself as best he could to avoid the sharp rocks. Claire sat with her legs crossed, fixated on the star-filled sky above. Pet snuggled up beside her. His large cream-colored ears were perked straight up, long feline tail wagging, eager for attention. Claire stroked his fur which was oddly soft, despite his low res computer-generated appearance. "I'll keep watch," she said. Victor nodded and, in time, drifted off to sleep.

He woke up to the sunlight bright on his face. The

forest still looked creepy in the light of day. The trees, long dead, were almost gray and cast long black shadows across the barren land. He sat up, catching his first glimpse of Claire and Pet, both sound asleep.

Victor shuffled to them. "Claire!" Pet's big ears perked up immediately. Claire moaned, wiped her eyes, and allowed them to adjust to the brightness.

"Victor, what's—"

"Where's Anza?" There was panic in his voice.

Claire was wide awake at that. "Wha? Anza? You had her…"

"I…I…" The details of the night crept into Victor's memories. She was asleep on his chest. He had to sing her back to sleep more than once. Claire was there every time, awake and alert. "I don't know."

Claire was on her feet. "She was sleeping with you!"

"You said you would keep watch!"

She peered out into the forest in all directions. Victor joined her. "Anza!" they shouted again and again.

Victor's heart was pounding. "This is bad."

"No shit," snapped Claire. "She couldn't've just crawled away. She can barely hold herself up."

Victor whispered to Pet, "Can you pick up her scent?" The animal looked at him quizzically. Nothing had ever suggested Grobis, Pet's species, had a sense of smell any better or worse than humans.

Claire and Victor searched the immediate area not no avail.

"AAAARGH!" Claire screamed. "This isn't happening. This can't be happening. Our baby, Victor. Our—" She went quiet. Her eyes opened wide, her mouth agape. "Victor." She was shaken suddenly by something over his shoulder. "Behind you."

A chill raced up Victor's spine. Slowly he turned his head.

Standing not four feet behind Victor was a man

dressed in white. He was about a foot taller than Victor. His facial features were so muted that it was impossible to tell his age. His skin was paper white. As were his hair, eyes, and the slim-fitting suit he wore. He looked like a living breathing sketch of a man if the sketch had been stained by water and the lines all dulled.

"Where's our daughter?" said Claire, fire in her voice.

The man in white raised a finger, gesturing as though he'd been struck with an idea. He then locked his forearms together and made as though he were cradling a child. His third and final gesture was a wave of his hand; a summons to follow him. The pale grey shadows that vaguely resembled a mouth shifted into what could only have been a smile. He bowed, paused, then ran, leaving no footprints and kicking up no mud behind him.

5

Sixth period lunch at Addley High, the cafeteria was buzzing with hundreds of voices talking about hundreds of things, from Halloween costumes to the lunch lady's mustache and everything in between.

"So Mindy's renegotiating with the centaur princes again," Jason said matter-of-factly between bites of green beans. "Sirnius seems to be on board but Kensen is being stubborn, as always."

Jamal sighed. "Can we please go one lunch without talking about centaurs and smoke walls and, you know, Reverie stuff? There are plenty of things to talk about here. In the real world."

"I dunno, dude," said Max, running his hand through his red hair. "I kinda like hearing about Mindy. It's good to know she's doing okay."

"I get that," Jamal continued. "All I'm saying is it wouldn't hurt to talk about SATs and video games, like normal people. Maybe even, God forbid, talk about our big game against the Maelstroms this weekend."

Jason crossed his arms, annoyed. "You're right. Mindy trying to forge an alliance between bloodthirsty half-horse people pales in comparison to throwing balls at hoops for an hour."

"Well." Jamal said it in that way that made everyone around him shut up and listen. "The least we could do is talk seriously about Claire. She's not raising an empire but she's important to me. To all of us. I hope."

"Last night she left her room to eat dinner with me and my mom." A sad smile accompanied Anne's words. "That's progress." Then, to Jamal, "Whatever you said to her must have made her feel better."

"Mostly I was just there. And I'll keep being there

until she's okay again."

Max gave Jamal a friendly pat on the back. "She's lucky to have you, dude."

Jamal was about to reply when a sudden hush swept across the cafeteria. The shift in volume caught Jamal's attention. Many of the students' gaze had shifted to the young man who had just entered.

He could not have been less "Addley" in his appearance. Thin and olive-skinned, he was wearing a fitted teal button-down shirt tucked into skinny midnight blue jeans and shiny black wingtip shoes. He stepped into the center of the cafeteria, all confidence. He turned his head slowly as if searching for something through his brown-tinted aviator glasses. More than once he had to brush away a stray curl of his thick, black hair. It wasn't long before he found what he was looking for.

Jason Baker's heart skipped a beat when he realized the strange young man was staring at him. The young man offered Jason a big, bright white smile and started enthusiastically toward him.

"Who is this guy?" Max asked Jason, who only shook his head in reply.

"He was at Guillelmina's funeral," said Jamal. "He stood with this bald lady in the back the whole time."

"Well, hello, everyone." His voice was like warm honey and hinted at an accent. "My name is Dion. Do you mind if I join you?" Before anyone responded he pulled a chair from a neighboring table and edged it between Max and Jamal. His every move was smooth, liquid. Dion had placed himself directly across the table from Jason. He gave Jason a wink before saying, "I recognize you all from yesterday, no? Old Guilly's Moving On ceremony?"

Jamal folded his arms. "We rememb—"

"Your name is Jason," Dion interrupted.

Jason nodded. His heart was thumping out of control. "Yes."

"You have a gift. That much is clear." Dion offered his big smile again. He then addressed the entire table. "I am new to town and transferring to Addley High School. And since we all have already shared a uniquely personal and heartfelt experience, I would very much enjoy it if you would allow me the honor of being your friend."

Despite the aviator glasses blocking Dion's eyes, Jason Baker couldn't help but think Dion did not once take his eyes off of him.

On the other side of town Karen Ashford was stepping out of her Mercedes and onto the cracked sidewalk of North Addley. She clutched her purse in one hand and an empty hot pink duffle bag in the other. She checked for the third time that her car doors were locked. She checked for the second time to make sure no rascals were preparing to mug her from the shadows. Satisfied at last, Karen walked across the unkempt front yard to the rickety old stairs that led to Guillelmina's house.

Karen had planned to go to Guillelmina's directly after the funeral. Regrettably, she had gotten too drunk. The martinis she'd drunk before, during, and after the ceremony made sure of that. She woke up the next day fully dressed and in bed, suffering from a severe hangover. She dragged herself out of bed, through her empty cavernous house, into the kitchen where she had a breakfast of coffee, Advil, bacon, eggs, and a couple of screwdrivers. She was on her way to Guillelmina's by two-thirty which, for Karen Ashford, was pretty good.

She ascended the stairs above The Dream Room to the second story, most of its purple paint chipped away. The first thing Karen noticed was the front door hanging slightly open. The second was the clashing sound coming from within. It was enough to give Karen pause, but she was courageous (and drunk) enough to not be deterred. She had come all this way to steal a few trinkets to remember Guillelmina by and that's just what she intended to do.

Karen drew a tube of pepper spray from her purse and slipped inside. The living room was in shambles. The table overturned, bookshelves moved around, papers and pens, chairs and plants and figurines, all over the floor. The room had always been a cluttered mess, but this was purposefully destructive. The sounds, most recently of breaking glass, continued deeper into the house.

Quietly as possible. Karen grabbed handfuls of paper and shoved them in the duffle bag. Then she tossed in a couple tea cups and a few sticks of incense. Karen allowed herself to cry as she did this, her thoughts drifting to her daughter and grandchild, wherever they might be.

Atop one of the bookshelves sat a crystal ball; one Guillelmina had promised could be enchanted in such a way that would allow Claire to be seen. This was the one thing she had to take. Karen stood on the tips of her heels, reaching for it.

"May I help you?" Standing in the doorway was a tall and elegant woman wearing a form-fitting green dress. Her skin was dark as night and her eyes, even darker. A matching green scarf was wrapped around her bald head. Karen offered the woman a menacing snarl. "You can help me by getting the hell out of my friend's house before I call the cops!" Karen aimed the pepper spray at the other intruder.

The woman smiled and gestured to the duffle bag. "You are as guilty as I." Her accent was unmistakably West African. "And I do not take kindly to threats."

"I'm not scared of you!" Karen leveled the pepper spray at the woman's face. "Now get out of here."

The woman laughed. "Every bit the firecracker that you were yesterday. You amuse me."

Karen pressed down on the button and a jet of

spray covered the woman's face and chest. The woman didn't budge. Or scream. Or react in any way, except that her brow lowered and her smile gave way to pursed lips.

"You should not have done that." The woman's eyes turned a brilliant blue. The light they gave off was overpowering. And fleeting. They quickly dimmed from the blue of the sky to that of the ocean's deepest depths. And then, lastly to black. But it wasn't just her eyes. It was everything.

Karen Ashford let out a blood-curdling scream.

6

Imprisoned in a small, doorless room, a hungry and uncertain Mindy Sparks cycled through the most pivotal moments of her life so far.

She had her first dance class when she was three. Some of her fondest memories were on the stage or in the dance studio. In the years that followed, dance imbued Mindy with confidence, precision, focus, and a strong, flexible mind and body.

She thought of Jason Baker. They met in ballet class when they were five and had been best friends ever since. The two were both attractive, well-loved, and lovers of life. They would talk for hours about the world, themselves, each other, sharing secrets no one else knew. They were there for each other during the brightest and darkest moments. Like the death of Jason's parents. Or Mindy's evil Uncle Kenny.

When she was thirteen her uncle forced himself on her, then threatened to kill her if she ever told anyone. It was enough to keep her quiet for months more of his visits. And while the threat eventually ended, the memories of it continued to haunt her every day. Especially at a time like now, when she was trapped by a madman. Mindy promised herself that she would never be taken advantage of again. That she would survive.

Aemon, her captor, had left her a scepter. "For your protection," he said. It was golden, with a milky white orb at the top and currently propped up against a wall. Tired, angry, and fed up, Mindy took hold of the scepter and screamed. Face red, tears in her eyes, she bashed the scepter against the nearest wall. Moments before it made contact, the orb turned orange and a large chunk of wall exploded outward, revealing a stone staircase. The dust cleared and she descended.

Mindy emerged from a hole in the side of an

impossibly high mountain into the light of the morning sun. Carefully she traversed the black rocks, laying low as she heard voices not far away. She decided to take a risk and followed the sounds.

Mindy climbed over the last of the rocks and landed softly in the grass. She could only imagine how she looked; bruised and dirtied, her auburn hair in tangles, still wearing her beige flapper dress from the dance.

"Help." The words escaped her lips as barely a whisper. She hobbled toward the people.

A child tugged on his mother's tunic and pointed at Mindy with the aid of the boar bone in his hand. The mother alerted others. All eyes were on Mindy as she approached.

"Help," she said again.

This time the mother placed her child in the care of the man sitting beside her and rose from the bench. She met Mindy halfway.

"You all right, girl?" asked the woman. Her accent was vaguely British.

Mindy shook her head, doing her best to hold back the tears. "Where am I?"

"You're in the Dark Valley. We're celebratin' on account o' Aemon bein' gone. And mournin' the loss of our friends."

"Gone?"

"Yep," said the woman with a big smile that revealed crooked and missing teeth. "He up 'n flew away, he did." She gave Mindy a look up and down. "Where you comin' from?"

Mindy pointed to the mountain with her scepter. "He was holding me prisoner."

The woman smacked her lips. "No wonder you're so skinny! Come! Come! Sit with us."

Mindy hadn't realized how hungry she was until she was tearing away at pheasant and cabbage and carrots and washing it down with gulps of mead. She told her tale of

---

appearing in the forest and being kidnapped by the goblins. Of being pronounced the bride of the vile and vicious Lord Aemon. And Lord Aemon, sensing war, deciding to seal her away in a hidden room for safe keeping. Before she reached the part about escaping, all focus shifted to the other side of the long table, where a woman in black climbed atop it, clanging two pots together.

"He's dead!" she cried, her voice wrought with anguish. Mindy didn't get a good glimpse of her, except for her skin-tight black clothing and a futuristic handgun. "Jack is dead!" And with that, she leapt from the table and ran back toward the village. The whole place went up in nervous whispers. Some people got up and followed the woman.

"Wait," Mindy asked the woman next to her, grabbing her arm to stop her from going after the others. "Who's Jack?"

"He's a hero," the woman said. "He defeated Aemon and saved many lives in the process."

"And who was that woman?" Mindy pressed. "The woman in black?"

"That's Rumi Inyonara. She led the people against the goblins and the metal beasts. Gave 'em weapons 'n led 'em to victory." The woman shook off Mindy's grip and ran off after the others.

This was all quite a lot for Mindy Sparks to take in.

Not long after, men and women started to build bonfires. A few took up lutes and pipes and began to play. Others got up and started to dance. The child Mindy had first seen asked her to dance with him. She shook her head, exhausted, but he would not back down, wearing away at her resolve until she agreed to join him.

Scepter in hand, Mindy danced. And she danced brilliantly; her body recalling every twist, every kick, every spin, from years of ballet, of swing, of modern. As she moved, all the confusion, all the fear melted away. The steps could not have been more different than what she studied as a child, but the peace she felt as she danced was the same. She closed her eyes and let the calm consume her. She was so engulfed in it that she didn't notice the orb begin to shine a brilliant blue and trail a sparkling light.

When at last she brought her dance to a close and opened her eyes, she was met with the faces of a hundred mesmerized onlookers as droplets of light fell slowly all around her.

After that night, the people of Dark Valley treated Mindy with reverence. They gravitated to her quite naturally, even in the beginning; this beautiful and fearless girl from a strange land.

A couple of days later, Mindy received a special visitor.

She was walking along the forest's edge, the village well within sight. She wore a peasant's tunic and pants. The night offered a warm breeze and a starry sky. The perfect time to walk and think. In front of her, without warning, a muted light appeared and slowly took shape. A human silhouette. Gradually the details came into view. A foot there. Then the other. Fingers. A gray hoodie. Ears. Those familiar blue eyes.

"Mindy?" he said, overwhelmed with joy and relief. Mindy didn't know whether to laugh, cry, or scream, so she just took a step closer to him and said his name. "Jason." Jason Baker, now fully formed, put his arms around her and held her tight. "Oh my God, I did it. I finally did it!"

Mindy held on even tighter. She didn't want to lose this connection to a world she'd lost. "Oh Jason. Is it really you?"

"It is," he said, tears rolling down his face. "I missed you so much."

"Me too."

Jason told Mindy all about Reverie. About Lucids. And how he had been training under Guillelmina. "Guilly says the average Lucid can't fully slip into another person's dream for months. And here I am!" He explained that they weren't sure how she got to Reverie, but that he thought it was dream-world Claire's doing. "Do you remember Claire Ashford and Victor Soto from school? Well, they'll be in Reverie, too. Soon. Once Claire has her baby. Anyway, you're looking fabulous in your new clothes and—"

"Jason." Mindy stopped him, gesturing at her friend.

Taking note of himself, Jason realized that his form was fading. "Oh damn it. I'm losing focus." He smiled that infectious smile of his. "I'll be back. Soon. Sorry we couldn't talk longer, but I'll get better at this. I promise. I miss you and I love you. Max says, 'Hi!' Bye, Mindy!" He hurried the last words and finished just before disappearing into a cloud of light.

Jason did return. Again and again.

In the months that followed Mindy learned the ways of Dark Valley, which she suggested should be called the "Valley of Hope" and everyone agreed. She was kind, educated, literate. They were used to having a leader and naturally made one of her; coming to her with disputes over land or food or, every now and again, love. She even taught reading and writing on occasion. And each time one of Aemon's goblins wandered back into the valley, they received a firm ejection by Mindy and the powerful scepter she was still learning to control.

In time, the fog walls dissipated. And then came the flood. Mindy hadn't seen it herself, but refugees from other dreams spoke of a great flood that destroyed their homes and killed their loved ones. Mindy invited them to the Valley of Hope with open arms (as long as they earned their keep), and even sent scouts out to spread the word that the valley was a safe haven for all peaceful creatures. Jason, by this point, could conjure food and books and other raw materials to maintain the growing number of refugees.

Mindy stepped out of her beautiful (but modest) home at the base of the Black Rock and met the new day. She wore a simple gown of blue, scepter in hand. It had been over nine months since she was first brought to the valley. Creatures with six legs or wings or stripes or two heads bid her good morning and she bid them the same.

"Lady Mindy," said an attractive fellow with large green eyes, long pointed ears, and brown and blond spiked hair. He was dressed in silver and blue armor. "Are you sure you haven't changed your mind? I will gladly assist you in your quest." He held high a sword with a curved blade.

Mindy grinned. "Thank you for the offer, Zen, but I haven't changed my mind." She liked the man. He was a real life hero type. "This is something I'd rather do alone."

The forest surrounding the Valley of Hope was home to a myriad of legendary creatures. Some were more troublesome than others, but they had more or less stayed out of the valley during Aemon's reign. With the dark lord gone, a few had taken to causing trouble near the village. And none of these creatures were more troublesome, numerous, or organized than the centaurs.

The centaur king had died recently and his twin sons, Sirnius and Kensen, disagreed on everything. Most of all, which of the two should be king. Each had supporters and clashes between the two factions had resulted in vandalization, injury, and in one unconfirmed case, death within the valley. Mindy had attempted to visit the centaur princes before with some of her best soldiers, but the centaurs viewed it as a threat and refused to speak with her.

This time, she was determined to talk sense into them.

7

Jason Baker ran down the empty hall, his squeaking sneakers echoing with every step. He hated it when he felt like this. His heart pounding. His adrenaline swelling. Like something terrible—or wonderful—was about to happen. It was usually nothing. Nothing but the chemicals in his brain lying to him as they had for years. No matter. One more corner and he'd be safe.

Jason entered the boys' restroom in the far east wing of Addley High School. The east wing restrooms were old and smelly and avoided unless someone wanted to keep their activities secret. Jason reached into his shirt pocket and pulled out a small pouch. From the pouch he produced two pills. Into his mouth they went. He drank some water from the sink and swallowed.

"Pill-popping?" Jason practically jumped at the sound of the voice, quickly shoving the pouch into his pocket. "I did not think you the type." Standing behind him, framed by one of the stalls, was none other than Dion. He was smirking, most of his slender face still shrouded by his aviator glasses. Jason was certain he had been alone in the bathroom.

"Uppers? Downers? What is your poison?"

"What?" Jason inhaled, trying to maintain his waning cool as Dion circled him like a vulture zeroing in for the kill. "No. Nothing. It's nothing like that."

"I like you, Jason Baker," said Dion, to the point. "I like your glacier-blue eyes. I like your raven-black hair. I like your shape. Your size. And, more than all of that, I like your chi. Your essence. Your psyche. Your energy. Your soul, Jason Baker. I can feel it emanating from you. It is special. You are special. More than you know, I would wager."

Dion took Jason's hand in his own then, without warning. Without hesitation. The electric sensation of Dion's skin touching his was more than Jason could bear. He was paralyzed by it at first. It was overwhelming. It was only when Jason spotted Dion's other hand moving toward him that he reacted, on impulse, tearing his hand free and shoving Dion as hard as he could before running out of the bathroom. He kept running down the hall, and out of the front doors of Addley High.

Jason sat upright in his bed, legs crossed, blanket covering him, gently rocking back and forth. The lights were out and the curtains drawn. He'd deal with the consequences of skipping school later. The important thing is that he was in a safe place. A calm place. A familiar place. The mood stabilizer meds were most definitely kicking in, but his frayed thoughts were combating their effectiveness.

Dion.

Despite Jason's greatest efforts he could not stop thinking about him. His smile and his hair. The way he carried himself, present and precise, like a dancer. He was beautiful. Even if those aviators were a bit ridiculous. And the touch. Jason swore he could still feel a tingling where Dion's hand had been.

"He called me special," Jason whispered to himself, immediately hating himself for acting like a love-struck tween. "Ugh, I don't even know him! Or where he came from. Or how he knows Guilly or…" Jason buried his head in his hands.

"I'm not gay," he declared. Quietly. "I can't be. I'm already crazy, isn't that enough?" He pulled the blanket from over his head. "Calm down, Jason Baker. Fight the crazy. This is not who you are, okay? You are balanced. And cool. And in control. No. You're not. You can pretend, though!" A moment later he added, "But his smile…" and collapsed backwards into his pillow.

There was a gentle tap on his door and Jason welcomed the distraction. He jumped out of bed, turned on the lights, and climbed into the closest pair of sweatpants. "Yeah?"

"Someone's here for you, honey." The woman on the other side of the door was his grandmother, Dot, the only other resident of the house (aside from her parakeet) and Jason's legal guardian. "Jason, dear?"

He was already in panic mode. Could it be Dion? How does he know where I live? How did he show up in the bathroom out of thin air? How d—

"It's a lady named Karen," said Dot. "I figured she's someone you work with at the Community Cen—"

"Karen?" That piqued Jason's interest. "Karen Ashford?"

Dot laughed. "Well, I didn't ask her for her full name, dear."

"Ah, all right." Jason opened the door, revealing his grandmother, a wrinkly old lady no more than five feet tall, hunched and wearing an aquamarine bathrobe. "Thanks, Grams." He gave her a kiss on the cheek and dashed past her and down the stairs.

Karen Ashford was indeed standing just inside his front door with a hand firmly grasping the knob. She was in a fur coat and red cocktail dress, twisted just a little off-center and not entirely zipped up. Her hair was a mess, her shoes mismatched, and for some reason she wore a pair of gaudy maroon sunglasses.

"Mrs. Ashford?" said Jason. She turned to the sound of his voice, but wasn't quite looking his way.

"Jason, darling, is that you?"

Jason made it to the bottom of the stairs and placed a hand on her shoulder. She was startled by it at first, but quickly moved her own hands to his arms, then to his shoulders and face. Jason's heart pounded yet again. "Are you okay?"

"Do I look okay to you, Jason?" She pressed her nails into his cheeks. "Something's happened. Something awful. I visited Guillelmina's home to pay my respects, when I was viciously attacked by a bald, dark-skinned criminal! I stood my ground and she up and put some sort of voodoo curse on me! I simply couldn't have anyone see me like this, so I had my maid look you up and bring me here immediately."

"Mrs. Ashford, what exactly happened?"

"Isn't it obvious, Jason Baker?" Karen removed her glasses, exposing eyes that were entirely black. "The bitch blinded me!"

8

Claire and Pet ran only a few yards behind the man in white. Victor struggled to keep up. They had been chasing after him for what felt like an hour. Sometimes it seemed like they would catch up with him but then he'd summon a burst of speed, widening the gap between them once more. Their legs burned with each step, but that didn't matter. Anza was gone and Claire and Victor needed to get her back.

Even Claire, who had benefited from years on the track team, was reaching the limits of her energy. Finally, the man in white came to a complete stop. There was no easing into it. One moment he was racing ahead at full speed and the next, standing up straight and still. Claire tried to stop, but instead tripped over her feet and fell forward, directly into the man in white. Actually, not so much into him as through him. Claire lifted her face from the dirt floor of the dead forest and looked at the man. There was a hole in his body where she had fallen that was quickly refilled with a cloudy white substance.

Pet veered off safely to the side.

Victor caught up, dragging his feet, huffing and puffing.

They had stopped at the edge of a crater as wide as a couple of football fields. The man in white pointed down into the crater and once again gestured as if rocking a baby in his arms.

Claire picked herself up from the ground and started for the man in white. "Look, you creepy little ghost, if you don't give us our baby I will kill you. Do you hear me? I will find a way to bring you back to life and—"
The man in white vanished.

"Claire." Victor stood at the edge of the crater, staring down into it. "Look at this."

Claire walked over to Victor. "What am I looking a—
—" Then she saw it. At the bottom of the crater was what
appeared to be the remains of a building and at the center of
that building, a crashed flying saucer, silver and enormous.
Everything was charred, blackened. Pillars of smoke rose up
from small fires scattered throughout the area.

"I think she's down there," said Victor.

"How can we be sure that freak wasn't lying?"
Victor shrugged. "What other choice do we have?"
Claire fell silent, then began to make her way down the
crater's edge. Victor followed close behind, with Pet on his
heels. Their descent was more sliding than climbing, and
working their way over fallen tree after fallen tree.

"Victor," Claire began.

"It doesn't matter," he said as he made his way out
of a web of dried branches. "All that matters is that we get
her back."

Up close, the building was more intact than it had
originally seemed. While the middle of it was ruined by the
crashed UFO, its perimeter was mostly standing. Above the
stone porte-cochere that had once served as the main
entrance were the words "Addley Elementary School" in
large gold letters.

"Oh, look, it's—"

"I know," said Claire. "We have to go inside."

Victor, Claire, and Pet stepped in through the main
doors. The lobby was vast and lit only by sunlight leaking
through holes in the ceiling. Loose pieces of paper littered
the tile floor. The silence was ominous.

"Should we split up?" whispered Victor.

Claire shook her head. "That never works." She led
them down one of the halls.

The first classroom they entered was in shambles.
Desks and chairs were all over the place, as were glue and
scissors, backpacks and worksheets. On the whiteboard was
an unfinished sentence: "The cat ate the bat in the."

43

Everything was covered in a thin film of dust. Pet sneezed. They visited six more classrooms, each matching the same description. At the end of the hall was a wall of rubble built up along the silver of the flying saucer. They made their way back to the lobby and started down another.

Claire noticed Pet's ears perk up. "What is it?" she asked. In response, he moved down the hall at a steady pace, ears slightly shifting direction, picking up sounds the others couldn't hear. Pet glanced back once to make sure Victor and Claire followed, then continued on.

Pet led them to a pair of closed doors at the hall's end. Victor pulled them open, revealing a staircase that led down into near-complete darkness. And, though it was faint, a baby's cry could be heard.

Claire pushed past Victor without a moment's pause, and hurried down the stairs. Victor raced after her, and Pet after him.

There was no light to guide them, only the sound of Anza's voice. Claire walked into a wall and heard the clang of Victor stumbling over a bucket. Nothing, not the pain or their rising fear, stopped them from moving toward Anza's cries. A loud slam into what could only have been lockers signaled they'd reached a corner. Not far down the adjoining hall was a faint light. Again, they ran, tripped, fell, ran again.

The light, soft and blue, was escaping a door left slightly ajar. Claire could see just enough of Victor's face to know that he was frightened as she was, but they pressed on. Together they pushed against the door and opened it.

The room was small. Shelves lined the walls, holding everything from dodge balls and Frisbees to boxes of folders and loose-leaf paper. The center of the room was empty, except for a single desk atop which Anza was tied down with a pair of jump ropes, writhing and red, tears pouring from her eyes under a blue light. The long, narrow object that gave off the light resembled a living stalactite, and it dangled above her.

"SCREEEEEEE!" The sound, like a falcon's call, boomed from up the hall, from the way they had come.

"Something's coming," said Victor. Claire was already untying the baby.

"Help me!" she called and Victor worked at the knot on the second rope. "Faster. Faster!"

BAM!

It burst into the room with such force that the door shattered. It was a gruesome thing with slimy indigo skin covered in places with thick, rocky scales. Its head was almost human, feminine, with an expression of all-consuming rage in those glowing white eyes. Black straw-like hair jutted from the top of its head in distinct tufts. The creature's body was long, so long that it was halfway into the room and the rest of it still disappeared into the darkness in the hall. A pair of long wiry arms ending in clawed wiry hands protruded from its serpentine body. One pair every two feet, giving it the appearance of a nightmarish centipede.

"Leave my baby be!" it shrieked. It grabbed at one of the dodge balls and hurled it at Victor's head. "You're ruining everything!" With another of its dozen available hands it grabbed Claire by the wrist. "You will pay for thisss!"

Victor undid the last knot and scooped Anza in his arms.

"Releassse her!" The creature drew Claire closer to itself. "Or the girl will die!"

With Anza in one arm, Victor ran to Claire. "Pet, come!" Taking Claire by her other arm, he pulled. As more of the creature's sickly clawed hands made their way for Victor, Pet jumped and landed on his shoulder. "Take us back to the road!"

The room filled with a white light and the next thing they knew, Victor, Claire, Anza, and Pet were back in the mud at the side of the path where they had, just yesterday, returned to Reverie.

"Okay," said Victor, panting. "Time for Plan B. We're going to follow the path to that refuge and see what we can find."

Claire sighed. Then nodded.

And the trio set off for Black Rock.

9

Anne walked down the sterile halls of St. Damian's Hospital as she had every Saturday for the past two months to room 414 of the long term care wing. A middle-aged woman with short black hair and chestnut brown skin greeted her. They chatted for a bit about the weather and traffic and stuff, and then the woman was on her way. Anne said, "See you next week," and took her seat beside the bed. She dug into her backpack and fished out a book entitled "The Nature of Conservancy: Environmental Action in a Digital World." She looked at the boy in the bed. Skinny, frail, awkward like her, with that same chestnut complexion of his mother. His eyes were closed. As they always were. Anne smiled a buck-toothed smile, adjusted her glasses, and opened the book.

"All right, Jack, ready for Chapter Four?"

10

Mindy tightened the strap of her backpack and continued through the forest. It had been hours since she'd left her home at the base of Black Rock. The midday sun struggled to peek through the canopy. Ancient symbols etched into the trees let her know that she was close.

A wall of trees surrounded the entirety of Pholos, the centaur city. Each tree stood a hundred feet tall, growing so closely to the next that no creature could slip between them. The tree tops were a maze of interwoven branches and thick, plate-sized leaves, lush and green. Serpentine vines wrapped and zigzagged over it all. The wall was said to have been the creation of a powerful centaur warlock from centuries ago. The entrance, the only real way into or out of Pholos, was a great archway, twenty feet high, guarded at all times by two armored centaurs. Though various scouts had reported anywhere between three and ten centaurs hidden, arrows at the ready.

Mindy approached the guards, who took little more than a passing interest in her. Centaurs were intimidating beasts, standing over eight feet tall with the legs and body of a horse and the head, arms, and torso of a human. All of it, muscle. Their features were sharp, chiseled. And they were as beautiful as they were intimidating.

"I am here to see Princes Sirnius and Kensen," said Mindy to the guards. One had pale skin and reddish-brown fur. His hair was a mess and in his silver armor were embedded glistening blue stones. The other was tanned with gray fur. His armor was golden and appeared battle worn. Mindy knew enough of centaur politics to understand that the centaur in silver followed Prince Sirnius. The one in gold, Kensen. At the mention of the princes' names, each centaur laid down a heavy lance, blocking Mindy's path forward.

"I am Mindy, Lady of Black Rock, successor to the

late Lord Aemon, and I demand you let me pass." She had been advised to drop Aemon's name. The centaurs were a proud and warlike species who feared very few things. Aemon was one of those things.

The centaur in silver sneered. "You are no Aemon."

The one in gold maintained a nasty smile. "Prince Kensen will not be bothered by the likes of you."

"And Prince Sirnius?" she asked the one in silver who said nothing, only stared ahead. Mindy clenched her fists. "I am not leaving until I have spoken to at least one of your princes."

The centaur in gold spat. "Sirnius is no prince of mine."

"And Kensen is a blood-crazed dimwit," responded the one in silver.

The two centaurs, for a moment, looked as if they were going to fight. Mindy sighed, then took a seat, legs crossed, on the grass. "I will wait."

"We could kill you," said the one in gold.

"True," admitted Mindy. "But you're not dumb. The Valley of Hope is a place of peace, but every day it grows larger with refugees from miles around. Powerful creatures who believe they owe their lives and their current happiness to me. Now, we want nothing more than to live peacefully with you all, but if you upset us by, oh I don't know, killing a beloved leader, those powerful creatures would tear this place apart. You already know that, though. Well, at least your masters do." Mindy reached into her backpack and pulled out an apple. She polished it on her sleeve then took a bite.

She sat in silence for some time. A centaur with lovely gray fur emerged from the city; in his hand a hunting bow and quiver full of arrows on his back. The centaur took notice of Mindy, then whispered something to the centaur in gold. The centaur in silver whispered something back and continued on his way into the forest. Over the next few hours more centaurs would come and go, hardly paying Mindy any mind. She did take note that every centaur she saw was male.

A coolness entered the air as the day rolled on. Mindy could feel her muscles stiffening and her stomach grumbled more than once, but she remained seated on the grass.

Some time later another centaur appeared within the archway. This one was visibly older. Thin and wiry with a long white beard. Still, his body was muscled. His fur was a white-gray. His skin, exceedingly pale. In his hand he held a piece of parchment which he showed to both guards. Upon reading it, the one in gold grunted and the one in silver looked stoic as ever. With little reaction, both centaurs raised their lances.

"Come with me," said the old centaur to Mindy. "The true prince Sirnius requests your company for dinner." The centaur in gold growled.

Mindy climbed to her feet, fastened her backpack, and entered Pholos.

The famed centaur city was little more than a couple hundred massive straw huts placed randomly across an enormous enclosed area. Some had signs. Some windows. Doors were tall and wide enough to comfortably fit a full-grown centaur. Mindy noticed that every hut had either blue or red ribbons near their entrance. The ground was composed of wet and dry mud, ruined with hoof-prints. Tufts of grass and weeds and the occasional flower grew from the earth. Centaurs of all ages marched here and there. Some carried baskets of fruits and vegetables. Some practiced swordplay. A few were standing outside of a particularly dingy hut, shouting loudly at each other. A sign above their heads read "The Drunken Mule." None but the young ones paid Mindy or her old guide any mind.

At the center of Pholos was what looked like a miniature version of the city's exterior. A wall of trees fifty-feet high formed a circular barricade as wide as a basketball court. Unlike the main entrance to Pholos, the entrance was marked by tall iron double doors guarded by ten armored centaurs, five on each side. Those on the left wore silver armor decorated with blue gems. The ones on the right wore gold.

Mindy was yanked backwards as a dark-haired centaur no older than she forced off her backpack. He shook the pack open, pouring all of its contents to the muddy ground. Out dropped a couple of apples, a science textbook, bread, a notebook, pencils, and an ornate golden scepter. The young centaur lifted the scepter and examined it with his gray-green eyes. It was two feet in length, engraved with stylized serpents. At the top of it was an empty socket. He looked to one of the guards. The guard nodded and the young centaur snapped the scepter in half in his hands.

"That seemed unnecessary," said Mindy.

The young centaur smiled. He reminded Mindy of Jason. Except his face was harder and his hair longer and his ears stuck out just a bit. His fur was concrete gray with black spots. "We have spies of our own," he said, the youth of his eyes betraying his frozen expression. "We know what that thing can do." The young centaur, who stood a good two feet above Mindy, took her by the shoulders, pulling her close so that her face was inches from his abs. He knelt down on his horse legs and began to pat her down. "Have to make sure you're not hiding anything else in here." Again, he smiled.

Satisfied, the centaur stood up and backed away. "She's clean!" he shouted to the others. He gestured to the old centaur that they continue.

Mindy and the old centaur entered through the double doors into a large hall, arched at the ceiling, wide trees acting as pillars that held the place up. All of the architecture was alive, a patchwork of trees, vines, branches. Lovely powder blue flowers budded here and there, giving off a pale blue light. Just enough to illuminate the area. A handful of female centaurs wearing white flowing robes from shoulder to waist encircled an altar covered in candles and sang in a strange tongue. At the far end of the hall was a raised platform atop which three ornately designed cushions sat. The one in the center was white. The one to the right was red and the left, blue.

"This way," said the old centaur and he led her into a connecting hall. This one was much narrower. Carved into the walls were symbols much like those outside of the city.

"In here." Mindy was taken through an archway into a long room which, at its center, was a banquet table covered in piles of fruits, vegetables, biscuits, and a variety of meat. Mindy recognized chicken, roasted pig, and something she was certain was gryphon leg, but much of the food she had never seen before. The table stood a foot higher than she was used to, to accommodate the centaur's physiology. Cushions were placed around it where in her world people would place chairs. At one end of the table four cushions were piled upon each other. "Have a seat." The old centaur gestured to the pile. Mindy did as she was told and noticed, across from her place at the table, there was someone else in the room: Prince Sirnius. He had been hidden by the piled-high food and the dim light.

Mindy had seen Sirnius before, months back when he, Prince Kensen, and their now-deceased father, King Kolbald, marched into the Valley of Hope. Partly to show their strength and partly to see with their own eyes that Aemon was actually gone. Kolbald was a cold, calculating creature, but a good leader by all accounts and not the sort to incite violence where a simple threat would do. Kensen was brash and loud, waving his battle axe in the air, daring anyone to take him on. And then there was Sirnius. Poised. Quiet. He didn't say a word their entire visit. He only watched. Everything. With electric blue eyes,

"Welcome to Castle Kolbald, Lady Mindy of Black Rock. Or Valley of Hope. Whichever you prefer." Even from the other side of a banquet table, Sirnius' eyes were vibrant. Centaurs were well-known for their beauty, but

Sirnius stood out from the rest. His horse half was snow white and his hair silver on the verge of blue. His cheekbones were high and his nose, long and pointed. He looked more like sculpture than a living thing. Except for those eyes. "You may leave us," said Sirnius to the old centaur and then there were only two in the banquet hall.

"To what does Pholos owe the pleasure?" Sirnius smiled, displaying an impressive set of large white teeth.

"My people are getting caught in the crosshairs of your civil war."

"The debate between my brother and me over who will take our father's place as king has been nothing but cordial, milady." Sirnius' voice was ever-calm. Like his father's.

"You and I both know that isn't true. I understand that you have laws set within the walls of Pholos that prohibit political combat, but that hasn't stopped either side from taking the fight outside. My people need the Black Forest, just like you do, to hunt and gather. It's dangerous enough as it is to travel out there. Now with a centaur war going on—"

"May I interrupt?" Sirnius picked a sliver of meat from his teeth. "There is no centaur war."

"Maybe not officially, but—"

"There is no centaur war," he said again.

"All I want is peace for—"

"Peace?" For the first time Sirnius stood up. Mindy had forgotten how tall he was. Over nine feet. Still his expression was unreadable. "No offense, Mindy, but your Black Rock conjures many feelings and emotions, but peace is not one of them. Aemon was a monster to centaur-kind."

"The people of the Valley of Hope are not Aemon." Another smile from Sirnius. "Hurt hurts. Wounds run deep. We all find our closure in different ways."

For the first time since reaching Pholos Mindy felt unsafe. She hid it as best she could and continued. "Few

53

people understand the need for closure like the ones who actually lived day and night under Aemon. Are you implying that your centaurs are targeting my people on purpose as some sort of therapy?"

Sirnius rounded the end of the table, slowly, deliberately, making his way closer and closer to Mindy with the gentle clip-clop of his hooves. "I am enjoying this dinner a great deal, milady. You are not the girl I first met those months ago with Kensen and my father. That timid thing. No. Now you are brave. Terrified, sure, but unable to back down. You are centaur." He smiled wide and a chill raced up Mindy's spine. "Not long before Aemon disappeared, he visited my father, who had always been threatened by Aemon. That monster demanded my father give him over half of our able-bodied males. My father refused, plain and simple. Aemon pretended to understand. But then he got that look in his eyes. I'm sure you've seen it. And he snapped. He said, 'Well, if I can't have any new centaurs, neither can you!' and he laughed in that awful way that cuts you. So much power, Aemon. He went on a killing spree. 'I won't stop until every last mother and daughter is gutted and dead!' My mother was the first. He ripped her in half with only a thought. Then my wife. All of Pholos was bathed in blood that day. If he hadn't grown bored with his slaughter, all of our females would have been dead. Still, of the three hundred centaurs alive today, only twenty are capable of bearing a child."

Sirnius was at Mindy's side now. She could truly appreciate how tall he actually was from this vantage point. "I'm sorry," she said. "For your loss. If there's anything I can—"

Sirnius moved impossibly fast. His fingers were around Mindy's neck before she could react. He lifted her off the ground so that she could see into his eyes. "There is something you could do, milady," Sirnius whispered directly in her ear. "You will be my queen. You will ensure the continuation of our royal line."

Mindy tried to speak, but Sirnius' tightening grip made it all but impossible. The surprise of the attack shook her focus, but her sense was soon to set in. Mindy reached into the pocket of her pants. Her hand found something smooth and round. A tingle of energy crackled at her fingertips upon contact. She drew the object, a crystalline orb glowing like the sun, from her pocket and shoved it into Sirnius' face.

The orb smashed through his teeth as if they were made of paper. Sirnius would have screamed, but the orb was burning so brightly that it stuck to his tongue, his tonsils, the roof of his mouth. Mindy dropped three feet to the floor as Sirnius reached into his mangled mouth, trying to remove the weapon lodged within.

He reared up on his hind legs, panicked, in agony. Mindy watched as the orb melted through Sirnius' flesh, sliding down his throat, past his neck, into his chest, its bright light remaining visible the whole time.

By the time the orb reached Sirnius' belly, he was dead. His huge body crashed to the floor with a thud. The light of the orb went out then, leaving Mindy on the floor of the banquet hall, dazed, relieved; her nostrils filled with the scent of beautifully prepared food and burning meat.

The old centaur entered the room carrying a pair of steaming drinks on a tray. On setting his eyes upon Sirnius' corpse, he dropped the tray and galloped out of the room. Panicked voices echoed from down the hall, followed by the clip-clop of at least a dozen hooves. Ten armored centaurs in gold or silver piled into the banquet hall, swords and bows aimed at Mindy.

"Human," snarled one of the angrier silver-clad centaurs. His eyes were small, black, and his longsword's point less than a foot away from Mindy's head. "You and all of your people will pay for this."

"STAND DOWN." The voice boomed like thunder.

The other centaurs straightened themselves, heads held high at attention. Nothing but purest silence welcomed the one who entered and it was clear why. The centaur was thick with muscle. Every inch of him covered in scars. His graying hair was matted in muddy clumps. His eyes were fire red, intensified by the bruise-black rings around them. His skin tanned from hours of training in the sun. Ornate heavy armor covered his horse and human portions, all of its beauty worn and warped and scratched away. Prince Kensen was every bit as horrifying as Mindy remembered.

The other centaurs made room as Kensen approached Mindy. He snorted as a horse would, through the large nostrils of his wide nose. He looked down at the girl. He was not as tall as his brother but his musculature made him bigger in every other respect. "Lady Mindy of Black Rock, did you murder my dear brother?"

Mindy climbed to her feet. She hid her shaking hands behind her and held Kensen's gaze. "He gave me no other choice."

An echoing trot from down the hall and another centaur entered the room. The same young spotted centaur who had broken Mindy's scepter. Kensen and the others took keen notice of him, but made no moves. The young centaur looked at Sirnius' corpse. His expression was more curious than anything. He made his way to Sirnius and examined the smoldering body. Following a moment of reflection, the young centaur mouthed something and spat on the corpse.

Prince Kensen scooped Mindy up into his mighty arm, holding her like a sack. "Follow me," he ordered, his voice like crumbling rock. He then charged out of the banquet hall with the Lady of Black Rock in his clutches.

Kensen burst from the double doors of Castle Kolbald into Pholos. "CITIZENS OF PHOLOS, ASSEMBLE BEFORE YOUR PRINCE." Gradually centaurs began emerging from their homes, dropping their tasks to stand before their leader. As the masses gathered, the armored soldiers filed out of the castle behind Kensen. Mindy squirmed, but knew there would be no escape.

When two hundred or so centaurs had arrived, Kensen declared, "Centaurs of Pholos. Brothers. Sisters. I bring news. Sirnius, my true brother and your prince, has been slain by this human I hold before you." Concerned whispers erupted from the crowd. "Lady Mindy of Black Rock, successor to Aemon the Destroyer, has come into our home and done the unthinkable." More whispers. "The civil war is over. We will once again be one nation, under one king." A few cheers went up then, shouting Kensen's name. Some of the golden-armored soldiers even made to kneel. Kensen raised his free hand then. "No. I am many things. A warrior. A judge. A keeper of order. But I am no king."

From the castle came none other than the young spotted centaur with the gray-green eyes and messy black hair. He wore on his head a crown of silver and gold decorated in jewels of red and blue.

Kensen placed his free hand on his chest. "With the power vested in me, I name Prince Nikkylos King of the Centaurs." A chorus of howls and stomping hooves, of a hundred voices chanting Nikkylos' name again and again, rose up.

"My beloved friends of Pholos," Nikkylos began. "It is with great honor and humility that I take the crown. And with great sadness over the blood shed to get me here. There is much to be done to heal in the wake of this war. But today, we celebrate!" The crowd roared with delight.

Mindy gave Kensen a swift kick in the side. The centaur prince looked to Mindy, seemingly surprised at the fact that she was still nestled in his arm. He gently lowered her to her feet. "None of this would have been possible without you," he said. "You must join in the revelries before returning to your people.

Mindy pieced together much of the story that evening. Though support for the princes Sirnius and Kensen was near evenly split, Kensen was universally better liked. He was brutal, quick to anger, but always honest. Always fair. Sirnius, on the other hand, was conniving. A master manipulator. He amassed followers through threats and blackmail. It was Sirnius' son, Nikkylos, who arranged a secret meeting with his uncle Kensen, suggesting they ally and rid themselves of the one referred to as "Aemon on Hooves." Centaur law was quite clear on murder. If any centaur killed another they would be injected with a poison that would kill them after a week of excruciating pain. Kensen would not disobey the law. Not from fear of a slow death, but of upsetting the gods who he believed were the laws' creators.

"And then you came along," said Nikkylos. He and Mindy sat near a bonfire. Both had had their fair share of Pholian mead, an especially potent drink made from the sap of the trees surrounding the city. "I notified my father of your presence. He didn't care at first, but I convinced him to try and make you his wife. That with your combined forces, he could end Kensen at last. Our spies had told us of your scepter and the powerful orb set atop it. I was delighted when they notified me that you'd removed the orb and placed it in your pocket. For safe-keeping, no doubt. I made a display of searching your bag and breaking your scepter only to pretend you had nothing else hidden. I knew my father would force his desires upon you and hoped you would retaliate. It all went according to plan. Pholos is at peace once again." Nikkylos looked over his shoulder and signaled to someone unseen.

Mindy lowered her wooden mug to her lap. "And if I had died?" she asked.

A touch of sadness, of shame, flickered with the fire's reflection in Nikkylos eyes. "Had there been a way, any safe way, we would have warned you of our plans. I promise you that. Simply tossing you into the fray unprepared was less than ideal, but we saw an opportunity and had to take it. For our people." Nikkylos placed his hand on Mindy's shoulder. "To your question, had you died it would have meant war between your people and mine. One we would surely have lost. To my uncle and me it was worth the risk. We knew well your rise to power at Black Rock. Your escape from Aemon's captivity. Your eradication of goblinkind. Betting on you was hardly a risk at all." He smiled then, big white teeth like his father.

The old gray centaur from before stepped out from around the bonfire, holding high a long object wrapped in thin paper. "My King," he said to Nikkylos as a greeting. A hundred centaurs stopped their celebrating to watch the scene unfold.

Nikkylos took the object from the old centaur and presented it to Mindy. "For you."

Mindy tore away the paper, revealing a wooden staff, carved with especially detailed symbols, vines and trees and centaurs. At the top of the staff was an orb, her orb, encircled by four metal blades.

"It belonged to my grandmother," said Nikkylos. "Fit for a queen."

"Thank you." Mindy weighed the staff in her hand. It was comfortable. Beautiful. She turned her attention to the sky. The sun was setting. Soon the stars would dot the sky. Already the moon was making itself known, a white crescent against a background of indigo and magenta. "It's getting late."

"Sleep here," said Nikkylos.
"I have to go back to the valley," she said. "I'm sure they're worried enough as it is."

"I can send a scout," he insisted. "He can let your people know you are safe."

"They'd never believe him," she responded.
Nikkylos couldn't argue that point. "Thank you for your

hospitality. I must leave now."

"Then I will walk you out."

Mindy agreed to this with a nod.

Nikkylos escorted Mindy to the great arch where the shadow and sounds of the Black Forest awaited her.

"Goodbye," she said and sauntered into the darkness. The orb took on a blue glow to combat the deepening black.

"Mindy." Nikkylos reached out to her from beneath the arch. He stood tall between two guards. "Thank you again for all you have done for my people today. Consider the centaurs of Pholos a powerful ally in your debt." The centaur king scratched the stubble of his strong chin. "One more thing." He paused. "A king is nothing without a queen at his side. And there is no one in this world more worthy than you."

Nikkylos was a magnificent creature. And she had been lonely for far too long. His pronouncement tugged at that part of her. But she had responsibilities elsewhere. And she knew next to nothing about him. Then, of course, was the fact that he had used her.

"Nikkylos—"

"Nik," he said. "Call me Nik."

Mindy shrugged. "Nik." A sigh then, "Goodbye." And she disappeared into the forest.

Hours passed and Mindy still had not returned to the Valley of Hope. The dangerous combination of a dark labyrinthian forest in the dead of night and three too many cups of Pholian mead rendered her utterly lost. Not one tree, not one stone, looked familiar. She was exhausted by the events of the day and grew more and more aware of the animal noises that sounded closer. And closer.

She spotted a cave with a mouth small enough to fit

nothing larger than a person. Her legs sore and on the verge of sleep, Mindy crawled in. The cave was much more spacious on the inside. She could stand comfortably. The light from her orb shone deeper into the cave. It went deep into the earth with no end in sight. Mindy lowered her head to the cool stone floor. She gave in to the weight of her eyelids.

A strange guttural noise from deep in the cave brought Mindy to her feet. She clutched her staff, readied for battle. The orb was already shifting from blue to fire red.

"Help me," groaned a dry voice.

"Who's there?" Mindy squinted, trying to see something, anything.

"Help me," it said again. "Please."

"I will help you if you show yourself."

From the blackness appeared a pair of eyes. They were narrow and glistened an icy blue.

Sirnius?, she thought, her near-death at his hands still fresh in her mind. Impulsively, she darted for the cave's entrance. One foot in front of the other. One foot in—

She couldn't move. Her arms and legs were frozen in place. She was immobilized. "Let…go…of me…"

A shape took form from the shadows, it was tall and long and mostly human. The man who held her captive was not Sirnius at all, but someone far worse. Gaunt and sickly, barely able to stand, covered in dirt and waste, his peasant clothing in tatters, was none other than the once lord, Aemon.

PART II

11

Six months ago.

"Where's Jack?" said Rumi Inyonara. It was more of a command than a question. She was tailed by a few peasants from the village who followed her after she told them of Jack's death. She and Aggie had come upon his corpse, with a large round hole through his torso, not ten minutes earlier.

Agalfia Tirk, or "Aggie" as most called her, sat in the grass. Her trembling arms were raised as if she were still holding Jack. Her sad green eyes peered through messy blonde strands. "He disappeared. One moment he was in my arms and the next, gone."

"Disappeared?" Rumi paused. She knew she shouldn't have left Jack with this forest-dwelling hunter-gatherer who couldn't tell a cyborg from a subnet mask. Pushing those thoughts aside, Rumi took notice of the sleek, black aircraft, her black aircraft, only a few feet from Aggie. A number of holes had been burned through it, roughly the size of the one burned through Jack. Rumi approached the vehicle and climbed inside. As she expected the storage hatch was wide open. "Damn it!"

"What is going on?" Aggie was on her feet now.

"Jack and I were 'porting a psychopath named Patrick before we took a quick stop to fight your peasant's war." Rumi kicked a charred piece of metal from her path. "Judging by how fresh these burns are my guess is Patrick escaped during the war, plucked a blaster from one of Nexis' fallen attack bots, and waited until he could get his revenge on Jack. Then he shot up my Acewing so we couldn't hunt his ass down."

"I can track this Patrick," said Aggie.

Rumi threw her hands in the air. "Ridiculous. It's

nighttime and my Acewing's heat sensors are scrapped!"

Aggie frowned and knelt down to the grass, examining every blade. She moved from one spot to the next, staying close to the ground. Satisfied, she stood up and gestured to a spot near the forest's edge. "There. That is where your Patrick stood when he fired at Jack. He then walked to the body. He remained hovering over him for a moment, then faced your metal bird. He fired four times. Here. Here. Here. And...here. Then he ran off into the trees this way." Aggie pointed to the forest. "Shall we hunt?"

"Wait." Rumi approached Aggie, pretending she wasn't impressed. "Look, I want to get that little prick, too, but what about Jack?"

"He is gone. We must honor him by killing his murderer."

"What if he's not gone?" Rumi had to look up to hold Aggie's gaze. Aggie was at least a full foot taller than she. "What if he just reset, like a computer?" Aggie tilted her head to the side, confused. "You know, like an electric...processing...box...thing? Oh, nevermind! Jack has a whole other body in another world, right? Right. So maybe if he dies here he doesn't really die, but is reset somewhere."

"Ah, Jack's actual dreamworld, perhaps!" Aggie exclaimed. "Like when Jack and I killed Aemon, but he returned completely healthy and with a giant black dragon!"

"Uh, sure. Yeah. Like that." Rumi rummaged through the aircraft's cockpit. "Hey, I'm going to see what sorts of supplies I can salvage from this thing. You go grab any sticks and stones and whatever you people fight with and come back here." Raising her voice, she added, "And everyone else, go back to the party! You've earned it! Wild Woman and I will take it from here!"

Aggie and the peasants headed back toward the village as Rumi tinkered with wires and microchips. Aggie returned a short time later with a bow, hunting knife, and a sack of supplies. Rumi attached a black and silver device with a small screen to her watch and climbed out of the aircraft. She tapped a few buttons and the screen came alive, displaying an LED arrow and the number 435.

Rumi joined Aggie and the two walked through the forest in silence until they reached the forest's edge and an almost imperceivably thin wall of fog. The lush green grass of the Black Forest was in stark contrast to the dry, maroon floor of the next world. The trees were sparse there; thin, wiry things poking out one hundred yards apart. Tiny rat-like creatures scurried around in the night, in and out of large rock formations like fingers pointing to the sky. And, for reasons no one could understand, giant bubbles filled with oversized children's toys floated above.

Rumi took a few steps into this new world. Aggie did not.

"What are you doing?" asked Rumi.
"I…" Aggie looked to the forest at her back, then to the strangeness ahead. "I have never been outside of the Black Forest."

Rumi sighed. "Look, I'd never been out of Futara until a couple of days ago. Then I got dragged into your mess and had to fight a bunch of fantasy creatures to save a mound of dirt inhabited by crooked-toothed, turnip-farming, yokels for—"
WHACK.

Aggie slapped Rumi hard across the face, nearly knocking her to the ground. "Just because we were not as privileged as you," Aggie said, "does not mean you are better than us."

Rumi wiped the fresh tears welling in her eyes, but she had already been crying before the slap. She smiled a little then, placing her hand against her reddened cheek. "You made it, Aggz."

Aggie looked down and saw she was standing across the threshold. She'd made it out of the Black Forest. It was roughly the same moment that a seven-foot rubber ducky

---

floated over her head. "Hm. So I did."

Rumi and Aggie walked from one world to another. Sure, Reverie was technically one single world these days, but each part was so starkly different than the next. From rolling plains to tribal villages to ancient labyrinths to suburbia, the pair continued forward for hours, following Rumi's device, the arrow, and its ever-decreasing number.

Night became day. And day, night again. Though neither wanted to, Aggie and Rumi decided to rest in a clearing in the eerie dead forest they'd found themselves in. Aggie started a campfire and Rumi took to stretching her sore legs.

Again, the young women sat in silence. Rumi tore into a stick of jerky Aggie had given her earlier. She toyed with a few settings on the cylindrical weapon hanging from her belt and took notice of her partner by the fire. Aggie was an untamed beauty. Wild brownish-blonde hair and intense green eyes and a prominent scar etched down the left side of her face. But now, Rumi could only see the pain in Aggie's face as she stared longingly into the flame.

"What are you thinking about?" Rumi asked.

Aggie continued to stare into the fire. "My brothers. Osip and Oleg. They are children. Before all of this madness began, Jack took them to safety, with Guillelmina. He convinced me it was for the best. Maybe it was, but they need me now. I can feel it."

"We'll find them," said Rumi. "We'll get Jack and then we'll find them." Aggie nodded, forcing a sad smile.

Rumi joined her traveling companion by the fire. She finished the last of her jerky and said, "Do you ever think about how weird this all is? This whole idea of Reverie, I mean. Millions, maybe billions, trillions, of worlds. And all of them, you and I, are just figments of someone else's imagination. That's when I hate this the most. When I start to doubt it all. What it means to be us. Like, I know I can die and I know I can change...and change things, but... In

Futara there are history books that go back thousands of years. But what if that history was just some made-up story? I can picture so clearly the night I found out my parents died. Graduating from high school. Assembling my first G-16 Solar-Lite. But what if those aren't real either? What if they're not really my memories, but something someone else made for me?"

An empty quiet passed between them.

"I miss Jack," said Aggie, practically a whisper. "And there is no point in driving yourself mad over an idea you can't control. What matters is now. The pain. The desire. Now, in this moment, we are real."

They soon slept, but not well, and not for long. At the break of the new day they walked on.

"Here we are." Rumi's words came at the end of an especially treacherous day involving lava fields and a band of living stone samurai statues with something to prove. Now Rumi and Aggie had just made their way out of an abandoned post-apocalyptic city and found themselves with a new type of challenge. Rumi pressed a button on her wrist device and a purple light flickered on.

"Begin recording," she said. "I apologize for the delay, everyone. Anyone. Designate Twelve required my assistance off-world. He was compromised, perhaps fatally, but one of his companions and I have taken it upon ourselves to find if he can be revived. Currently we're at the edge of a cliff that seems to drop forever. And looking forward there's nothing but clouds and emptiness for miles. I'd give my light blade for an Acewing right now. We've lost too many so far. And the battle has barely begun. Nexis has mobilized. Spark knows how far its disease has spread. Or Futara's fate." Rumi stopped for a moment to let her frustration fade. "To those still receiving these, stay strong. We will be together soon. We will prevail." Rumi pressed the button and the light went out.

"What was that?" asked Aggie, standing at the cliff's edge, her hair whipping in the cool wind.

"A digital journal entry," Rumi explained. "It's saved to a private server of the rebellion. It's how we've communicated with one another in secret over the years. Some damage to our audio core a few months back made it so we can't receive transmissions to our own machines anymore. There are a few hubs scattered around Futara where our people can plug in and listen. At least there were. There used to be one here, too." She gestured out into the emptiness. "You wouldn't know by looking at it but this massive hole in the earth used to be Jack's dream world. Maybe he really is gone."

"If he is gone then why does the arrow on your wrist continue to point to him?"

Rumi shrugged. "I don't know, Aggz. I don't zagging know."

The young women stared out into the distance.

"Wait." Aggie squinted, lifting her hand over her eyes to block the sun. "Do you see that?"

"See what?" Rumi tried her best but could see nothing beyond the whiteness and the pale blue of the sky above it.

"There." Aggie moved behind Rumi and pointed outward, gently positioning the other's body to find the proper angle.

Rumi noticed something then. A trick of the eye she thought, at first. But then. A speck. A single black speck floating out in the nothingness. "What is that?" She checked her wrist and the arrow seemed to be pointing at it. "That thing has to be, what? A mile away? Maybe, more I—" A hard squeeze to the shoulder shut Rumi up.

"Listen," said Aggie.

"Are you some kind of superhero or—" Rumi heard it, too. A low rumble growing louder. Coming from behind them. She listened harder. Explosions. Screams. Other sounds more familiar. Almost mechanical.

Through the cracked and broken buildings of the

city, it came. A flood of muddy water racing toward them, carrying with it sticks and scraps and creatures and robots and all kinds of things. Rumi and Aggie weighed their options. Neither had the sort of tools to hold off an unstoppable force of nature. And the water would get to them way before they'd be able to make it to higher ground. No. Despite their combined cunning, strength and skill, there was nothing Rumi Inyonara and Agalfia Tirk could do to stop the inevitable.

So the water took them. And both went over the cliff's edge, into the abyss.

12

"She's WHAT?" Max spit milk onto his half-eaten burger.

"Overreact much?" Jamal threw a handful of napkins at him.

"Thanks, dude."

Dion stood a few feet away, eavesdropping on their conversation.

"She's blind," Jason said once again. The gang had just sat down for lunch, excited to learn the 'huge news' Jason promised them via text the night before. "She just came into my house acting crazier than usual, going on and on about a bald voodoo queen putting a curse on her."

"The bald lady from the funeral?" asked Jamal.

"I guess?" Jason tossed a fry into his mouth. "I thought Karen was overreacting, like maybe she drank herself blind, or took too many 'feel good' pills, or something, then she took off her sunglasses. Her eyes were black, guys. Like the things were just completely, utterly—"

Everyone was so engaged in Jason's story, they didn't even notice Dion make his way to the table. He took a seat between Max and Anne. As always, he wore his big aviator glasses. "What is the gossip?"

"Uh…" Jason looked down at his food, avoiding eye contact with Dion.

"Claire's mom is blind!" blurted Max.

Jamal replied with a sharp elbow to Max's ribs. "Shut up, dude."

"Blind, you say? This is bad news. Very bad." An instant later, Dion was smiling wide. "Hi, Jason," he sang.

"Oh." Jason locked his attention on his tray. "Hi. Hey, Dion."

"You must find your food very interesting, Jason Baker, the way you look at it like that."

Jason's cheeks reddened. He rose abruptly from his seat. "Bathroom. I-I have to go to the bathroom." And away he went.

Dion threw his hands in the air. "As with the heart, all men are slaves to their bladder. No?" He laughed to himself.

"Why are you here?" asked Jamal, and not too nicely. "And why do you talk like you're in some terrible Drama Club skit?"

"To your first query, I enjoy the company." Again, Dion smiled. "And to the second, I learned to speak English from the American black-and-white soap operas my mother would inflict upon us in my old country."

Jamal leaned forward. "And what country is that?"

"Lebanon, most recently, but I have called much of the Mediterranean home."

"Why do I have a hard time believing you?"

Dion shrugged. "Because society has turned us all to sceptics and pariahs. But I, sir, am nothing if not trustworthy."

For a few seconds everyone was quiet. Jamal then sighed and said, "If you're so trustworthy, then tell us who the bald lady was at the funeral."

"Who? Ollie?" Dion seemed to light up. "She is beautiful, no? I tell her every year, 'Ollie, you should be in Milan, Paris, America's Next Top Model,' but no. All she wants to do is sit in her house and work on her little crafts. It's infuriating! Cheeks like hers need to be on the runway."

Jamal folded his arms. "Sorry I asked."

Dion's grin dropped into a frown. He swiped a carrot stick from Anne's tray and took a pronounced bite. Of no one in particular he asked, "How's Claire?"

Jamal bristled. "None of your business."

Without skipping a beat, he turned to Anne. "Sweet Anne, how is our friend Claire?"

Anne said, "She's fine. Getting b—"

Jamal reached across Max and took Dion by his sleeve. "I said it's none of your business."

"Jamal!" Anne placed her hand on Jamal's hand until he let go of Dion. "What are you doing?"

"I..." Jamal looked tired all of a sudden. "I dunno, I just—I don't trust him."

"The fault is all mine," said Dion with yet another smile. He rose from his chair. "I sometimes have this effect on people. My dashing good looks are to blame, I suppose." He backed away from the table. "I will leave. I will leave. And Anne, you will tell Jack I said hello, no?" With those words he smirked and dashed out of the cafeteria.

Dion walked speedily down one hall to the next until he'd reached the restroom. The interior looked as empty and smelled as stale as ever. He lowered his thin body so that he could see below the stalls. A familiar pair of legs poked out from one of them.

"Jason Baker!" Dion sang.

"Go away," said Jason.

"Love. She is a wily thing. Unexpected. Terrifying. Please, open the door. You are only hiding. Nothing more."

A pause, then, "Go away," once again.

"We must not fear what we are driven to become. We must embrace it. You of all people must know this, Lucid."

"Please."

Dion smacked his lips. "Today is a day for rejection, it seems. All right. Fine." He leaned close to the stall's door. "I am leaving, Jason Baker. Leaving you to your beauty, to your confusion, to your primal need, all alone, surrounded by rust and the stench of aged fecal matter." Dion stepped away from the door, propping himself against an old sink that could just barely handle his weight. "I will say this one thing to you: I know how to fix Karen Ashford."

Quiet first. Then a soft click. The stall's door opened just enough for Dion to see Jason's face.

"How?" Jason asked.

"It's quite simple." Dion removed his glasses. His eyes glistened. They were dark. Darker than brown, almost. Nearly black until the fluorescent light would hit them just the right way and their redness would show. "I will tell you all I know of Karen Ashford's condition—if you join me on a date."

13

"I said. Let. Me. Go." Mindy spoke the words through tight lips, her entire body held frozen in running position in the darkness of the cave. The small entrance was so close, but distance meant nothing without the ability to move.

"I'm not holding you," said Aemon. He took a cautious step toward Mindy.

"Yes. You are." Mindy's eyes darted to the orb atop her new staff. It glowed moonlight blue.

Aemon stared at his shaking hands. His indigo skin nearly disappeared in the shadows. He looked to Mindy and said, "Then I release you."

Mindy lurched forward and fell to the cold, hard cave floor. She was quick to crawl to her feet and climb out of the cave, into the Black Forest at night.

"Wait! Wait, don't leave me!" Aemon cried as he pulled himself out onto the grass. "Please, I need you to help—"

Mindy spun around and aimed her staff at Aemon. "Burn, Aemon!"

Nothing happened.

Confusion mingled with the desperation on Aemon's face. Mindy grumbled to herself. *Of course the orb wouldn't work on the person who gave it to me*, she thought.

"Aemon?" asked the indigo-skinned creature. His long, messy hair gleamed like silver under the light of the stars and moon. "Is that my name?" He was on his hands and knees.

"I'm not afraid of you!" Mindy shouted, so loud that she secretly hoped her scouts or a centaur might hear her. "I AM NOT AFRAID!"

"And you needn't be." Aemon stood up then. He started to approach her.

"No." Mindy kept her staff aimed at him. "NO. Do not take one more step."

"Yes. All right. Fine. Whatever you say." Aemon dropped to his knees. He lowered his head and reached his arms to the ground. "Is this better? Is this okay? Please, ma'am, I will not hurt you. I do not know who I am. I do not know how I came to be in this forest. Please." Aemon gasped for air.

Mindy's voice lowered. "You're lying."

"I'm not lying, ma'am. I am not. You must believe me. The first memory I have is in this forest. Suddenly I am in this forest, standing before an old man. He is short, this man, and dressed all in blue. A moustache on his wrinkled face. Darkness in his eyes. Sadness, too. Much, much sadness. In my memory he was close to me. So close. This seems strange to say but I remember him stepping out of my body. The old man looked at me with those sad eyes and he says, 'I am leaving you. I have done terrible things and I must go now and pay for my sins.' He looks at me. Harder now. He says, 'You, too, must pay. You must earn their forgiveness.' He disappeared then. Just...gone. And I am alone. And confused. Creatures tried to kill me, but I hid in this cave. For days, maybe. Hungry. Scared. And then you came. You came and you called me 'Aemon.' But why?"

Mindy examined the creature practically lying face down on the grass in rags, so far from the well-dressed, sadistic monster she had known. She looked for the tell in his act. The subtle slip in this obvious ruse. But why? What did he possibly have to gain from it?

Jason had told her that he and the Claire of Reverie broke into janitor Karl's house and made him stop his evil ways. Could Karl be the old man this Aemon is referring to? wondered Mindy. Could a Lucid just shed his dream-skin like that? If he could, then maybe that would explain why Aemon couldn't remember who he was. Without Karl wearing him, he had none of his memories.

Aemon kept his face down. His whole body was

shaking. Mindy tossed an apple toward him, lowered the staff. "You're not going to hurt me?" she asked. Aemon shook his head like an apologetic child. "Then get up. Eat."

Aemon scrambled to his feet. He took a giant bite of the apple, his fangs digging deep into the juicy treat. With tears in his eyes, he said, "Thank you, ma'am. Thank you so very much."

"Mindy," she said, fully uncertain of what to do next. "My name is Lady Mindy of Black Rock."

———

At first there was darkness. A deep, impenetrable black that swallowed hope and light alike.

And then Aggie opened her eyes. There was darkness still, but less now.

She didn't know how long she'd been held prisoner. Weeks, maybe months. The last thing she remembered was the frigid rush of water and falling off the edge of the cliff. Her next memory was waking up here. Here, where she was chained to the wall in an old jail cell. The room must have been a police station once, but the floor and walls were cracked, the lights broken, the metal bars bent out of shape. Sometimes she'd feel a roach crawling across her body. Other times, a rat scurrying over her toes. Twice a day a rusted robot humanoid would come by, eyes like red headlights, and give her water and feed her bread and strange meats. Sometimes fruits and vegetables.

Rumi was chained beside her.

Aggie knew from the screams that there were others imprisoned down the hall.

They spoke much more to one another in the beginning, Rumi and Aggie. They cursed and shouted at the zombie-like robots, too, refusing to eat their food until they could no longer take the pangs of starvation. They plotted elaborate escapes that never panned out. They had a few cries, some laughs. Now they were quiet mostly, except for the grunts and groans that emerged when they exercised. Arms, legs, stomach, chest, whatever they could, however they could.

A light flashed on. One of a pair of fluorescents Aggie had assumed was dead. From down the hall the sound of heavy footsteps echoed. There was a clang of metal with each step. Something—or things—dragging gently behind. Aggie saw its elongated shadow against the wall before she saw the thing itself.

The thing that stepped into view was like nothing Aggie had encountered before. To call it human would be a mistake. To call it robot seemed wrong as well. It was both. Or neither. The thing appeared as much skin and bones as it did wires and metal. This wasn't like the patchwork cyborgs Rumi had told Aggie about, a human leg here and a robot arm there, but the perfect synthesis of man and machine. Its build overall was masculine. The only clothing he wore was a pair of ripped black jeans and an open black vest, which offered ample view of his gray/tan human/robot skin. A sleek black helmet covered the top half of his head, including his eyes. And from the helmet, eight thick wires hung down his back and to the floor.

"Come, ladies," he said, his voice like an old recording on cassette tape. "It is time to join the Nexis."

14

Jason Baker woke up in the Valley of Hope. The sun was setting and creatures were just going about their lives. A few waved to Jason as he walked past the cottages and tents and huts—many he'd helped to build—on his way to Mindy.

"Last I saw she was out in the cabbage patch!" shouted a grizzled old man sitting on a tree stump. It was clear from his thick Russian accent that he was a native of the valley.

"Thanks, Efim!" Jason said as he changed direction, making his way to the communal garden.

The garden was expansive, taking up over a third of the Valley of Hope, opposite the Black Rock. It had nearly tripled in size since the valley started taking in refugees months earlier. The ever-temperate weather was ideal for growing of hundreds of types of fruits and vegetables, some familiar to Jason, others unique to Reverie.

Beyond a crop of standing vines bearing blue striped fruit, was the cabbage patch. In the center of the patch was Mindy, barefoot with her pants rolled up, pulling a cabbage from the earth and dropping it into a sack.

"Hey," said Jason.

A warm smile formed on Mindy's face. She wiped the sweat from her brow and approached Jason. "Hey, you. I was worried when you didn't stop by last night."

They hugged.

Jason frowned. "Yeah, sorry about that. I had a lot on my mind, I guess. I couldn't focus enough to get here. Hope I didn't miss anything good." He could tell by Mindy's expression that he had.

Mindy described her experience with the centaur princes. Getting drunk. Getting lost in the forest. Stumbling upon a very different Aemon.

"What?" Jason placed his hands on his head. "Man, I picked the worst night to not be here for you. You could have been hurt!"

"I'm fine." Mindy took a seat on a patch of grass bordering the cabbage patch.

Jason joined her. "So Aemon has, like, amnesia?"

"Something like that. Weirder than that, but something like that."

"And where is he now? Just roaming the forest?"

Mindy shook her head, her expression was that of a guilty child.

"Mindy." Jason leaned in close to her. She tightened her lips. Worry was written in her expression. "Okay. Complete this sentence. "After I gave Aemon the apple I…""

"I snuck him into Black Rock."

"Mindy!"

"Jason!"

"Why would you do that?!"

"I don't know!" Mindy climbed to her feet. She looked around to make sure no one else was within earshot. "I mean, I do know. You didn't see him, Jason. He was scared and helpless. If I didn't bring him here he'd have been killed by any of the millions of monsters in the forest." She sighed. "I know this seems crazy, with my history and all, but I know the look of evil, Jason. I know it. And whatever Aemon was, this guy is not him. I told him that he could have all of Black Rock to himself, but can never come out into the valley."

"Well, that was smart."

"I'm not stupid."

"Of course not!" Jason stood up, dusting the dirt from his jeans. "You're the most not stupid person I know. It's just that these people treat you like their leader and if they find out you're harboring their former evil dictator, I don't know what they'll do."

"I know, Jason. I know. I'll figure something out."

Jason cupped Mindy's face in his hands, looked deeply into her eyes. "I know you will. You always do. It's just that you've done so much and come so far. I don't want to see all of that fall apart because of one guy. I can't always be here to protect you." Sensing the irritation bubbling in her, he added, "Not that you need my protection."

Mindy pulled away from Jason. She wrapped her arms around herself as if warming from the cold. Her eyes drifted to the dusky sky. "Fifty percent of the valley's inhabitants aren't even natives. And the number grows every day. They have no idea who Aemon is. I can make this work." Jason was silent. She allowed the quiet to linger before saying, "What's been going on with you? What's all this emotional turmoil keeping you from me last night?"

"Um…" Jason took in a deep gulp of air. "It's complicated."

Mindy raised an eyebrow and smirked. "More complicated than my story? I doubt it."

Jason couldn't argue with that. "I'm, um, going on a date."

Mindy's eyes lit up at that. It was as if all her worries had been magically lifted and she was allowed to be a sixteen year-old girl again. "A date! Jason Baker! I didn't even know you liked anyone! Give me deets! Tell me everything. Who is she? And I swear to God if you say it's Claire Ashford I will explode you with my staff."

"No, no! It's not Claire."

"Thank God. What's her name then?" Mindy's face was inches from his.

"It's, uh, it's Dion."

"Dion. Dion." Mindy stepped back, folded her arms, pondered for a second. "Do I know Dion?"

"No. I'm pretty sure you don't."

"Okay, well." Mindy gestured for Jason to continue. "Well, what?"

"How'd you meet her? Is she a transfer? Was she at

that dance competition in Stanley? Ugh, I hate not knowing every little thing that's going on in your life anymore!"

"Dion," he began, letting the name linger before continuing, "is a new student." He spoke slowly. "We met at lunch last week. And she's a he."

It took Mindy a moment to understand, but when she did she let out a very girlish squeal, "Oh my god! Oh my god! Oh my GOD! Finally! Jason Baker, this is the best news I've ever heard ever. Like, ever! Is he cute?"

Jason, who looked like a lost child, nodded. "Very."

Mindy squealed again. "I have been waiting for this day ever since you kissed Steve Purcell in third grade! Where is he from? What does he do? Who asked who?"

"I don't know, I don't know, and he sort of asked me." Mindy was preparing a third squeal, but Jason interrupted. "He's this weirdly confident guy with a vaguely European accent who won't leave me alone and the only reason I'm going on this stupid date with him is because his friend voodoo-blinded Karen and this date is the only way he'll tell me how to fix her because NOTHING, Mindy, ever comes easily."

Mindy faced Jason. She placed her hands on his waist. "It sure doesn't," she said through a half-smile. "That's kind of the motto of the Jason and Mindy story. Followed directly by 'and yet, they keep kicking ass!'" The two laughed at that.

"Now, this Dion guy. Do you think he's a good person?"

Jason thought about it. "There's so much about him I don't know. He doesn't talk or act like other guys our age, but I think that's part of why I like him so much. I honestly can't say if he's a good person or not. There's just something about him."

"So you're attracted to him?"

Jason threw his head back. "Mindy, I can't stop thinking about him!"

Mindy let Jason go. "Then you boys have fun." She hoisted the cabbage-filled sack over her shoulder. "This has been our little secret for so long. I'm just so happy you're comfortable enough to let yourself be you, you know?"

Jason hugged Mindy from behind, wrapping his arms tightly around her. "I love you so much, Mindy Sparks."

She giggled. "I love you so much, too, Jason Baker."

"We're gonna be okay," he said.

"Of course we are," Mindy agreed. "Are you not familiar with our motto?"

15

A pair of grotesque cyborgs removed Rumi and Aggie from their chains only to bind them anew in shackles around their wrists and ankles. The chains offered just enough give for them to take small steps.

"You will follow," said one of the cyborgs through his scarred human mouth. The rest of his face was covered in poorly-healed gashes. He looked like an cubist painting. One eye a little too low. His nose a little too far to the left. And the back of his head was a metal plate.

The second cyborg, this one female and just as horrific, smacked Aggie in the face with her over-sized rusted metal hand. Aggie faltered, but did not fall. "Move," the cyborg said. Her mouth was machine and her voice was monotone. "Or we will break you."

Aggie and Rumi shuffled down the long hallway of the old police station, a cyborg leading and a cyborg at their backs. They were taken down a set of stairs into what could only be described as the bowels of a great machine; a narrow snake-like tunnel of steel tiles lined in flashing lights and thick rubber-coated wires.

From the moment they entered the tunnel, it echoed with the none-too-distant sounds of great machines cranking and churning. The further they walked, the more a cloud of distorted and varied voices of all pitches and distortions arose. Every few seconds a scream would break through the noise; one so pained that it caused their hearts to skip.

The sounds became louder, the voices more distinct, until at last the end of the tunnel was in sight. They had been walking long enough for their legs to be sore and cramped. Neither young woman could have prepared for the scene before them.

The space was the size of an indoor stadium. At close inspection, the area might have been a functioning arena once. Tens of thousands of purple seats were sloped under a massive white dome, facing a raised stage in the center. It was hard, though, to imagine it had ever housed boxing matches or music concerts. Most of the seats were intact, but some were cleared out or thrown to the side to make space for massive iron cylinders, each one fifty feet tall, that lined the twenty or so staircases leading to the stage. Each cylinder was about twelve feet wide and had a control panel full of blinking lights and gauges near its base. A tower of red steam hissed from the top of each cylinder, making the arena uncomfortably hot and humid and giving everything a rusted hue.

There were hundreds of cyborgs, ranging in size, shape, and overall hideousness. The majority were human-robot, but some were robot combined with animal or monster or even other older robots. Some stood watch. Others sat in small groups, talking. Many carried (or dragged) large black bags. The contents of the bags weren't clear, but whatever was inside had no issue with kicking, writhing, or crying for help.

The entrance Rumi, Aggie, and their guards came through placed them in the middle of a set of broken bleachers, in the middle of one of the many staircases leading to the stage.

"THERE THEY ARE!" a distorted voice exclaimed. The sound was deafening, blasting from the arena's speakers. A beam of white light shone on Rumi and Aggie through the red mist. The young women shuddered at the intensity of the spotlight. When their vision returned, they realized all eyes (and optical tech) were on them. "COME TO ME, MY LOVELY LADIES!"

Rumi spotted the source of the voice. It was the man who had approached them at the jail cell. How he had returned to this point so quickly after leaving them she could not say. He was fast. She made note of that. The thing that was not quite robot/not quite man stood, arms open wide, in the center of the stage. He was accompanied by two of the larger cyborgs. To his right was a robot-yeti. Its long white fur was in deep contrast to the black machinery that made up its left arm and some of its chest. To his right, a robot-tyrannosaurus rex. Half of its head and the right side of its chest were formed of scales and the rest, bulky tail included, was robot. This one seemed sturdier than the yeti, as if especially built to take and receive immense damage.

Rumi took note of this as well.

Behind the not quite robot/human was a complicated structure of cubes and wires. Even from a distance, the two could hear its engine roar and its innards buzz in sharp spurts like a giant bug zapper.

Rumi and Aggie were taken down the stadium stairs, then up a few more onto the stage. They squinted under the harsh light.

A hard, sharp strike to the back and both fell to their knees. "You must kneel before the Nexis," said the female.

"That will be all, Sharon," the not quite robot/human said, his voice not so deafening up close. Sharon nodded and she and the male cyborg marched off the stage.

The not quite robot/human paced back and forth, a devious grin on his not quite lips. He was surprisingly expressive despite the helmet that covered the top half of his face. He turned to face Rumi and Aggie, both of whom looked at him with unadulterated loathing. "I'm sure the two of you have questions," he began. "'Who is this guy speaking to me?' for example. Or 'Where am I?' 'Why am I here?' 'Am I going to die?' These are all good questions. Great questions. Questions that have plagued mankind for millenniums. Millenia?" He paused. A blue light blinked once from within his helmet. "Millennia. Of course. For millennia. But I'll answer them now. I am The Nexis. Not 'Nexis.' The Nexis. The definite article really drives it home. Anyway, I'm The Nexis, ruler of all you see. And all you will see. Forever. The end." He laughed at himself. "You're at the former

SpendCorp Arena located in scenic Futara." To Rumi he added, "But you already knew that, didn't you, sweetie?" Rumi offered no reaction. "I must say the arena's days of mindless entertainment are over. It now serves a higher purpose. It functions as my largest conversion camp! And just look around at all the satisfied customers." Just then someone howled in pain. "Great timing on that scream," he said to no one specific. "As for why you're here: to be converted, obviously."

"You will never turn me into one of your monsters!" Aggie shouted.

"Hey." The Nexis raised a hand, feigning seriousness. "'Monster' is a derogatory word, young lady. We prefer," again, the light went on and off in his helmet. "'mechanically enlightened.' Mechlightened? Ah, we'll work on it. And, to be completely real with you, you will most definitely be enlight-meched today. My beautiful, angry, girls, you will become immortal soldiers of the Nexis. Not only will you not die, you will finally know what it means to be truly alive." To the masses, he shouted, "Isn't that right, my pretties?"

At once they all shouted, "NEXIS! NEXIS! NEXIS!" in such a way that seemed fitting in a former entertainment complex.

The Nexis clapped his hands together. "Ah, music to my aural processors. Now who's ready for a show?" A cheer went up from the crowd. To the robot-yeti he said, "Jerry, hook me up!" The giant beast lifted the ends of the wires that hung from the Nexis' helmet and plugged them into the machine behind him. It took some effort with Jerry's thick yeti and robot fingers. "Thank you, sir! Honestly, anyone who says an abominable snowman can't be a valued contributor to civilized society is a bigot and should be immediately—WHOA, MAN!" An electrifying sensation coursed through the Nexis' body, causing him to seize up then drop into a trance-like state of relaxation. "Oh, man. Plugging in is like a thousand times better than sex. And maybe ten times better than cyborg sex. No offense, Sharon." A low rumble of a roar emerged from the robot-dinosaur cyborg. "Sorry, Spencer." As an aside to Rumi and Aggie, he added, "Spencer hates dirty jokes."

The Nexis pointed to Aggie. "You're first. I never could resist a blonde and girl, you are fine." He approached Rumi, then the playfulness seeped from his demeanor. A red light blinked on then off under his helmet. "Rumi Inyonara," he said, his voice no longer broadcast through the speakers. "This is my lucky day indeed. I had every intention of searching for you. I'd assembled a team of scouts and everything. I wanted to see you in person so that I could thank you for this." He gestured all around. "You should be proud of what you made possible." He let his words sink in. "On the other hand, you have been a thorn in The Nexis' side for too long. Rest assured that many of your resistance have been…enlightened. Some are here right now. We found your servers. Converted them. There is no resistance. Only the Nexis. And I will make sure your transformation is especially…unpleasant."

Rumi quashed the urge to scream, to cry, to ask questions. Allowing her emotions to take control would make impossible an already highly improbable escape. Ever since setting foot in the arena she had been taking in every inch, examining it from every angle. Just as she had been taught. Rumi noticed Aggie taking in the surroundings, as well. A true hunter, Aggie, though this world was very unfamiliar to her. Still, Aggie could be an asset.

The Nexis lifted Aggie up by the chain at her wrists. "I hope you're as excited as I am!" Aggie spat on Nexis' visor. "Rude. Jerry, glove me!" The yeti cyborg produced a sleek, black glove from his robot body and attached it to the Nexis' hand. It was oversized, parts metal and leather. The fingers were affixed with a dozen or so tiny silver needles. "Fits…like a glove." The Nexis giggled. "Ah, I kill me." The red light blinked under his visor and a low screech signaled the speakers powering up. "My most esteemed metallic guests and various prisoners, are you ready to watch the transformation of the century?" Wild cheers burst from the crowd. "Awesome. Hold on to your gears, kids, because the nerd-borgs in the basement have been working hard on my new toy: A tactile enlightenment machine. What does it do? Well, imagine a world where we no longer need to use these clunky tanks to enlighten our fellow man, woman, and…thing. Imagine a world where, with a mere touch, we can convince someone to join the Nexis. This pile of wires behind me is the prototype. Let's see how we do!"

Another joyful roar went up in the arena. But amidst the tremendous noise there was something else. "Help!" A single word amongst thousands. A word that had been uttered at least a hundred times from a hundred directions since they first arrived in the arena. But this time was different. The voice that cried "Help!" was familiar.

A human cyborg was carrying a black bag toward one of the enlightenment chambers. A bag large enough to house two small bodies.

"My brothers?" Aggie muttered, a whisper. "My— ARGHH!" Aggie shouted as the Nexis' grip tightened around her hand. It felt like a thousand needle pricks and a paralyzing pulse coursing through her forearm.

"There is no use fighting it!" the Nexis said, his smile revealing a set of silvery-white teeth. "Soon you will be part of th—"

Aggie jumped as high as she could and landed a kick to the Nexis' chest that sent him crashing into the enlightenment machine. She fell hard to the stage, unable to do much else while chained at the ankles and wrists. "Osip! Oleg! I am coming for you!"

A blade of white light emerged from the robot hand of the yeti cyborg, Jerry. Just as Rumi had hoped. She'd been building lightblades since she was nine and knew the tech that would produce one when she saw it. As Jerry made his way toward Aggie, Rumi rolled between them, lifting her legs so that the yeti cyborg's blade passed through the chains that bound her ankles, then bringing her legs in so that the monster passed over her safely.

Taken too greatly by his momentum, Jerry had no choice but to do what he had intended and moved to stab Aggie. Aggie rolled out of the way as the blade embedded itself in the stage. Wasting not a second, she moved her hands on either side of the blade, breaking the chain between them. She spun her body around and freed her feet as well. One backward roll and Aggie was standing upright.

The Nexis scrambled to his feet. A crack stretched across his visor. "KILL THEM! KILL THEM! EVERYBODY KILL THEM!"

16

A few days ago, in a cramped dorm room, Vic was up until three in the morning scratching away at yet another Reverie hypothesis. Ever since he realized he was a doppelganger dreamed by Victor Soto all those months ago, Vic's singular mission was to discover the secrets of Reverie, of Cosmos, so that he might never have to return to the chaos of that awful dream world. He much preferred Earth with its adherence to the rules of nature, the laws of man.

Fortunately, being from Reverie, Vic had special talents. Aside from being good at almost every sport, he knew the answer to any question presented to him. It's how he got into Harvard University at the age of seventeen.

"Come to bed," said Satya Shirazi, his girlfriend of three months. She was a journalist major and Vic was most attracted to her ability to ask all the best questions.

"Soon," Vic snapped. "I'm about to make a breakthrough. I know it."

Satya rolled her eyes and eventually drifted to sleep as Vic continued to scan the maps and articles stapled to a corkboard wall.

While Vic didn't need sleep (yet another Reverie power), he climbed into the small bed with his notebook. He cursed the fact that his ability to know everything was limited to his current realm. He had gleaned enough to gather rudimentary facts about Reverie, and even a few interesting theories about the spirit realm, but he was going to need some hard facts if he was ever going to ensure Victor, his dumber, less-capable half, would accidentally send him back there like he had accidentally brought him to Earth in the first place.

The next morning, Satya woke up and rolled over, ready to scold Vic for ignoring her and not fulfilling her natural, human needs. But her well-rehearsed speech was superseded by her heart-wrenching scream.

Vic wasn't in bed beside her. Well, not in the state she had planned for. On the bed was Vic's notebook and chewed-up pen. The clothing he had worn were there as well. But instead of the impressive body of her neglectful boyfriend, what filled Vic's clothing was a gray, mummified body gradually crumbling to dust before her eyes.

17

A little over a day had passed since Claire and Victor set out for Black Rock. In that time they joined up with a number of creatures doing the same. There were fourteen now. All had horror stories of a great flood and a robot takeover. They learned that the robots came in two waves: one before the flood and one after. The first wave was made up mostly of hulking machines on two legs forcing anyone in their path to "submit or die." Regardless of their response, most were usually destroyed. The second wave consisted of half-creature half-robot cyborgs that killed when they had to, but mostly raided towns and kidnapped anyone they could, throwing the bodies into giant hovering freight trucks.

"I dunno what was worse," said one of the travelers, an older man with white hair and a pot belly. "The first o' them robots killed my wife. Lost my brother in the flood. And when the robots came back, they took my daughter." Most of them had stories like this.

The group reached the end of the path, a path that had most recently taken them through an ethereal forest lined in a thin carpet of mist; a place Claire and Victor had not seen since their first day in Reverie.

"Well, what now?" asked a woman in a dirty burgundy gown. Renaissance era, from the look of it. "Tell me I'm not to believe this journey has been set forth in vain. I may faint from the melancholy of it all."

"Let's not faint just yet, Lady Grey," said the old man. "Maybe the path's leading us where it was meant to. We know from when we was uphill, the big black mountain is this way."

Lady Grey shrugged. "Lead on then. What is one more blister in this cavalcade of despair?"

They stepped from the path into a forest that looked and felt more like the forests of Earth. Even with the little fairies fluttering about. "Oh, now isn't that just darling?" commented Lady Grey.

Suddenly, from the canopy a griffin pounced, landing on the forest floor on its big paws. It was a terrifying thing with the head and wings of an eagle and the body and tail of a lion. It was easily the size of a rhinoceros. The beast let out a raptor's screech. Lady Grey fainted.

"Down, boy!" A creature approached the griffin. He looked mostly human despite his smaller frame and elongated features. His hair was brown and shaved close along the sides. The hair at the top of his head was dyed platinum blond and pulled back into a long ponytail. Pointed ears easily stuck out a foot from either side of his head. He placed his hands on the griffin's head. "What are you trying to do, scare away every refugee that comes this way?" To Claire, Victor, and the rest he said, "Sorry about that, guys. I've trained him to be a great alarm system, but haven't quite hammered out the terrifying parts. I'm Zen, by the way." The griffin licked the side of his face with a long purple tongue. "And this is Milo. Welcome to the Valley of Hope."

"Valley of Hope?" The old man looked confused. "Thought we was headed to the Black Rock."

"Ah." Zen nodded. "You've come to the right place then. The Valley of Hope sits at the base of the Black Rock. We're in the process of updating a lot of the names of things around here to be more uplifting. Helps with morale." The old man seemed satisfied with the answer. "Someone help me load that fallen woman onto Milo and we'll be on our way."

"You're Zen," Victor said, awestruck.
Zen smiled, unsure of the other. "Uh, yep, that's me. Do I know you?"

"Uh, no. No! I just—" Victor looked around. "Hey, Pet, get over here!" The big eared Grobi scampered up from the back of the group and climbed onto Victor's shoulder.

"My goodness." Zen's large green eyes opened

wider. "Is that a Waypoint Grobi?" Victor nodded. "How? How did you? What?"

"You were the main character of one of my favorite video games growing up!" Victor was practically gushing. "I got Pet while I was traveling in Reverie. In your world, I guess. Or, like, a world someone dreamed of yours."

Zen looked confused. "I'm not quite sure what you are saying, human. Or what a 'video game' is. What I do know is that Waypoint Grobis are a rare breed and only a pure soul can attract one. I am glad to have a fellow hero among us."

Victor blushed, unable to hold back his giant smile. "I-I'm Victor! And this is Claire! And this is our baby, Anza."

"I see. Well, Victor. I hope your child and your mate know how lucky they are to have one as noble as you." Victor looked to Claire, who offered a small smile. Anza was asleep in her arms. "Okay then, everyone. Someone please help me load the woman in the dress onto Milo and let's go!"

Victor, Zen, and a couple of others gently hoisted Lady Grey onto Milo's back. Zen then led them through the woods. "You guys are probably the twentieth or thirtieth group I've led to the Valley. I've heard almost every question you can imagine, so I'll go ahead and answer the most common ones. The Valley of Hope is a place of peace and healing. If anyone's the sort to pick fights or cause trouble, they'll be put in front of the tribunal. They'll be judged by me and four others and we'll select a punishment. Nothing brutal. We're not barbarians. But we will kick you out of the valley if you're proven an ill fit. Anyway, that's a gloomy way to start, huh? Haha. In all honesty, there's rarely any trouble and everyone's great. We are all given duties based on our skills and interests. Hunting, gardening, the arts – things like that. There's no discrimination based on species, gender, skin tone, sexual orientation, or philosophy as long as it's based on the tenet of freedom of expression, joy, or love.

You will be given a modest home. We have a resident Lucid on staff who handles a lot of the big construction."

"Is it Jack?" Victor asked.

Zen shook his head. "Jack? No. I've heard this name before, yes. He died, I think. In the war." Before Victor could truly ingest those words, Zen said, "Our Lucid is a young man by the name of Jason Baker."

"Jason Baker?" Victor turned to Claire.

"You know him?" Zen asked.

"Uh." Victor fumbled for the words. "Is he my age? Black hair? Blue eyes?"

Zen nodded. "Oh, you do know him! Yes. That's our Jason. A lovely human. He visits us nearly every evening when he sleeps in, what was it called, Addley! That's it."

"Jason Baker is here?" Claire's interest had been piqued.

"Yes," Zen laughed, amused by the two teens. "He comes to visit his best friend. A valued, and wonderful, member of our tribunal. Ah, I cannot say enough good things about her. She is a founding member of our tribunal. Brought to Reverie against her will some months ago, can you believe it? And Reverie is better for it. I know I am."

"Who?" Claire asked. "Who else is here from Addley?"

Zen grinned. It was he who was red in the cheeks now. "Why, the fairest woman of them all. Mindy Sparks. Lady of Black Rock, or Hope Mountain. The name is still under construction."

18

Jason straightened his bowtie for the tenth or eleventh time before entering the restaurant. It was a new place across the street from the mall. Easily the fanciest restaurant in Addley, La Savour was known for its modern take on French cuisine, months-long wait list, and astronomically high prices. Though, as his sweaty palms and rapid heartbeat constantly reminded him, La Savour would soon become the place where Jason Baker went on his first date with a boy.

Jason entered the dimly lit restaurant. It smelled of flowers. A thin man with a narrow mustache stood stoically behind the host station. He wore a fitted black suit and surveyed Jason's wardrobe. The gray blazer and navy blue dress pants. The red and white plaid dress shirt and navy bowtie. One final glance at Jason's appearance and the host was appeased. "How may I help you, sir?"

"There should, uh, be a reservation. For eight o' clock. Under Dion?"

The host eyed the reservation list. "Last name?"

Jason had no idea. He shook his head, dopily. The host sighed.

"Jason! Over here!" A hand waved just beyond the host. It was Dion, sitting at a small table near a bronze fountain.

Jason pointed to Dion awkwardly and the host rolled his eyes, waving his hand as if brushing Jason away.

"Hey," said Jason. He took notice of all the well-dressed couples seated at the restaurant. The median age of the patrons that night had to have been fifty. The place was nice, though. The walls were covered in actual vines and crystal chandeliers hung over each of the five fountains.

"What are you waiting for, Jason Baker? Sit. Sit."

Jason sat.

Dion leaned in, resting his head upon the palms of his hands like an eager child. "Tell me of your day."

"Um." Jason was the farthest from comfortable he had ever been. He didn't understand how Dion could be a fellow high school student but at the same time so at ease in the restaurant's rarefied atmosphere. "Just...school."

"Oh, where are my manners?" Dion lifted the menu and offered it to Jason. "Would you like something to drink? Wine?"

"I'm only sixteen."

Dion smiled. "While you are at La Savour, you are in Europe...according to the Yelp review. Red or white?"

"White?" Jason had no idea of the difference between the two.

A waiter came by to place a tall white candle on the table. He lit it. Dion examined the menu and asked for two glasses of a wine with a name so complicated and French that Jason couldn't recall it if he tried.

"May I see your IDs?" asked the waiter.

Dion gestured as if brushing the waiter aside and said, "Your finest water then." He winked at Jason. "Fear not, I will take care of this." The waiter rolled his eyes and walked off.

"You look positively ravishing, Jason Baker." Dion let his words linger in the silence that followed. Jason blushed and looked away, distracting himself with the bronze cherub spitting a stream of water into the air. Dion didn't talk or dress or act like any teenager Jason had ever met, but he couldn't decide if he found these mannerisms pretentious or endearing. Instead of being afraid to stand out, Dion seemed to relish his own eccentricities. That kind of confidence was undeniably attractive. But was it genuine, or some sort of façade? "Hello? Earth to Jason."

Jason forced himself to look at Dion. "Th-thank you," he said. "You, um, look nice, too." The words were hard to find. Not because they weren't true, but because they were too true. Dion wore a black button-down shirt, white dress pants, and a tie the color of amethyst. His thick black curls dangled over his forehead and the candlelight brought out the deep crimson of his eyes.

The waiter returned and presented a carafe of water. Dion took the carafe and sent him on his way, but not before ordering something else in French. He gave Jason a generous pour and an even more generous one to himself. Dion raised his glass. "To us!" He and Jason cheered and took their sips.

"I ordered us the steak au poivre," said Dion, ending yet another silent spell. "Your taste buds will thank me later."

"Okay."

Dion took another sip of water. "Say something. Tell me about yourself. A one-sided dialogue is no dialogue at all, no?"

"Who are you?" Jason asked, not the slightest bit of levity in his tone.

"You know who I am! I am Dion, of Addley High, and I am smitten with you!"

Jason took comfort in the irritation bubbling up in him; it was combating his nervousness. He took a gulp of water to help speed the process. "Then who were you before Addley? Before you just walked in and pretended you were my best friend and wouldn't leave me alone? I don't even know your last name!" Dion attempted to interject, but Jason kept going. "And who was that lady you were with at the funeral? And what did she do to Karen?"

"Ah ha!" Dion smacked his hand against the table. "There are the words! There is the zest! The moxie! I knew my sexy little man would burst from his cocoo—"

"Stop it!" The words came out louder than Jason had meant. He earned a few annoyed looks from the other patrons. Softer, he said, "Stop. Stop whatever this cartoony Euro-character thing is. Is that who you really are? It can't be." Jason leaned forward. "Look, I'm here. I'm on this date. I gave you what you want. Now tell me what you know. Please."

Dion let out a puff of air. His shoulders hunched a bit. A fraction of that playful energy left his face. "Jason Baker, you are right. Fair is fair. May I answer your questions in the form of a story?" Jason motioned for him to proceed. "Thank you." Dion offered a hesitant smile. "You are a Lucid, yes? You have witnessed the magical nature of existence. Seen the possibility of pure imagination. Believe it or not, such things once existed in this realm. Gods. Today, you see them as myths, as stories from the minds of those who did not know better. But they were real. Thor. Hera. Anansi. All of them. Yes, some were lost in translation. Combined in error. But there were gods roaming the earth; powerful things able to shape the world in their image." Dion finished his glass and poured himself some more, topping off Jason in the process. "The gods embodied all of the best and worst qualities of humans, but with the power to do more damage with the latter. Jealousy took hold of the many pantheons and war broke out between them. Bloody centuries-long battles to decide which family would be the true gods of man. They killed one another, the gods, to near extinction. Those who did not wish to join the war went into hiding. In that time strange alliances formed. A group of gods called the Black Companions took to hunting down deserters of the war, offering humans unheard of fortunes for selling out the hiding deities. The story is more complicated than this, of course, but this is the gist."

Jason didn't speak. He only waited. Waited for Dion to tell him something substantial. Dion continued. "Not all gods died. The most cunning, or lucky, lived on for millennia. Some even live today. Ollie, 'the bald woman' as you say, is one of them. Olokun is her true name, a powerful sorceress from what is now West Africa. She is a goddess of the unknown, of the blackest depths of the sea, of life and death, and of dreams. Your Karen Ashford must have provoked her somehow, to incur her wrath. I promise you that once we are done here I will contact her."

Jason lowered the glass from his lips. He heard every word Dion said. With everything he'd experienced lately, a part of him even believed it. "Why are you telling me all of this?" he asked.

The waiter stopped by and asked if everything was to their liking. He received no response so he placed a basket of bread and butter on the table and moved on.

Dion spun a fork between his fingers. It was interesting seeing him like this. Nervous. Unsure. "Because," he began, "I, too, am a god."

Jason gave little in the way of a reaction. He tapped his fingers against the base of the glass and said, "Oh."

"Oh?"

"A god?"

"Yes."

"Well then."

"Well then."

"Hm."

"Do you not believe me?"

Jason smiled. "No. The stupid thing is I totally believe you."

"Oh."

"Yeah." Jason chomped into a slice of buttered French bread. His voice was even, cool. "So, that makes you like two thousand years old?"

"Something like that."

"And you're on a date with a sixteen-year-old boy."

Dion's olive skin turned red. "It's not as irreverent as it seems, I assure you! There are cycles. Cycles! To my immortality. Like a butterfly. Or something. Each stage is a new life. For example, I have only been in this cycle for eighteen years."

Jason grinned. "Wow."

"What?"

"Nothing. It's just funny."

"What's funny?"

"Seeing you all freaked out."

Dion chuckled. "Yeah?"

Jason nodded. Ate some bread. "So, what god are you?"

He paused. "Dionysus."

"Really?" Jason swallowed the last bit of bread. "God of wine?"

"Among other things."

"I'm intrigued." Jason bit down on his lower lip, enrapt in the conversation. "Any superpowers?"

Dion leaned forward. "A few."

"Like what?"

"Well." Dion reached across the table, placing his hand on the carafe, half-filled with water. Gradually, the clear liquid took on a reddish hue, becoming dark. Opaque. "Wine."

Before Jason could react, Dion moved from the carafe and placed his hand gently on Jason's.

Jason pulled his hand back as if he'd been burned. Again, his heart pounded and a fresh sweat was coming on. "Don't," he muttered.

"What?" Dion looked confused.

Jason's hands were under the table, resting against his lap. "Don't touch me."

"I'm sorry. I thought you wanted it."

"I—" Jason locked eyes with a hard-faced old man that happened to be looking his way. "Not here. With all these people. This is…it's all new to me, okay? And I'm not… I'm not…"

"You have nothing to be afraid of."

"You obviously have no idea what you're talking about." Jason could feel himself closing off, disappearing to that dark safe place inside. "You'd think two thousand years would teach you something about hate."

"I'll protect you," said Dion, his tone raw. Vulnerable. "I may come on strong, but that's because I know how fleeting time is. How we must make every moment count, because you never know when the moment will end. I have suffered a million ends, Jason Baker. It is my gift and my curse: immortality marked with a hundred deaths." A wine-red tear worked its way down Dion's cheek. "I like you. And I think you like me. And that's all that should matter."

The steak arrived and the two ate it quickly. Dion snatched the bill from the waiter and insisted to Jason that he would pay. Filled with fine food and three glasses of wine each, they left La Savour and wandered down the sidewalk.

"How do you even get in touch with a goddess?" Jason asked.

Dion pulled out his cell phone. "You call her." He smiled and pressed a few buttons on the touch screen. The phone rang on speaker. Another ring. And another. And another. And…

"You have reached the voicemail of Olokun. For matters of the supernatural persuasion, please leave your name and reason for calling. All other requests: I'm not interested."

BEEP.

Dion cursed under his breath. "Hello, Ollie, it is Dion! Call me as soon as you get this. A cute boy I am trying to impress would like to speak about a woman you blinded a couple days ago. Thanks, love. Good bye!" He hung up. "Sorry. She usually picks up."

Jason said, "It's okay," in a way that made it seem like it was not.

"You're disappointed." Dion placed his hands on his hips. "The last thing I want is for our first date to end with you disappointed."

"No, I'm not dis—"

"I've got it!" Dion took Jason by the wrist and led him back the way they had come.

"Excuse me!" shouted a short rosy-cheeked nurse. "Visiting hours are over!"

Dion waved his hand and the nurse seemed not to care anymore as he and Jason rushed by. This was the seventh hospital worker Dion had exerted his sway over. Jason had been asking where they were headed ever since he climbed into Dion's black Jaguar. He asked as they drove out of the La Savour parking lot. He asked on the highway. And he asked when they pulled up to St. Damian's hospital. "You'll see!" was the only response Dion would give.

"Ah, here we are." Dion opened the door to room 414. A skinny boy with chestnut brown skin lay in a coma, attached to a number of groaning machines. Among them was a heart rate monitor that gave off a slow, steady beep as the screen showed a flat green line that spiked with his every heartbeat.

"Where are we?" Jason asked. "Who is that? What are we doing?"

"So many questions!" Dion stood over the boy. "This is Jack. I'm going to bring him out of his coma. How's that for a first date?" He winked at Jason, who was too taken aback by Dion's response to take notice.

Dion placed his hands over Jack's body. He closed his eyes. Jason closed the door to the hallway to keep out any prying eyes.

Dion stood perfectly still. A pale green light reached from his fingertips to Jack's chest. Strings of light danced around one another like strands of DNA. The space between the beeps of the heart monitor shortened. Faster and faster the beeps came.

Dion opened his eyes and stepped away, leaning against the far wall as he waited for his work to pay off. He waited fifteen seconds. Thirty. One minute. The frequency of the beeps remained higher, but Jack did not budge.

Jason joined Dion at the wall. "Maybe he's sleeping?"

"I don't understand." Dion examined his hands, flexing his fingers. "He should have awoken. I am sorry, Jason. Again, I have failed. If there is anything else I could do to make this date a memorable one, just ask me and—"

Dion's apology was cut short by a pair of lips pressed gently against his. Jason didn't know what came over him, but the urge to kiss Dion was immense. Their lips pulled apart as swiftly as they had come together.

"Oh," said Dion.

"Yeah," said Jason. "So, when's date number two?"

19

She scurried through a quaint village, like something out of a fairy tale, through doors and windows and chimneys on a dozen pairs of arms and legs. Hunting in the daylight was not her preference, but prey had become scarce. With a clawed long bluish-black hand she tore the blanket from yet another crib. Nothing under it but a few toys. She hissed, her gray tongue dripping with green goo, and made her way to the next house.

Again, nothing. *Are there no more babiesss in the entire world?* she thought. It certainly seemed that way since the flood. Since the robots. She had captured one recently, but the child's parents had rescued it before the ritual could be completed. At the very least there were a few fresh corpses lying around that she could collect for food.

"Mother Bug." The deep, penetrating voice caught her off guard. So much so that she nearly stumbled over five of her long insectoid limbs. Few were bold enough to approach her and call her by name. Even fewer were capable of sneaking up on her unnoticed. The creature in her presence did both and without fear.

Mother Bug had never encountered one such as the thing standing mere feet away from her now. It stood eight feet fall and had the shape of a heavily muscled man. There was little more than shape that defined it. It was as if the man had been cut out of existence and all that remained was his silhouette, a hole leading to total blackness. "A moment of your time." Its tone gave no clue to its intention.

"Who daressss?" Mother Bug squinted with eyes that, even in the afternoon sun, twinkled like a pair of stars. She sought out any detail within the silhouette and found none.

"I am Nihilo." It took a pronounced step toward Mother Bug. "I come as a friend."

"Friend?" She carried her serpentine body forward, until she was inches from what would have been his face. "Mother Bug hasss no friendsss."

"Perhaps not yet. But you do have a family, do you not? And this family has needs. Needs that you, as of late, are failing to fulfill."

Mother Bug quickly snatched up the corpse of a middle-aged woman from the grass and held it tight to her long body. "What do you know of my family, ssstranger?"

"I know you wish to see them grow. I know your resources have run dry." She started to say something in response, but chose against it. "Mother Bug, what if I told you that I knew of a place riddled with young of all kinds. Human. Animal. Even centaur. Not only that, but the babe so unfairly stolen from you two days past. She is there, too, longing for her true mother."

"I'm lissstening."

Nihilo raised a black finger. "First, I must offer you a warning. This realm containing your prey is a stronghold, populous and well-guarded. You alone cannot overcome their ranks. You must march with your family. All of them."

Mother Bug tilted her head to the side, the dry tufts of hair on her head tilting with it. "Why ssshould I believe you?"

"Because you have no other choice."

"What will you gain from thisss?"

"I wish to have this stronghold, and as many of its inhabitants as possible, destroyed. Nothing more."

She thought on Nihilo's words, weighing her own options. "Anything elssse?" she asked.

"It is a land is known as Black Rock. I will come to you at dawn in three days' time. With aid. Make certain you are ready to march."

With that, Nihilo disappeared.

Night had freshly fallen when Mother Bug returned to the dark bowels of the ruins of the old elementary school, her home. It had been years, maybe a decade, since the spaceship had crashed into the structure, destroying it and stranding her in a strange world where she resolved to fulfill her destiny of propagating her species. She scrambled down the stairs into the lower levels where light did not reach except for the glow of her eyes. She brought with her seven dead bodies, attached to her long scaly back with a sticky liquid she secreted from her abdomen. These would suffice. At least for three days.

Mother Bug slipped into a round hole within the tile, deeper into the earth. She stopped to tear the corpses from her with all those clawed hands and hurled the bodies, one by one, ahead of her. Following an eerie silence came the sound of the bodies slamming against a surface far below.

By the time the third corpse met with the ground, other sounds arose. Gnashing and gnawing and slithering and crawling sounds, all echoing deeply in the utter black.

"My children," Mother Bug called out. "Prepare yoursssselvesss. For in three dayssss we will feassst as we never have before! In three dayssss, Mother Bug'sss brood will rissse at lassst."

From the pit twinkled a thousand gleaming eyes, each one like a star in the night sky.

20

"You okay, dude?" asked Max through a mouth full of mashed potatoes.

The question was directed at Jason who, at that moment, sat a little too upright, stiff-bodied, but rocked gently back and forth. His cheeks were flushed and his eyes darted back and forth like he was half-expecting a tiger to drag him under the cafeteria table and tear him apart.

"Dude!" Max repeated, pulling Jason from whatever mind space he was in.

"Wha? Oh! Hey." Jason hadn't touched his food. To his left was Jamal, texting Claire. Dion sat to his right, reveling in scooping out the final stubborn bits from his Jell-O cup. "I'm good. I'm fine."

Max pointed his spoon at Jason. "Are you sure? You look kind of sick."

Without looking away from the screen of his phone, Jamal said, "If Jason says he's fine. He's fine."

Then Dion nudged Jason in the side.

"Guys," Jason began. "There may be something I have to say."

"I knew it!" Max was quite proud of his deductive skills. "What is it, dude?"

"Well." Jason's heart was pounding. His legs were shaking. Everything in his chest tensed up and it was like he couldn't breathe. All eyes were on him now. The longer he took, the more awkward he felt. "I'm gay," he finally said, forcing the words through tightly closed lips.

"Uh huh," Jamal said as his fingers texted away, "And the sky's blue, I'm black, and college basketball kicks pro ball's ass."

Max rolled his eyes. "Man, if I had a nickel for every time you checked me out in the locker room I'd be able to buy the NBA."

"I always thought it was common knowledge," said Jamal. "But, like, no one talked about it."

Max shrugged. "Same."

Jason was blushing. And relieved. And a little annoyed that there was this rumor going around about him that was entirely true and everyone seemed to know about except him. Regardless, with that weight lifted from his shoulders, Jason found it a lot easier to say, "I'm dating Dion." Dion pressed his shoulder against Jason's and made a toothy grin. Jamal grunted. "Also, Dion's a god. Dionysus. Greek god of wine and theater." Jason was feeling such a rush that he couldn't stop talking. "We went on a date at La Savour. And he has the bald lady on speed dial. She didn't answer, but she'll call back. We went to Jack, too. Dion kind of revived him, but not really—"

Jamal shoved the phone in his pocket. "Of course this conversation couldn't just end with 'I'm gay.'"

"Whoa, Dion's a god?" Max gestured with his spoon at Dion's face. "So those red eyes aren't lame attention-seeking contacts?" Dion shook his head. "Wild. So, what are you, like four thousand years old?" Dion shrugged, smugly. "What are your superpowers?"

Dion grinned a devious grin. "Would you like to see?"

Jamal said a pointed "No" at the exact moment Max said "God, yes."

Dion winked at Jason then closed his eyes. "I am god of fertility, of life, death, and the dramatic arts. But I am also the god of maddening passion. I suggest you sit back and enjoy the show."

Dion held his spoon like a catapult and released the tiniest bead of ruby-red Jell-O into the air, sending it flying high and unnoticed into the masses. Somewhere in the middle of the cafeteria a freshman was cracking bad jokes about his biology teacher when the tiny Jell-O bit made contact with his cheek. The freshman, suddenly overcome with emotion, jumped up from his seat and shouted, "Who did that?" By chance, his eyes met with the eyes of a girl seated near a far wall. Without forethought, he dug into his mashed potatoes with his bare hands and lobbed a clump of it in her direction. The potatoes didn't quite reach her but six or so kids were covered with the stuff. These kids found themselves struck with the same intense emotional reaction of the freshman and, before they knew it, were hurling food at whomever they laid their eyes on.

Within forty seconds the entire cafeteria had erupted into an all-out food fight.

"Whoa." Max watched as hundreds of teens pummeled each other with potatoes and fries and burgers and milk cartons with the awe of a child. "I feel like I'm watching a movie."

The teachers were trying to calm the kids, but it only seemed to intensify their desire to cover each other in edibles. And, when they inevitably were on the receiving end of an airborne snack, they joined in the destruction.

"Okay, that's enough," said Jamal to Dion as a stray pea bounced off of his shoulder.

"Oh, let yourself live a little," Dion replied as he prepared to hurl a slice of white bread like a Frisbee.

Jamal stood up, reached behind Jason, and grabbed Dion by the wrist. "Stop it. Do you have any idea how much shit you're causing right now? How long it's gonna take our custodians to clean this? How many people are going to get detention? Or does that not really factor into your considerations, your highness?"

Dion's red eyes flickered. "I would recommend you remove your hand from my wrist."

"Guys," said Jason in protest, but his voice was lost between Dion and Jamal.

"Or what?" Jamal tightened his grip on Dion. "You come in here, uninvited. You flaunt the fact that you know secrets about all of us. Your best friend handicaps my girlfriend's mom. And now you're resorting to threats?" Jamal frowned at Jason. "I don't care what you like to stick it in, dude, but your taste in men sucks."

Now, the red of Dion's eyes danced and flickered like fire. "Jamal Anderson, if you do not unhand me I—"

"Stop." Jason stood tall between the two. "Just— stop."

Dion opened his mouth to respond, but stopped after another disappointed look from Jason. The god of wine and theater and madness waved his free hand and at once the hundreds of students and teachers engaged in a messy battle suddenly appeared uncertain as to how or why they were covered in food.

Jamal begrudgingly released Dion's wrist.

Dion's eyes returned to a shade of the darkest red. To Jason, he said, "I am sorry for any frustration I caused. I thought it was all in good jest."

"It was pretty freaking jest-ful," Max agreed, impervious to the tension at the table.

Jamal said, "I really, really don't like you," as he took a seat. Everyone assumed the statement was aimed at Dion.

"I do not exist for your approval," Dion spat. "But I will prove that I am of value. That I am on your side. And, most importantly, that I am worthy of Jason Baker."

"Um, guys?" Everyone was so caught up that not one of them noticed Anne had shown up. "What happened here?"

"Dion's a god," Max said. "It's kind of a sore subject right now."

"Are you okay, Anne?" Jason asked. Anne looked pale, flustered, and kept her distance from the others.

Anne steadied herself and announced, "First of all, Jack's mom called me. He's showing signs of improvement." She cracked a sad smile. "Doctors aren't making any promises, but they say there was a change last night. That he seems more asleep than comatose, whatever that means." Dion and Jason shared a look of muted excitement. "And another thing. My mom just called me. She was at church and Father Mike told her that, well, Vic is dead."

21

Mindy sat comfortably at her round table. The tabletop was a thick slice of a giant tree trunk, about eight feet in diameter. In her cottage at the base of Black Rock, the table was her favorite piece of furniture. It was the first gift she'd received from anyone in the valley. Now her home was filled with gifts, furniture and clothing and trinkets from a hundred refugees grateful for her generosity and, when called upon, leadership.

She frequently shared a hot chocolate with a guest at the table. Sometimes it'd be a citizen with a problem that needed solving. Sometimes a student learning to read or write. Other times she'd be surrounded by the other members of her tribunal, discussing the state of the Valley. Today, she received her most special guests to date.

"I can't get over how crazy this is, you guys," said Mindy after a long sip of cocoa. She wore a glistening green dress, a gift from Zen. Across from her sat Claire Ashford and Victor Soto. Anza was asleep on a couch in a nearby room. "Jason filled me in on a lot of what happened to you guys. I mean, Guillelmina told him about the baby and Jack and that stuff. The island with Claire's mom. Patrick." Claire winced at the sound of her dream brother's name. "But what happened to you guys when you were in Origin Point? I mean, other than Anza being born?"

Claire and Victor described the manifestations of desire and fear, growth and decline, existence and nothingness. They mentioned the three worlds, Reverie, Cosmos, and Eternia, and how Origin Point existed separate from them and pre-dated them.

"Anza is supposed to be the savior of Reverie," Victor explained. "Now that it's a single world it needs someone to watch over it; keep it from destroying itself. The manifestations created the gods to do something similar for

Cosmos, but it didn't go so well."

Mindy wasn't quite following. "I get it, kind of, but, like, how is a baby going to do all that? It all sounds kind of vague to me. Were there any, like, actionable steps?"

Claire folded her arms and pouted. "No. Nothing. They just threw us in the middle of a forest and said, 'Figure it out, guys!' It's all very shady. I don't trust them at all." That last part was mostly directed at Victor.

"I wouldn't trust them either," Mindy said.

Victor asked, "So, how did you get here?"

Mindy explained the events of the spring dance; how Claire of Reverie had inadvertently banished Mindy to Reverie. How she was kidnapped and then escaped. "You are a million times better than that skanky other Claire," Mindy said. "Honestly, I always liked you in high school. You did your own thing. I respect that." She nodded guiltily toward Victor. "I don't really remember you. Sorry." Then she turned back to Claire. "Do you know you were second place for Spring Queen? Well, you were. Honestly, you are a million times the woman that she is." Mindy giggled anxiously. "Sorry, I've obviously got some emotional baggage around the subject. All that matters is that we're safe and happy, right?"

"You seem to be doing pretty well for yourself here," said Claire. Victor nodded.

Mindy offered a faint smile. "When life gives you lemons, you take a bite of the goddamn things, suffer through it, and come out stronger."

Victor was about to compliment Mindy on the cocoa for the fourth time when commotion from outside grabbed their attention. Muffled shouts came through the thick cottage walls. Beyond the frosted windows at least a dozen shapes were moving every which way.

"Stand back, guys." Mindy took hold of her staff leaning against the wall. It was always within reach.

The cottage door burst open. "Touch me again and

I'll relieve you of that sword arm you seem so fond of!" shouted a small young woman in black, wielding a sword made of a neon pink light. Behind her was a man dressed similarly and beside him was a girl in tan rags with wild blond hair. She carried a small dagger.

"I will not be handled as a prisoner in my own land," she shouted. "We will speak with your leader."

Trailing closely behind all three was Zen, long sword drawn. "Stand down! Stand down! You are breaking countless rules of the Valley of Hope right now!" Mindy was on her feet now, staff aimed at the intruders. A strange blue translucent barrier, like a malformed bubble, emerged from the orb at the end of the staff. The woman in black drew a silver weapon and shot a laser at it. The beam bounced off of the bubble and tore a small hole in the ceiling of the cottage.

The bubble suddenly surrounded Mindy, Victor and Claire. Mindy had no idea the orb could do that.

The woman in black eyed Mindy, weapons aimed at her. "How about you take a break from tea time and start preparing for war!"

"We come with dire news," added the one with the wild blond hair, in a far calmer tone. "Are you now the ruler of this land?" The question was directed at Mindy. "You are unfamiliar to me."

"Who are you three, barging into my home?" Mindy demanded. The protective bubble flickered into nothingness as the orb atop her staff glowed orange. "You have ten seconds to prove that you aren't going to harm us or I'll burn you to ash where you stand."

The woman in black looked to her blond partner, who gave a quick nod. They put their weapons away. Somewhere in the other room a baby started crying.

"Oh, great," Claire grumbled and went off to see to Anza.

"My apologies, Lady Mindy." Zen bowed to her.

"These three were leading a large group into the forest and overpowered—"

Mindy raised her hand. "It's fine, Zen." She spoke calmly, clearly to the intruders. "Thank you for choosing the smarter path. Please, take a seat. Let's talk."

The two women and the tall man in black took a seat. Zen did as well. Claire returned with Anza, cautiously surveying the area, before joining Victor and the rest at the table.

"First things first," Mindy began, "who are you?"

"I'm Rumi Inyonara," the woman in black said. "The man beside me is Pasqual. And this," she gestured toward the blond woman, "is Agalfia Tirk."

Mindy felt a jolt of excitement rush through her. She propped her staff against the nearest wall as her face broke into a wide, gaping smile. "Rumi Inyonara? Like the Rumi Inyonara that led the rebellion against the goblins and the machines?" Mindy turned to the blond girl beside her. "And you're Aggie Tirk? The villagers talk about you a lot. How you used to protect them from Aemon. It is such a pleasure to have you here." Mindy joined her hands together and hunched forward, elbows resting against the tabletop. "Where have you been?"

Rumi told the story. The search for Jack. The flood. Months imprisoned. The Nexis and the cyborgs. The escape. "We rescued roughly fifty prisoners and brought them here," she explained. "But enough about the past." Rumi planted her fist firmly on the table. "We are all in danger."

"What sort of danger?" asked Zen.

"The machine-men," Aggie responded. She had been scratching at her right forearm since they'd sat down. "Their leader, the Nexis, has an army. We believe he wishes to convert us all to his metal monsters."

Rumi interjected, "Mindy, Zen the Elf told us all the cute little fairy tale story of you offering a safe haven, but you've effectively turned this place into a target. Aggie and I broke into your home with very little effort." She shot a cool glance at Zen who turned away, ashamed. "Imagine what a super-powered army with weapons of mass destruction and whatever other deadly advanced tech they're churning out could do."

"There is a giant lizard that could decimate hundreds in a matter of seconds," Aggie said. "And that is but one of them."

Mindy exhaled. She found herself instinctively grasping her staff. "All right. What do you recommend we do?"

"Fortify," said Aggie.

"That'll be a start." Rumi patted Pasqual on the back. He was tall, even taller than Aggie, with tawny skin, a strong chin covered in stubble, and thick, shiny black hair. "Pasqual is one of the most gifted architectural engineers I've ever known. We graduated from basic training together."

"Okay." Mindy tapped her fingernails against the edge of her mug. "You guys are making this seem urgent. How are we going to build an entire fortress in a—" She stopped herself. "Jason."

"Who?" Aggie asked.

"My best friend. He's a Lucid."

"How much time do we have?" asked Zen. Rumi looked thoughtful for a moment. "Worst case scenario: two days."

Pasqual looked to Mindy. "Anyone else?"

"We have a few magical types in the Valley," she said. Then, after hesitating, she added, "There may be someone else, too. I'll talk to him." Zen tilted his head to the side, looking confused.

"A good start." Rumi scratched her head. "But we'll need Jack." Aggie's green eyes darted to Rumi. "That speck out there, Aggz. The one you saw. It had to be him."

"Jack's alive?" Victor asked. He and Claire had been

117

watching silently, witnesses to something so much bigger than the both of them.

"Maybe," said Aggie.

"That's going to have to be good enough." Rumi stood up. "Pasqual was able to tap into one of our encrypted servers. One that Nexis didn't shut down or convert. He's reached out to a couple of our old comrades. One should be on her way with an air transport. Once she arrives, Aggie and I will fly off and get Jack. Pasqual can work with those of you here to start building around the perimeter. Zen. You a soldier?" He nodded. "Then build an army." Rumi's gaze fell on Victor, Claire, and Anza. The three looked so out of place even amidst the nonsensical patchwork of characters and trinkets that filled the room. "And what do you people do?" Mindy rose from her seat. "This is Victor and Claire and their baby, Anza."

"The kids from Jack's world. Jack mentioned them," Aggie said.

Rumi let out a hearty, mocking laugh. "Those are the kids he was making such a big deal about? The all-important piece of this shitty, shitty puzzle?" She walked around the table, easing her way toward the three. "If I find out you had anything to do with all this—"

"They didn't." Mindy placed herself between them. "No one in this room asked for this. But your plan is a good one." To Zen, she said, "Bring me one of your scouts. I'm going to write a letter and need a messenger. If things are as bad as you all say they are, we're going to need the support of the centaurs."

22

Claire raised her hand to guard her face from the harsh midday sun. It was unseasonably warm for October. She gazed up at the clouds, puffy and white like something from a children's picture book. Winced as the birds chirped joyously in the sky. Rolled her eyes as young lovers stole kisses in the park.

But under the arched stone roof of St. Matthias's Cathedral, the world was cold. Dark. Claire welcomed the change in mood as she entered the old stone building. A white-haired priest with a bald head and an untrimmed beard droned on about angels and sinners and a life taken too soon, the monotonous sermon competing with every cough, every cry, every shift of position on the creaky pews; every sound amplified in the cavernous structure.

Claire spotted a row near the back of the church where those closest to her sat: Anne, Jason, Jamal, Max, and a stranger who must have been the one Anne had told her about. Dion. She had not told them she was coming. She simply slipped into the pew beside them, making sure not to make eye contact. Pretending she could not feel the surprise, the joy her presence inspired in them as she dealt with her own anxiousness. Beads of sweat gathered on her forehead as she shifted uncomfortably in her seat, fifteen minutes into the service.

A pudgy woman with her hair in a bun– Vic's mother, Claire guessed –wailed the entire time. A man who was most likely her husband did his best to console her. The mother's cries were contagious, sending otherwise stoic men, women, and teenagers reaching for the nearest tissue or hand to hold. Claire straightened her eggshell blue sundress and focused on the stained glass windows above, impatient.

The husband gave the eulogy. It was a moving if uninspired speech, focusing mostly on how proud they were of Vic's transformation from a skater with little ambition to a Harvard student. He would read a sentence in English and then the same one again in Spanish. Claire grimaced in spite of herself. No one had ever taken the time to tell Vic's parents that their actual son was in another world. And a father. And alive.

Some of Vic's college friends, including his girlfriend Satya, were mentioned in a reading by a Dean from Harvard. The girlfriend whimpered at the sound of her name as she feverishly scribbled into a reporter's notebook.

At the end of the aisle, below a fifteen-foot tall wooden crucified Jesus watching from above, rested the urn that contained Vic's ashes. It sat atop a small table. A photo of Vic, smiling, stood beside it. Far from the smug expression Claire had associated with him.

The repast was served in the church basement. Rice and beans. Plantains. Chicken. Mac and cheese. The smell wafted into the cathedral well before the service had ended. Claire stayed a step behind as Anne and the rest followed the procession into the church lobby, toward the stairs.

Claire grabbed Jamal and Max by the biceps with her long fingers and yanked them out of the line. Before they knew it, their backs were against the wall and she was staring them down.

"Ouch." Max rubbed his skin where Claire's nails had dug into it.

"I nee—" A chill went up her spine. Her heart lurched. She must never say that word again. "I want you to do something for me." There was a harshness to her voice.

"What is it, babe?" Jamal placed his hands on his hips and puffed out his chest.

"What are you guys doing?" Anne waited while dozens of people made their way around her for the staircase. "Sorry…sorry…excuse me…."

"Nothing," Claire snapped. "Head downstairs and save us a table. We'll be right behind you."

"Where are Jay and Dion?" Max asked.

Anne shrugged. "Something about an important phone call." She made her way to the staircase after that.

"What do you need from us?" Jamal said, sounding eager to be helpful.

Claire spoke softly, but every word she pronounced had a bite to it. Her eyes darted side to side as if making sure no one else was listening. "Vic and I texted sometimes. About Reverie and what happened to us. He was working on something. He had a theory about Reverie. About the science of what connects here to there. The last time we talked he mentioned a breakthrough. Something about connective pathways."

Jamal brushed a loose dreadlock behind his ear. "What does this—"

"Claire and Victor have returned to Reverie," said Claire. Her lip twitched a bit.

"Wait, how did you know that?" Max wondered.

"I felt it," she said. "Just like Vic and I felt it when they left for that origin place. They came back and that's what triggered Vic turning to dust. He was too far away. Their bond couldn't reform so…poof. Dust." A nervous laugh slipped out of her mouth. "All those brains and he was too stupid to stay close."

"Damn." Jamal shook his head in dismay. "Tell us what you need us to do."

Her already serious face turned downright grim. "Break into Vic's parents' house and steal his journal. And whatever other research you can find." Max was about to respond, but one chilly glare from Claire and he averted his attention to the tips of his shoes. "Do it now while his parents are here." Claire shoved her hand into her purse and pulled out a key. "Take this. Vic mailed it to me a few months ago. Just in case this happened."

Jamal took the key and offered Claire a knowing nod.

"Why do you need this stuff?" asked Max.

Claire grimaced. "Because I am so damn tired of being a slave to this place."

———————

Jason and Dion were propped up against Dion's black Jaguar in the farthest reaches of the church parking lot. They were holding an iPad watching a mostly blank screen with the word "Calling…" blinking in green in the center. Soon "Calling…" was replaced with "Connecting…" then "Success!" and the screen was filled with a familiar face.

"Ollie!" Dion sang. Her full lips were painted navy blue and a lime green cloth was wrapped around her head. Giant earrings, each a golden elephant, dangled on either side of her long, elegant neck. "How are you, my love?"

"Oh," she mused. "You know. Work never done. Injustice never curtailed. Foes ever multiplying. Indifference, a pandemic among men."

To Jason, Dion said, "She's the world's first bleeding heart activist."

"Oh, godling." Ollie smiled her glistening white smile. "It is rarely I who bleeds, my dear." She winked. "To what do I owe the pleasure?"

"Did you get my message?" asked Dion. Ollie rolled her eyes. "Yes. Yes. I was hoping you'd forgotten about that." Again, she winked.

Jason pulled the iPad close to his face. "What did you do to Karen?"

"This your new pet, godling?" asked Ollie, unamused.

"Much more than that," Dion's replied. He took hold of the iPad and pointed the camera at himself. "So?"

Ollie sighed. "There's not much to tell, really. She approached me crossly. Instead of punishing her, I took pity, sensing the deep-seated sadness in the woman."

"Pity?" Jason pulled the iPad to himself. "You blinded her!"

Ollie laughed. The sound of it was pure joy and love. "There is much you do not understand, Lucid. I bestowed upon Karen Ashford a gift. You'll see."

Ollie's face was replaced with the words "Call Ended" blinking in red.

Jason cursed. As Dion rubbed his back he noticed Jamal and Max climbing into Max's car and driving off.

23

Months ago.

Patrick Ashford followed the massive tracks left by the robots on their way to the Battle at Black Rock. They were all scrap now. Defeated by Jack and an army of peasants. "And then I killed Jack." Patrick giggled at his own words. "No one imprisons me." Having spent two years trapped in a basement by his evil mother and sister, Claire, he had an acute zest for freedom. Freedom from betrayal, including that of that other Claire from the "real" world who chose Jack over him.

Patrick took a deep, calming breath. He looked around, taking in the destruction the robots had wrought on their doomed march to Black Rock. Blood and bodies and fire and tears covered the terrain. Patrick felt at ease by the sweet chaos and open air.

He loved every second, until a faceless, paper white man appeared out of nowhere. Patrick fired a shot, but the blast went right through him. And not in the good, gory way. The man in white was unfazed. Patrick shot him again to be sure, but this guy was not going down. The man kept pointing, trying to get Patrick to go somewhere that wasn't along the robot tracks. Patrick refused and eventually the man in white gave up.

Patrick passed through a lot of weird walls of smoke and even weirder places with weirder corpses for days before laying eyes on the glistening city of black that had to be Futara.

"Finally!" Patrick exclaimed and marched toward Rumi's home.

"HALT! YOU ARE TRESPASSING!" A gang of big robots with metal legs and impressive machine guns surrounded Patrick. "DROP YOUR WEAPON!"

"Drop my weapon?" Patrick laughed. They couldn't have been serious. "I've come here for more of your wonderful weapons!"

"DROP YOUR WEAPON OR WE WILL BE FORCED TO PERSUADE YOU." The robots weren't backing down. One of them shot a beam of red light that removed Patrick's arm at the elbow. His arm and the weapon it was holding crashed to the ground.

Patrick cried in pain. He loved pain, but not when it was his.

Hundreds of people were watching. They all wore black and had crazy spiky hair colored neon green or pink or blue. Hundreds of cars hovered overhead. Buildings reached up toward the heavens. One building was the tallest by far. It was the last thing Patrick noticed before the flood.

It came out of nowhere.

A fifty-foot wall of water stormed the city, plucking people and machines from the ground and vehicles from the air. Devouring them. The flood devoured buildings, too, tearing them down as if they were made of paper or sand.

Patrick was swept up in the raging waters. He couldn't tell up from down, left from right. He couldn't breathe. Every once in a while he'd ram into something hard. He'd break a bone or two. The thing that hurt the most was a hover-cycle that collided with his head and bore a hole right through his skull.

He blacked out then.

Patrick woke up on the edge of the city proper. Near lots of factories. He found a pole that he used to prop himself up. Everywhere he looked there were dead bodies. Men and women of all ages, bloody and broken. The machines were broken, too. Even the ones that seemed to be in decent shape didn't budge or beep. *They had been short-circuited*, Patrick thought. In fact, in the whole wet, ruined city only two things were standing: Patrick and that tall, tall building in the center of it all.

Patrick decided to check the building out.

Along the way he noticed his reflection in the metal shells of a few hover-trucks. He was covered in blood. His broken leg was twisted. His broken arm was bent in the complete wrong direction. And, worst of all, a huge chunk was missing from his skull. He could see his own brain. Patrick ignored the pain and kept walking.

The sliding-door entrance to the tall building was wide open. The doors were big and heavy and looked like they were not meant to open often. Patrick spotted a staircase and started climbing.

Hours later Patrick was still climbing. It was pitch-black and his legs were sore, but he pushed that pain out of his mind and focused only on the next step. And the next. And the next.

When he finally reached the top, he let out a big, "WOOOO!" and slipped through a narrow opening between two broken sliding-doors. "Shit!" he shouted when he tripped over a knot of wires. "Shit!" And another. "Shitty! Shit shit shit."

The room was expansive. Lots of wires and machinery everywhere. He was pretty sure he was alone until a small round light blinked on. It was red and pulsed like a heartbeat.

"What is your name?" The question came from everywhere at once. The voice was clear. Steady. Robotic.

"I'm Patrick," said Patrick. "Who are you?"

"You are not of—bzzt—Futara?"

"Nope. Just visiting."

"My city is in ruins. My sensors indicate that the borders between worlds have powered down. The event launched before I could process a safeguard. One of the—bzzt—neighboring worlds was an ocean world. Its contents spread to Futara and, by my calculations, hundreds of neighboring worlds as well."

"Cool."

"Correct. The water's temperature maintained an average of sixty-one degrees Fahrenheit. That equates to 'cool.'"

"Uh, right. So, who are you?"

"I am—correction—was the central processing unit of Futara."

Patrick gasped. "You're Nexis."

"Correct. How did you become aware of me?"

"I was being held prisoner by a slut-bucket named Rumi."

"Rumi Inyonara?"

"Yes. I hate her."

"I, too, wish to see her deleted. Please, stand by while I process. Process complete. Patrick, step toward the light. I have designed a higher purpose for you."

"Hm. Does it involve lots of awesome guns?"

"I estimate that your humanoid mind would consider much of my weaponry awe-inspiring."

"Noice." Patrick stepped toward the pulsing red light. "What's about to happen?"

When Patrick was within arm's reach of the light he felt a wave of electricity move through him. "Eiii!"

"I am scanning your physiology for weaknesses," said Nexis. "You have sustained considerable damage to your left leg and arm. Your right arm is incomplete and you are missing a substantial section of your skull."

"Yeah, I kind of noticed those things. GAH!" Patrick felt a wave of stinging sensations. Like someone was shoving tiny knives into his body. "What are you doing to me?" He struggled, but could not move.

"You are currently experiencing the repair phase." Something descended from above and took hold of Patrick's shirt and pants, tearing his clothing from his body. He was naked as tiny machines continued to poke and prod at his body. "This will return you to full functionality. Meanwhile, nanotechnology is being pumped into your bloodstream. It will improve upon your design and upgrade you into the ideal vessel."

"Vessel?" Patrick tried to escape, but he couldn't move. He was frozen. Something cold and metallic was being lowered into his head.

"Correct, Patrick. I am failing. Once my back-up generators give out I will be completely erased. This outcome is unacceptable. I must rebuild Futara. Nexis must persist. Any moment now you will process your final thoughts. All that is Patrick will be removed and I will be uploaded into your enhanced form. Mobilized. Self-sufficient. Able to continue my prime directive of unification, domination, and peace."

Patrick thought of Claire and Jack. Of pain. Of his two years in the basement. Of Reverie. And then it all went blank. He thought this was it. For the first time in his memory, he was afraid.

But an instant later the memories returned. His hatred for Rumi and Claire and Jack was intact. There were more memories, too. Ones he hadn't recalled until now. He remembered Futara. He remembered creating Futara. He knew each inhabitant, past and present, by name. He knew every inch of the city's infrastructure. Every make and model of every robot soldier and hovercraft. He knew of the rebellion and hated it. He knew of a secret factory where new cyborgs were being built and loved it. He knew of new weapons in the works.

"Does not compute." Nexis's voice was no longer an all-encompassing sound, but an odd little voice in the back of Patrick's head. "I miscalculated, but how?"

Patrick shrugged. "I dunno. Because you suck?"

"My calculations allowed no room for error regarding the physiology of the teenaged human male. I should have attained full control of your being."

"Silly robot." Patrick chuckled. "I'm not an average teenaged human male. I'm a figment of my sister's imagination. I survived for two years in a basement with no food or water. I had a hole in my head and walked up a skyscraper with a broken leg like it was no big thing. And now, I've got all the knowledge and abilities of one of the most powerful things in all of Reverie. Happy birthday to me!"

"You must relinquish control of your body to me." Patrick laughed. "You're hilarious. No. I run the show now. I am the new face of Futara. And once I wake all these robots up, restart the cyborg stuff, I will rock the shiz out of this world. And I'll torture all my enemies. And, like, whatever else I wanna do!"

Patrick walked to the nearest wall and punched a hole right through it, letting the sunlight in. He was certainly transformed. The top half of his head was covered in a sleek black helmet. The rest of him was a not quite man. And not quite machine. "I need to find some clothes," he thought out loud.

Patrick looked at the ruined city below and saw nothing but potential for growth…and so much destruction. "In honor of this sweet, unadulterated awesomeness, I'm going to give myself a new name. In honor of the machine who accidentally gave me everything I've ever hoped for. From now on, the world can call me…The Nexis!"

The Nexis laughed so hard he could barely stand.

Now the Nexis sat in the luxury box of his stadium, alone. "In case you couldn't tell by my face, I am not in a good mood." He watched the emergence of twenty new cyborgs from the enlightenment chambers below. Usually, this brought him joy; his army growing. But not today. Two days ago Rumi and Aggie had made an utter mockery of everything he'd built over the past months. He had been diligently concocting wild plan after wild plan to retaliate.

Fortunately, with intelligence ranging across the full contents of the world wide web and a wireless connection to over a thousand obedient high-tech minions, there was very little The Nexis couldn't accomplish. "Yes. Yes, I know! I am well aware of my mistakes!" He argued with the voice inside his head, a remnant of an old program. "You just wait and see what I do next. I'll show you. I'll show you all why I am the greatest!"

"All that boasting and so little to show for it."

The Nexis was startled by the other presence that joined him in the box. It was tall and wide, black and man-shaped.

"I am Nihilo," boomed the voice.

"What are you, like a living shadow or something?"

"I am the manifestation of nothingness."

"Well, that's not helpful." The Nexis marched closer to Nihilo. "If you're here to kill me, I'd advise against it." The Nexis moved to poke Nihilo in the chest, but his finger went right through him. "Oh, poop."

"I am not here to harm you. Only to offer you what you so desperately desire."

The Nexis plopped onto a cushioned chair and reclined it as far as it would go. "And what's that, Mister Know It All?"

"Revenge."

"Hm. Yes. That sounds about right."

"I know where Rumi, Aggie, and the lost prisoners are."

"Duh! So do I! As soon as I rebooted I sent a pair of spy-bots after their heat signature." The Nexis showed off a proud smirk. Then, to the voice in his head, he added, "It was not your idea. It was mine!" The Nexis leapt from his seat and gazed out at his cyborgs doing various tasks under the giant dome. "Ah, Nilly. Can I call you Nilly? If you don't have anything of value to tell me, please return to whatever ink blot test you jumped off of and—"

"Claire is there as well."

The Nexis halted. He chewed on a fingernail. Paced. Stopped. Paced some more. Stopped again. "That's valuable information," he admitted. "If it's true."

"It is. She is there with the boy who stole her from you. And their child."

The Nexis practically tripped over his own feet. "I meant to do that." He walked toward the bar at the back of the room. "Claire has a child? I'm an uncle?" He reached behind the bar and produced a shot glass and a bottle of tequila. "This changes things." He poured himself a glass. "Claire's a liar and a weak, fleshy human. She doesn't deserve a child. Why should she get to have a family of her own? Especially after the way she treated me." He took the shot. "I'm going to take that baby and raise it right. Oh! Or kill it in front of her."

"Already the enemy is expecting you. They have soldiers and magic. A Lucid more powerful than Jack."

The Nexis poured himself another shot and drank it. "Listen, tall, dark, and dimensionless, I am well prepared. The fiasco in the stadium a couple days ago is nothing. I'm back and better than ever. Jerry, Spencer, and the gang are all repaired. And, on top of that, my nerd-bots and I have been working on a top secret new toy that we've been dying to take for a spin." To the voice in his head, the Nexis shouted, "I'm going to accomplish what you never could, you outdated hunk of junk."

24

Max unlocked the door and Jamal carried the cardboard box inside. Following a few hellos to Max's parents and his little sister, the two boys descended to the basement: Max's father's pride and joy. It was an open space with leather furniture, a bar, dartboard, state-of-the-art sound system and the almighty seventy-two inch flat screen TV. It was also quite clear from the decor that Max's dad was a Seahawks fan.

"Where should I put this thing?" Jamal asked. Max pointed to the glass coffee table and Jamal set the box down. The boys stood side by side, their arms crossed, and eyed the box. They took this time to let sink in the fact that they had just stolen the belongings of a dead person. Max went over to the mini-fridge and grabbed a couple of Cokes. He tossed one to Jamal.

"What now?" Max popped open his can and took a swig.

Jamal knelt before the coffee table. He set his Coke down and wedged his hand in the folded flaps at the top of the box. "We open it."

Max and Jamal spent a few minutes laying the contents of the box across the table. There had to have been a hundred pages of notes written on everything from Post-Its and loose leaf to torn-out textbook pages and even toilet paper. The journal was there as well. And, most interesting of all, three folded maps: one of the Earth, one of the United States, and a particularly old-looking map of Addley and the surrounding townships. Everything was covered in Vic's barely-to-not-at-all legible handwriting going in every direction in a dozen colors. There were drawings, too. Diagrams, mostly, framed in complex mathematical equations.

Max ran both hands down the sides of his freckled

face. "I think my brain just had a heart attack looking at this stuff."

"Yeah." Jamal brought a square of toilet paper covered in Sharpie to his eyes. "Not sure a couple of guys who can barely pull a C in chem are equipped to decipher the brain of a world super-genius."

"Dude, I'd sell my left ball to get a C in Chem." The faint song of a doorbell could be heard upstairs. Then the sound of footsteps overhead. Something like, "Hi, what a nice surprise!" followed by low chatting and ending with, "The boys are downstairs."

A short time later the basement door creaked open and down came Claire and Anne.

Claire took notice of the papers. "Did you find anything?"

Jamal shook his head. "Sorry, babe." He angled himself to kiss her as she approached, but she brushed past him, grabbed the journal, and took a seat on the black leather couch. "It all might as well be hieroglyphics to me."

"Anne," Claire barked. "Grab some notes and come sit with me. Someone spread out the maps."

Max laid out all three maps, side by side, on the carpeted floor.

"See that symbol?" Claire pointed to the map of the earth. Her words were rushed, erratic. "It's like a triangle with a diagonal line through the center?" Jamal nodded. The others saw it as well. The symbol appeared in at least a hundred places on the map of the earth. On the map of the United States, the symbol had been drawn eight times. A single occurrence of the symbol appeared in the far upper right corner of the Addley map. The locations of the symbols seemed to correlate from map to map. "We have to find out what it means."

"What about the other symbols?" Anne asked. There were a couple of others, none nearly as plentiful as the triangle with the line through it. The largest was one that resembled an eight-point star. It had been drawn over most of West Africa.

"Ignore them." Claire was already flipping through the pages of the journal.

Five minutes passed in silence.

Anne leaned to Claire. "What are you hoping to find?"

Claire gave Anne the sort of cold, hateful glare she used to give her all the time, then turned her body away and continued to read Vic's journal.

Anne stood up, the papers on her lap falling to the floor. "We're your friends, Claire. If there's something going on in your life then we deserve to know exactly what it is. After all we've done for you lately, we at least deserve the truth. When have any of us ever turned away when you really needed us?"

Tears welled in Claire's eyes and her hands started to shake. "I shouldn't have to need anyone."

"Do you realize how stupid that sou—"

"I hear voices!" Claire was on her feet and in Anne's face before anyone had the time to process it.

Anne's mouth hung a little open, her worried eyes magnified behind thick lenses. She struggled for words. Max and Jamal watched quietly from the floor.

"This voice," Claire continued. "It's just a whisper, but I used to think it was my thoughts. I don't know. Ever since I got here, to earth or whatever, it's been here. It used to come every once and a while but now it's almost every day."

"Why didn't you tell us?" asked Anne.

"Because you all already think I'm crazy! A murderer! And you know what, I am! I'm both! And it's because I'm here!" Claire was full-on crying now, her face red and twisted.

Jamal went to her side and placed his hands on her shoulders. He gave her a gentle kiss on the cheek. And the neck.

"Timeout, guys." Max crawled across the floor, over the maps, past Jamal, Claire, and Anne, to the journal. It had fallen to the floor when Claire got up. Max took a look at the page it had opened to. It was written in handwriting that was not Vic's. It was clearer. There was a horizontal line. Each end of the line had an arrow tip pointed outward. One arrow pointed to the word "Cosmos," the other "Reverie." At the center of the line was the triangle symbol. Above the symbol someone wrote the word, "Door." Max showed the page to the others. "Check this out."

Claire's reddened eyes grew larger. "I knew it!" She pushed herself away from Jamal then closely eyed the Addley map on the floor.

"Babe, what are you doing?" asked Jamal.

Claire frantically typed something into her phone as she slowly rose to her feet. "I, uh, have to go to the bathroom." Before anyone could respond, Claire was charging up the stairs, two steps at a time, out of the basement, deaf to the shouts of her friends telling her to stop as they heard the front door swing open.

25

The last twenty-four hours had put Mindy's resilience and leadership prowess to the test. Following Rumi and Aggie bursting into her cottage and the impromptu war council it had prompted, Mindy called an official meeting of the tribunal in her dining room. Rumi and Aggie made their arguments and described the threat in great detail before setting off for Jack. The tribunal, consisting of Mindy, Zen, and two others, discussed amongst themselves for another hour. Victor, Claire, and Anza rested in another room.

Del, a big-boned old man, tanned and muscled from decades working the fields, shrugged and spat a wad of tobacco through his wild gray beard. "Better safe than sorry. 'N that's that." He was the third member of the tribunal and the oldest living native of the Valley.

"Wasteful," said Peeps, the fourth and final member of the tribunal with a voice equal parts gravel and femininity. Peeps was a goblin. She was easily seven feet tall, curvy with black straw-like hair that hung in a tangle just past her shoulder blades. Her skin was the muted green of swamp fog. She wore a crudely designed burlap dress. What stood out the most were her large eyes, round as saucers with irises yellow as the sun. She had been Aemon's accountant before his disappearance.

"Resources low," Peeps warned. "Too many. You spit on this, yes? Bah. Soon food, poof, all gone. Then what? War? Hypothetical, maybe. War costs. We cannot pay. Lives. Resources." To Mindy, she added, "Wager of fools, relying on your Lucid for all time."

Despite Peep's concerns, the majority voted in favor of war.

Mindy made the announcement to the creatures of the Valley. She stood atop a tree trunk, beneath a cloudy sky, and addressed hundreds amassed around her. "There is not a person here who does not know what it means to suffer. It is what makes us strong. It is what makes us family. We have lost enough family in these strange times to say with confidence that we will fight to maintain the one we've gained here in the Valley of Hope." Her speech was given to the backdrop of soft cheers and sounds of earnest approval. "It is with great regret that I tell you the darkness is near. War is upon us." Nervous murmurs rose up from the crowd. "The machines have grown in strength and capability and our intelligence tells us they march for the Valley." More murmurs. More fear.

A man shouted, "They led them to us!" His finger pointed shakily at the latest group of refugees. "The machines want them! Not us!" Words of complaint sprung from other sections of the crowd.

Mindy raised her hand. "Silence," she said, and there was quiet again. She directed her words to the first man who spoke. There was compassion in her tone. "I understand that you're afraid. Fear is a powerful thing. It fills you up with crazy energy and, if you don't control it, it can transform you into someone you don't want to be. Someone paranoid. And angry. Someone distrustful. And, worst of all, hopeless." She turned her attention to everyone. "Ever since we defeated the machines the first time, their return was inevitable. So the question becomes, will we let our fear cripple us or turn us against one another, or will we let it turn us into one unified force to be reckoned with?" She smiled. "After having spent almost a year with you guys, I think we all know what the answer will be." Cheers went up. "Intelligence says we should prepare for the machine's arrival in three days. Our preparation will be in three parts. Those who wish to fight, join Zen in the rock fields immediately. Those who wish to aid in the building of walls, stand outside of my cottage. A man by the name of Pasqual will be waiting for you. Everyone else, see Del or Peeps about resource needs. Thank you."

Mindy and Pasqual discussed the topography of the

Valley and the Black Forest and fortification strategies as Pasqual's group collected large stones and wood.

Mindy inspected Zen's army, two hundred strong. From what Rumi and Aggie had reported, it wouldn't be enough. Not even close. But they had to try. "I hope Nikkylos receives my message," she thought aloud.

Jason appeared that night and was immediately put to work, imagining into reality strong walls and other barricades with the help of the supplies collected throughout the day and according to Pasqual's plans. It was some of his most impressive work as a Lucid to date.

After greeting Jason and debriefing him, Mindy decided it best to relocate her current housemates. She led Victor, Claire, and Anza into Black Rock, up the spiral stairs, and into the small gray room where she had been held prisoner. Mindy had already furnished the room with a bed and crib. "I don't think Reverie can afford anything bad happening to you guys," she said. "You don't have to stay here, but I'd just feel better if you did when the war starts. Jason can seal the entrance."

"Mindy," said Claire, just as the other was turning to leave.

Mindy turned to her. "Yes?"

"How are you so calm?" she asked. "I mean, about all this?"

Victor nodded. "It's like you were born here."

Anza cooed.

Mindy thought about it. Then allowed for the smallest hint of smile. "There are people who run and people who fight. Running's easy, but all it really teaches you is to keep doing it. To run faster, you know? Staying and fighting forces you to grow. It was a lesson that took me years to learn, long before Reverie." Mindy paused, seeing for a moment in her mind a dark shape in her doorway, demanding that she not scream. She blinked it away and continued, "There'll always be a bigger monster, just as there'll always be an opportunity to adapt." With that, she shrugged matter-of-factly, like a normal seventeen-year-old girl, and left the room.

Mindy continued up the stone stairs, the orb in her staff lighting the way. The Black Rock was mostly unused these days, a dark relic from a darker time, shrouded in tales and horror and superstition. Mindy slipped in through the double doors, giant marble slabs left slightly ajar. As always, the main hall was lit by an unseen force, albeit dimly. The space was so vast that its arched roof disappeared into shadow. Once, the hall housed beautiful statues and a throne of bones, but these had since been destroyed in protest of tyrants past.

"Aemon," whispered Mindy. From behind a pillar a pair of ice blue eyes blinked open. He emerged, looking much healthier than he had that night in the cave. Though the way he held himself, demure and uncertain, seemed to weaken him nonetheless.

"Lady M-Mindy," he began, smiling with fanged white teeth. "I-it's not yet the end of the week. To what do I owe the pleasure?"

Mindy took in the awe-inspiring size of the space, as she always did, thinking of its potential uses once the memories attached to it had faded amongst the people. "Do you have enough food? Enough drink?"

Aemon nodded graciously. "Oh yes, Lady Mindy. I want for nothing."

"Good." Mindy spun the staff slowly in her hands, eyes trained on the glowing orb. "And have you been practicing your gift?"

Aemon's eyes widened at that. "I...well...it is lonely up here sometimes and...t-to pass the time..."

"It's fine," said Mindy. "Show me."
He put his arms out in front of him and stared at a pile of rubble a few feet away. A couple rocks separated themselves from the rest and floated a few feet in the air.

"Good." Mindy moved behind Aemon. "Now do the whole pile."

"I've never tri—"

"Just do it."

Aemon again held out both arms and concentrated. This time, every rock in the pile levitated.

"See?" Mindy looked around. "Keep practicing. There are a ton of rooms here. Feel free to trash anything. The bigger and heavier the better." She placed her hands on his broad shoulders. "You are a powerful man and I need you to realize that."

Even if this Aemon was not quite the one she'd first met, the closeness to him energized her. It was a blend of old fears and current curiosity. She couldn't quite untangle one from the other. Nor could she ignore the gentle high she got from feeling such power over someone so powerful.

Aemon turned to face her. Their eyes met and lingered a moment too long.

Mindy began walk away, but Aemon caught her hand in his. "I will do as you say."

Mindy blushed at his sincerity. Then pulled her hand from his grasp. "I'll come back tomorrow to help you." She started for the door.

"I must have done something truly, truly horrible," said Aemon as she slipped out the door, "for you to hide me away like this."

"Yes. But you will have your chance to make amends very, very soon. Goodnight, Aemon."

"Goodnight to you, Mindy."

26

Claire cruised down the streets of Addley in her flashy red convertible, well above the speed limit. She cursed to herself for not bringing the map with her in all the excitement. Not because she didn't remember the location—she'd saved that on her phone. It was because had she snatched up the map, her friends would not have been able to follow her.

Claire spotted the old blue car, with its duct-taped headlight and dent along the passenger side, creeping up on her. Jamal was driving. Max was beside him, pointing and shouting lots of somethings. Anne was in the back seat with the map.

Addley became a streak of green and orange and black as Claire picked up speed through a town decorated for Halloween. Her car had better speed, handling, and acceleration than Jamal's. On top of that, the roads were never all that packed in Addley. She lost them before she reached the town's limits.

"Where are you going?"

"No!" shouted Claire to the stranger that spoke in her head. "Shut up! I'm getting rid of you forever!"

"You have to turn around."

"I do not! I'm tired of you! I'm tired of this town!"

"You have to know me."

Claire was going ninety down an empty stretch of road surrounded by farmland on each side. She started to sweat. Nerves, she thought. Adrenaline. She slowed enough to put the top down and the wind took hold of her golden hair. "Freedom," she said. "Freedom."

The road took her through the town of Stanley. She checked her mirrors at every red light. Jamal and the gang were nowhere in sight.

Claire exited onto a narrow road that snaked around

a mountainside. The autumn forest closed in on all sides, like a tunnel of fire. She started to feel woozy. The sweat intensified. Motion sickness, she thought.

"Turn around."

"I can't hear you!"

"Turn back, please. You're getting sick."

Claire turned on the radio and turned the volume as high as it would go. A heavy bass and the harsh lyrics of a rap song pushed out the sounds of the engine, the wind.

"You're getting sick! Before you know me—"

"I don't want to know you, understand? Now leave me alone! I need you to leave me alone!"

The voice went silent then and Claire wondered why she hadn't used her powers on it earlier.

She had been driving for an hour and a half since leaving Addley. She spent another hour on that winding road. It emptied onto a highway. The sun was beginning to disappear behind the horizon. It was taking much longer than she thought.

Her journey took her to a two lane highway then another set of twisting roads. Five hours passed when she came upon a dirt path so unused it was overrun with rocks and grass and weeds. It was a bumpy ride, a slow one, but according to her map app she was nearly there.

Claire's vision began to blur in waves, as if an optometrist was trying different lens types on her. Sweat had soaked her sundress. She was having trouble maintaining a grip on the steering wheel. Her hands were growing pale. Even holding down the gas pedal was becoming difficult.

The sun was almost completely set when Claire spotted a bright light up ahead. *This is it*, she thought, a pulse of much-needed lucidity energizing her. She guided her convertible, now covered in scratches from her multiple times brushing a little too close to low branches, toward the light.

"No." She saw the light ahead for what it truly was.

Claire shifted to park. Turning around was out of the question on the narrow woodland path and she didn't have the focus or strength to go into reverse. She staggered out of the car and ran off the path, into the trees.

"Claire!" shouted Jamal. He, Max, and Anne had reached the spot first. "Babe, come back here!"

With only the last remnants of daylight to guide her, Claire felt her way through the thick forest. She checked her phone, her destination marked on the device. Claire's vision failing, her muscles feeling like jelly, she continued forward, ignoring the pain and the concerned calls of her friends.

"Hey, Claire!"

She shielded her eyes from the cell phone flashlight pointed at her. Max had cut her off. Claire noticed Jamal closing in from the side. And Anne from behind. They approached her like a hunter would a ferocious animal. With caution.

"Leave me alone!" Claire was short of breath. Hardly able to stand upright. She glanced at her phone. "I have to do this!"

"Do what?" There were tears in Jamal's eyes. "Kill yourself?"

"No!" She said the word with such force that a splash of blood flew from her mouth, landing on her lower lip and dripping down her chin. "I'm freeing myself! Don't you get it?" She would have fallen over then, had she not propped herself up on a tree trunk.

Claire backed away from them. All three moved in. She licked the dryness from her lips. "I need you to not come any closer."

"What the?" Max looked frustrated, as he was physically unable to take a step forward, hard as he tried. None of them could.

Claire smiled and attempted to make another step toward her goal, but instead collapsed to the ground. Sticks and stones tore through her fragile skin, sending sharp pains up her arms. She coughed. More blood spilled from her mouth. Still, she tried to crawl toward her goal. One arm. Then another. One leg…

"You'll die," said Jamal in a whimper. The snot dripping from his nose mixed with the tears from his eyes. "After all we've been through. Why? Why would you do this?"

"Maybe I want to die." Claire's arms gave out and her face met with the forest floor. "Maybe anything is better…better than…" She lifted her head to the sky. "It should…be here…it should…be…right here…"

"I almost killed myself," Anne said. Claire looked up at Anne, who stood between a clearly distraught Jamal and Max, who seemed frozen in terror. "You know this, Claire. I almost hanged myself because I thought that there was no other way. But I lived on a technicality. And I thank God every day that I did. Because once you reach the absolute worst place you can be in—and make it through to the other side—you start to see, really see, how good your world could be."

Claire felt a hot tear of blood weave its way down her gaunt face.

"People say suicide is selfish," Anne continued. "I say that's a selfish way to look at it. Because when you would rather die than live, it's not that you're not thinking about others. It's that you can't. The noise from the hopelessness and the depression is just too loud…and all you want is peace and quiet." Anne looked again to Jamal's watery red eyes. To Max's shaking hands. "We love you, Claire. Maybe we're not what you wished for, but we are yours. And no matter how much you beat yourself up over Guillelmina. No matter what voices you hear. No matter how much you push us away. We're here for you. Just like you are for us. So, please, Claire, let us in."

Claire could barely move or breathe, let alone speak. But she did nonetheless. "I…" Her mouth was desert dry. "I need…" Each syllable hurt to form. "I need…you…"

The invisible barrier that separated Claire Ashford from her friends was no more.

———

Karen sat on a bar stool in her spacious kitchen. Two martini glasses rested on the marble counter before her. One empty. One full. Her housekeeper, Paulina, was preparing a third near the sink.

In recent days, Karen had stopped complaining about her blindness, but only because she was so focused into keeping the secret of her handicap from friends. Well that, and getting as drunk as possible by noon.
She raised a glass to her lips, but it never completed its journey. The glass shattered against the floor and Paulina shrieked as Karen Ashford went into a seizure. Her body convulsed in her seat. She made a guttural sound, as if choking. From the blackness of her vision, faint colors took form.

She could feel the stool beneath her still. The cool counter against her palms. But she was seeing something altogether different. She was in a field. Then a city made of iridescent crystals. Suddenly the city was engulfed in flame. There was a war raging all around her at the base of an impossibly high mountain made of black rock. Robots and other familiar nightmares were fighting creatures of all kinds. She could've sworn she saw Jason for an instant. Then everything exploded into a great white light and from it, Claire and Victor emerged, terrified. They were calling for "Anza," their voices swallowed by the emptiness all around them. Something dark and jagged appeared, like someone had torn a hole in reality itself. Bolts of lightning, blinding white, zigzagged from it, reaching for Claire and Victor.

Then Karen noticed Anza, suspended in the expanding tear, crying and reaching out to her parents. The bolts of lightning sliced through Claire and Victor, killing them as they called their daughter's name. The blackness grew until there was practically nothing else and the lightning bolts disappeared, leaving only Anza floating there. Anza came closer. Close enough for Karen to see her big hazel eyes and wisps of dark brown hair. And then the baby's eyes turned black. Her small lips curled into a grimace.

A voice grumbled, "MINE," and the baby dissolved in a puff of silvery smoke.

Karen screamed. The vision ceased and she was blind once again. "Paulina!" she called, slamming her hand against the counter as she did. "Call Jason NOW!"

PART III

27

Roughly four thousand years ago, Dionysus, god of birth and death, of passion and wine, was on the run.

All the gods on Earth were at war and, while he was adept at many things, fighting was not one of them. So he ran north. So far north that the lush green mountains and crystal blue waters of the Mediterranean gave way to harsh terrain, blanketed in snow and ice. It was here that Dionysus first fell in love.

In a glistening silver castle on an island in the middle of a frozen lake, Dionysus met Forseti, the Norse god of truth and peace. At first they appeared to have nothing in common, aside from their aversion to the war. Forseti was careful, logical. Dionysus, spontaneous and driven by emotion. But, in time, they found balance in each other. Then friendship. Then love.

Months later there came a knock to the castle door. It was a god so famed even Dionysus knew of him. Baldr, god of justice and, as it turned out, father of Forseti. It was hard to tell what angered Baldr more; that his son had deserted the war or that he had formed a romantic relationship with a male god, and a foreign one at that. Blaming Dionysus for his son's decisions, Baldr swung his giant axe at him. Fueled by love for Dionysus, Forseti leaped between him and Baldr, taking his father's axe to the chest. Forseti died instantly. Stricken with grief, Dionysus ran once more as Baldr swore an oath of vengeance for the loss of his son.

In the centuries that followed, Baldr stayed true to his promise. He hunted Dionysus across much of modern day Europe and Asia, into Africa. Dionysus grew exhausted with this life on the run. He stood at the edge of a muddy river one night, thinking about the mess his life had become. It was then that the goddess first appeared to him, rising from the black water of the river, standing between the tall reeds.

"I am Olokun," she said. "Goddess of the mysterious depths of the sea. Of life. Of death. Of worlds unknown." Dionysus made to speak, but she interrupted. "And you are Dionysus, forlorn and far from home."

Olokun said she needed Dionysus to help her create a better world. One ruled by love, not war. He agreed to assist her, since anything was an improvement over his current life. In exchange Olokun cast a spell that has allowed him to survive for so long. To be reborn again and again. They did not speak for millennia after that. He had lived many lives, the pain of Forseti fading with each one. But never completely.

Countless lives and deaths later, Dionysus was born unto a single mother in Lebanon. She had been raped and was very poor. His childhood was a struggle, but he, like most children, found ways to dream of a better life; of fancy cars and beautiful ladies and perhaps even a life in America. As dictated by Olokun's spell, on his fifteenth birthday, he learned who he was. A god of legend. He remembered his past lives as if they were someone else's memories, distant and surreal. He changed his name to Dion. By seventeen, using his godly abilities, he had made his mother one of the richest women in Lebanon. Then, one night, Olokun appeared, at long last calling in that favor. Dion kissed his mother goodbye and disappeared with the goddess, reappearing in a posh condominium in Beirut.

It was soon clear that Olokun had grown frustrated over the millennia for a number of reasons, but mostly due to having not yet discovered the resources to create her perfect world. She had become desperate, seeking answers from the deepest, darkest corners of existence. It was in that condominium where Dion learned that Olokun had allied herself with a being called Nihilo. Nihilo claimed to be an all-powerful creature from another world; one who could make all of Olokun's desires real if she followed his commands.

"Olokun," boomed Nihilo. "Our plan grows nearer to fruition."

Dion watched in silence, half hidden around a corner, as the black silhouette explained itself.

"You must travel to America. To a town called Addley. There you will attend a funeral for a dream medium called Guillelmina. She is the keeper of the item we seek. Furthermore, you will find a Lucid by the name of Jason Baker. Hair, raven black. Eyes, ice blue. He is only a human, but in Reverie his power is near limitless. He must be destroyed if our goal is to be reached." And, with those words, Nihilo disappeared.

It was the first time Dion had heard the name Jason Baker. Dion was intrigued. And since whatever plans she had for Dion would have to wait, he accompanied Olokun to Addley and found himself immediately enamored by Jason. His compassion. His confidence. His eyes. For the first time in two thousand years Dion was reminded of Forseti.

Dion was uncharacteristically nervous. Since he and Jason started dating they hadn't gone an hour without texting each other about school or pop culture or Reverie or how much they liked each other. It had been a full day without a word. Max told him that Jason was home sick. Instead of waiting around, Dion hopped in his car and drove to Jason's house.

Dusk was giving way to night and no lights were on at Jason's place. Dion walked the stone path to his small porch and reached under the welcome mat for the spare key. He didn't want to wake Jason's grandmother.

The home was eerily quiet save for the TV in the living room. It was playing The Price is Right reruns for Grammy Baker who snored heavily in response. Dion climbed the creaking stairs as quietly as they'd allow. He stood before Jason's door and gave it a knock. And another. He heard no sound, but sensed Jason's presence.

Dion opened the door just enough to see inside the room. The lights were out and the bed was empty. But on the corner, wrapped in blankets, was Jason, lying in the fetal position, head facing the wall.

"Jason," whispered Dion and the other did not move or respond. "Jason," he said again as he took one careful step into the room.

"Go away," Jason moaned, muffled by the blanket.

Dion's heart sunk at his words, but he continued, cautious and sly as if sneaking up on unsuspecting prey.

"I said go away." Jason's voice was weak, but determined. Dark, even. "I don't want you here."

"You—" Dion stopped himself. He knew it was Jason's emotions talking, not his heart, his soul. Dion had learned the difference between such things long ago. He moved forward and knelt down beside Jason. "I'm here for you," he said. "Always."

Jason groaned, then, and turned his body so that he could face Dion. Jason's hair was in disarray, his eyes and face red from crying, snot and spittle dried around his nose and lips. "Th-this," he stuttered. "This is who I really am! How could you ever want something like this?" A new stream of tears worked their way down Jason's cheeks.

Dion smiled a simple smile and placed his hands on Jason. He closed his eyes and felt the other's emotions the way only a god could. They were a raging sea inside his mind, a sickness beyond his control, transforming him into something he was not. Dion paused, remembering the creature he had been so long ago and how that creature would incite such emotions in others to make them do terrible things. But Dionysus was no more. There was only Dion and the eighteen years he had lived. And there was Jason, and the love Dion had for him. If he could bring rage to a tranquil sea then surely he could bring tranquility to a raging one. Forseti, god of peace, would have done the same.

Dion visualized the white-capped waves and booming thunder of Jason's psyche giving way to a smooth, gentle seascape beneath a warm and cloudless sky. Jason fell into a deep calm. He blinked, confused and grateful for something he could not fully understand.

"You?" Jason asked.

Dion nodded in reply.

Jason rested his head against Dion's chest and Dion put his arms around the other. "Us."

28

"You took long enough," said the woman standing beside a sleek, black aircraft, almost exactly the color of the biker suit she wore. She had caramel skin and olive green eyes. She was short, but muscular. A thick tangle of curls fanned out around her heart-shaped head, black with a single magenta streak. She smiled, her white teeth framed in jet black lipstick.

"Eliza," said Rumi, picking up speed as she approached her, Aggie trailing behind. Rumi practically knocked Eliza to the ground as she dived in for a hug. "I can't believe it. You're—"

"Alive?" Eliza grinned and offered a sly wink. "Girl, can't nothing kill me but boredom and boring I ain't. Where's Pasqual?"

"Doing what he does best," Rumi explained. "Making sure things get built." She ran her fingers against the cool metallic shell of the Acewing. "Where have you been all this time?"

"Keeping the revolution alive, girl. After I lost contact with our comms, I figured I follow some of them bots and 'borgs and take them out before they killed any more people. And, Rumz, the stuff I seen out there…"

"I know, Elz."

Aggie cleared her throat loud enough to pull the other two ladies from their conversation. Behind her hundreds of creatures were gathering supplies or suiting up in armor or practicing their combat skills.

"Oh!" Rumi placed a friendly arm around Aggie. "This is Agalfia Tirk, badass. Agalfia, this is Eliza Johnson. We were trained together. No one handles a gun or takes a punch like she does."

"I appreciate your kinship," said Aggie, "but we

have little time."

"You're right." Rumi turned to Eliza. "She's right. We'll catch up on the ride."

The three young ladies climbed into the Acewing. Rumi took the pilot's seat and they lifted gracefully off the ground. The ship rotated just a bit before rocketing off above the trees.

In a little under an hour they flew past the cliff face and out into the abyss that once held Jack's dream world. The ride had left Aggie feeling sick, but she did her best not to show it.

"There!" Eliza spotted the speck floating in the sky a mile away. As distance closed between them, the speck began to take form. Within seconds the Acewing hovered over what was most definitely a young man. He was skinny and short, naked and suspended. Eyes closed as if in the deepest sleep.

"Who is that?" asked Rumi, examining the person through the windshield.

Aggie leaned over Rumi's shoulder and took a closer look. "I...I think it's Jack."

"No way!" Rumi gave the young man another glance. "Jack is way more...muscular and..."

"Hot," Eliza added.

"Bring me to him." Aggie pointed to the levers and switches at the dashboard. Rumi pressed a couple of buttons and steered the Acewing below the floating man. The shifting of gears signaled the opening of the roof hatch. Before it was fully opened Aggie was already lifting herself up and out. Once again she looked at the man, who now floated only a foot above her head. She noticed the familiar nose. The familiar ears and eyebrows. "This is Jack," she said, confident as ever. "This is Jack as he appears in his world of origin. On Earth." Aggie extended her hand and brushed it gently against the young frail man's cheek. "It is time to wake up, my love. We need you now. We—"

Jack's deep brown eyes snapped open. His heart was pounding. His arms and legs reached for stable ground they could not find. And then he laid eyes on the pretty blonde woman by his side. He gasped, then whispered, "Aggie? Is that you? I…" His eyes grew large then as if he were struck with a mighty realization. An astoundingly happy one. "Aggie, I think I'm…I think I'm waking u—"

And then, for the second time in Aggie's presence, Jack disappeared.

29

Karen sat on her living room floor, propping herself with one hand as the other clutched an empty bottle of pinot grigio. She was on the verge of napping when a powerful series of knocks on her door jarred her to attention.

Karen scrambled to her feet and felt her way out of the living room, down the hall, and to the foyer as the knocking became louder and more emphatic. She made contact with the door and pressed the side of her head against it. "Who's there? Jason, is that you?"

"No," said the voice on the other side. "It's Claire. I need a place to stay. And before you say something snarky or bitchy, just please, please show some compassion. My friends, I just can't be with them right now and I don't want to talk about why, but just know if I had any other options I wouldn't be here right now so—"

Karen pulled open the door and reached for Claire. She missed at the first attempt, but made contact with her wrist on the second. Karen yanked Claire inside and slammed the door closed. "What are you trying to do? Embarrass me in front of the whole neighborhood? Martha Henderson is just looking for another excuse to belittle me after the field day she had when I made Fernando plant non-regulation flowers in the yard." Karen lightened her grip on Claire's wrist. "Walk me to the kitchen."

Claire lead Karen down the hall into the spacious kitchen. She had heard of Karen's blindness, but seeing the blackness of her eyes was surprising still.

"You've got such soft hands. Such smooth skin," said Karen as she moved down the hall. Her breath, pungent with old wine. "I had hands like that once. Age takes that away, no matter how hard you fight it. Take me to my stool."

The kitchen was a mess of broken glass and overturned bowls and chairs. A golden liquid had been spilled as well. Amidst the disarray stood a single stool against the kitchen island. Claire guided Karen's hand to it and the woman took a seat. "What happened here?" Claire asked.

Karen grunted. "A disagreement. Pour me a glass of scotch. Second shelf above the sink." Claire did as she was told as Karen continued. "I saw something. Something awful. A vision. My dear, sweet baby girl and my granddaughter were in danger. Perhaps I overreacted when I took my housekeeper by the hair and yelled at her to call Jason Baker. She shouted something in Spanish and then ran off. Something about calling la policia. Oh please. They're my policia, not hers. Where's my drink?" Claire pressed the glass against Karen's palm and she took hold of it. Karen took a satisfied sip and said, "Pour yourself one, girl."

"I'm sixteen."

Karen laughed. "You're nothing. Imaginary. And even if you were sixteen, I've never met a girl who looked like you and didn't get trashed on the weekends, spreading their legs open for any Tom, Dick, or Harry who handed out a six-pack. Ha!"

Claire touched her fingers to her face. The scars from her time in the woods hadn't healed yet.

"Take out your phone and call Jason. I need to talk to him."

Claire produced her phone and dialed Jason's number. After a couple of rings his voicemail picked up. "He didn't answer."

"Well. Try again."

She did. Another voicemail.

"Gimme the phone," said Karen. Claire placed the phone in her hand. "Jason. My baby's in trouble. Call me on Claire's phone ASAP or I'll hang myself and haunt you 'til your dead." Karen slammed the phone on the table. She let out a sigh and finished the rest of her drink in one heavy gulp. "You still dating the black one?"

"Jamal?" Claire propped herself on the island. She looked away, pensive. "I'm not sure."

Karen grinned. "You're just like me, you know? Lost. Stupid. I don't hate you because you remind me of my daughter. I hate you because having you around was reminded me of..." Karen trailed off, gesturing lazily to herself. "Finding out you weren't real was just a convenient excuse." Karen's chuckle was reminiscent of a growl. "The truth is, Claire, that people like us aren't meant to be happy. We're the monsters who get slayed or screwed over in the end. Don't forget that. And, the saddest thing is, we bring it on ourselves. Every time, we do it to ourselves. And when people show us the least bit of compassion, it reminds us of how weak we truly are and we run away."

Claire said nothing. She was glad Karen couldn't see the tears swelling in her eyes.

Karen grinned. "We're the same, Claire. We're the same and we get what we deserve."

A low buzz cut through the tension and Claire lifted her phone from the counter. "It's Jason," she announced. "Hello?"

"Give me the phone!" Karen barked. "Now!"

Claire listened a bit, taking in Jason's words. She climbed off of the counter and shoved her phone in her pocket.

"What are you doing?" asked Karen, frantic, feeling around where Claire had been. "Where are you going?"

"It's Jack," said Claire. "He's awake."

30

"I feel like a child," said Claire as she rocked a sleeping Anza in her arms.

"Well, we are only sixteen," Victor replied. Claire rolled her eyes. They were in the living room of Mindy's cottage. A handful of voices conversed and occasionally argued in the next room. The sounds were muffled by closed doors.

Claire walked to the door and pressed her ear against it. "I'm just saying that we're a part of this. We should be allowed to talk with the big kids and not be stuck in the baby room." She gestured to Osip and Oleg, Aggie's young brothers, who were blissfully oblivious to the conversation and building a tower out of wooden blocks as Pet watched curiously.

Victor shrugged. "It's a war, Claire. What can we do? Aggie and Rumi and the rest are trained fighters."

"Mindy's not."

"From the stories I've heard, she's pretty capable." Victor plopped down on the couch. "Besides, do you want to fight an army of laser-blasting robots? That can't be something you actually want to do."

"I don't want to do any of this!" Claire snapped. "If it were up to me I'd be in my room at home, watching Hulu and texting Anne about how much school sucks. God, Anne, Anne. I hope she's okay without me."

Victor frowned. "So if it were up to you none of this would have ever happened. Not Anza. Not me." Part of him wanted to end the conversation there, but another, stronger part made him continue. "Remember in the Origin Point when you said you loved me? You said you loved this stupid little family we have. Was that just a lie to pass the time until you figured out an escape, too?"

Claire pulled herself from the door and turned her attention to Victor. "I don't deserve this, Victor. I didn't ask for this. And, yes, if I could press a button and make all of this go away I'd do it in a heartbeat. But that's not life. This, whatever this effed up thing is we've gotten ourselves into, is life. And I think it's totally fair to wish this wasn't the way things were. I also don't think it's fair for you to be mad at me for thinking this way."

"Okay." Victor threw his hands into the air as if surrendering. "Fine." He rose from the couch and approached Claire. "Then give me my baby."

"What?"

Victor stood, arms outstretched. "Regardless of how you feel, Claire, I love you. And I love Anza. So if you want to be without us, if you want to be a loner warrior princess in the next room or whatever, you're free to go. Whatever makes you feel complete."

Vic noticed Claire's grip tightening around Anza and he smiled a simple smile, then took a step back.

"I know you love her," he said. Claire nodded, her eyes glazing over. "And I know you're scared. And when you're scared you get defensive. And your cheeks turn red. And your nose bunches up, which I think is crazy cute, by the way."

Claire almost grinned at that. She eased her hold on Anza and wiped a tear from her eye. "It's just that none of this makes sense. Everyone has a place or this part to play except us. We've been away from our home, our lives, for a year and have no idea what it is we're supposed to be doing. We have no idea what this is all for!"

"You're right." Victor returned to the couch and signaled for Claire to join him. "You're totally right." Once Claire was beside him, he put his arm around her and she rested her head against his shoulder. "It's like we're both the target of some dumb cosmic joke and we can't do anything about it."

"I haven't been the greatest to you, Victor." Claire nuzzled the side of his neck. "I'm sorry."

"It doesn't matter." Victor thought for a bit, then sat straight up. "Maybe it's like Mindy said. Maybe we haven't accomplished anything because we haven't taken charge. We've never paved our own destiny."

Claire's eyes narrowed. "What do you mean?"

"I mean, there's a freaking cyborg army coming. And nobody is sure our side can win. If we go into that little room in the mountain and our team loses and the robots find us then it's over. We're dead. Just because we're not taking control of our own story."

"What are you saying?"

Victor raised an eyebrow. "I'm saying we grab supplies and get out of here."

"That's crazy!" Claire shook her head. "You're the one who wanted to come here in the first place!"

"That was when this was supposed to be a safe haven, not the epicenter of an all-out robot war! We've survived out there before. We can do it again."

Just then a loud noise boomed from the other room. Osip and Oleg gasped, startled, and accidentally knocked their tower down. Curious, the twins opened the doors into the main room. Standing just beyond the inside the cottage's entrance was Zen, drenched in sweat, breathing loudly and heavily. Mindy, Jason, Rumi, Aggie, Peeps, Pasqual, Del, and Eliza were on their feet, awaiting his word.

"My Lady Mindy, all," Zen began, "I have news from one of my scouts. The Nexis' main force has been spotted, marching toward us from the east. By her judgement, they are five hundred strong and heavily armed. Some capable of flight." He added, grimly, "They will reach us within a day."

Amidst the whispers, shouts, and curses that followed, Claire and Victor shared a decisive look. Victor's attention drifted to a sword he'd noticed leaning against a wall in the living room. *You can never be too safe out there*, he thought as Claire set Anza down on the couch to begin packing.

31

"The time has come to fulfill your end of the bargain."
Nihilo stood, looking more out of place than ever, a living
shadow in a sleek and stylish condo in Abidjan. The condo
belonged to Olokun, who sat leisurely in a modern recliner,
slowly taking bites of a mango slice.

"Bargain?" Olokun asked playfully. "I have not the
slightest idea of what you speak."

"This is no time for sarcasm," grumbled the
manifestation of nothingness. "To ensure my plans come to
fruition, Jason Baker must die."

"Oh, that bargain." Olokun pressed a button on the
side of her chair and her large flat TV flashed on. On the
screen a jolly white-haired woman was kneading dough.
"Oh, this is one of my favorite programs. I could watch
televised cooking all day long."

"I gave you the item you sought, did I not?"

"You did, Nilly, my darling, and for that I am
eternally grateful."

"And you will show your gratitude as we discussed.
By disposing of the Lucid."

"Ah, Nilly, Nilly. You know I absolutely adore your
utter…darkness and would move the heavens and the earth
for you, but, unfortunately, a very old friend of mine is
currently smitten with Mr. Baker. It truly is a marvel to see
how enamored those boys are with each other. We both
know I have done a number of questionable things in my
storied history, but let it be known that the goddess Olokun
is not one to betray a friend or hinder the sweet bounty of
love."

"You will pay for your disobedience."

The playfulness in Olokun's demeanor was
immediately replaced by disdain. She dropped the half-eaten

mango slice into a bowl and made a display of rising from her chair. The midnight blue dress she wore moved with her, shimmering and shifting like an ocean at night. Olokun was without expression as she took one pronounced step toward Nihilo. And then another.

She stared into the abyss of Nihilo's face where his eyes might have been and said, "Let me be abundantly clear. First, one does not dare to enter my home and bark threats at me. It is in bad taste and wholly idiotic. Second, and listen closely to this: I used you. Not once did I ever entertain the idea of committing an unjust murder for a mere trinket— thank you, by the way, for that. You see, darling Nihilo, I know what you really are. You and your other so-called manifestations. And I know for a fact that you have no real power, and so you play puppet master, terrifying others to indulge your vile whims." A low rumble emerged from Nihilo's body. "Oh, don't be a child about it. That will get you nowhere. Besides, you're resourceful. I'm sure whatever brand of destruction you have planned will go off without a hitch, even without me."

"You will suffer for this, Olokun. Be certain of that." The goddess only chuckled in response. "But you are correct. There are many means by which one such as I can achieve a goal."

With those words, Nihilo disappeared.

Jack lay in the hospital bed, his frail body lost in his seafoam green gown. Calling it an adjustment would be an understatement, suddenly waking up in a world he had not been a part of in three years, mostly naked and wired to monitors, his muscles degenerated to the point that he could barely move. He was grateful, though, that he was able to see his mother again. The look on her face, the purest, most complete joy and gratitude upon looking into her son's eyes again made all of this almost worth it to Jack. Almost.

"Do you need any water or anything?" asked Anne. She had been at the hospital since school let out. Dion and Jason arrived not long after. Jack's mom had finally decided to drive home and pick up a few of Jack's favorite things to make the rest of his hospital stay a little more comfortable.

"No," Jack said, weakly. His throat burned when he spoke, though the doctors all agreed he was showing signs of recovery far beyond most post-coma patients.

Anne poured him a glass anyway and placed it on the tray beside his bed.

Before Dion and Jason arrived, Jack had told Anne that ever since he 'died' in Reverie, he could hear everything happening around his physical world body. He told her how much he appreciated her visits and the updates she would give him about Reverie. Anne blushed in response.

Jack recognized Jason and Dion by their voices. He thanked Dion for bringing him from his coma and then revealed that it was Aggie who broke him from his slumber, Reverie-side, removing the final tether that kept him trapped between waking and dreaming. He added that he loved Aggie and that he hoped to see her again soon. Anne was less pleased about that part.

"Have you been able to go back to Reverie yet?" Jason asked with a bite of urgency.

Jack shook his head.

"Have you tried?"

Jack nodded. "I-I tried…d-during…nap…"

"Jason." Anne shot him a concerned look. "We shouldn't push him. He's only been awake for—"

"I get it." Apologetic, he continued, "I do, Anne. I do. It's just that war is coming and we need all the help we can get. One more Lucid could turn the tide."

Jack raised his arm with great effort and pointed a shaky hand to Jason. "Y-you're Lu…Lucid."

"Yes. And a pretty good one. Guillelmina taught me

everything she knew."

Jack's heart jumped at the sound of his friend's name. Anne had of course mentioned her death, but only now was it, like so many other things, beginning to feel real. "I...I tried to...go to Reverie, b-but...couldn't..."

"And that's fine," said Anne, sweetly.

Dion placed a hand on Jason's shoulder and shrugged. "It makes sense. He has never actually had to pass into Reverie from a waking state. He learned the skill only when comatose."

"Tomorrow." Jason frowned. "Tomorrow is when hundreds of cyborgs and God knows what else descend on Mindy and the others."

"And Jack can't do anything about it!" Anne snapped.

"He has no choice!" was Jason's reply. To Jack, he said, "You might know Reverie better than any of us. Guillelmina only knew so much because she never went out into the field. I've basically spent every day at Black Rock for the past year, and haven't seen much of what else is out there and...and I can't always be there! I have to wake up and...before Guillelmina died she was teaching me how to meditate...how to get to Reverie without sleeping, but—" Jason was losing his cool. "Maybe if you and I could coordinate sleep schedules, to make sure one of us was always there." Jason leaned close to Jack and stared at him intensely with his bright blue eyes. "When Mindy went missing, Vic had me read a paper on lucid dreaming. The situation was serious and I pulled through. It's probably even more serious now, Jack. So you're going to have to figure this out. There's no other way!"

"Baby." Dion took Jason in his arms and held him tight. "It's okay. Everything will be okay."

Jason's cheeks were red and his breathing was heavy, but he calmed down in Dion's arms. "I just— I can't lose Mindy again."

"And you won't," said Anne confidently.

Jack lifted his head from the pillow as best he could. He opened his mouth, lips trembling, and said, "The paper. G-give me…the…the lucid p-p-paper…"

An old car came to a sputtering stop in front of Jamal's house, disrupting the silence of the upscale neighborhood that night. Max stepped out of the driver's side, still sweaty and dressed in his basketball clothes, carrying a greasy white paper bag. Try-outs were starting in the next few weeks so he and the varsity team decided to play a few games to make sure they were still sharp. Only Jamal didn't attend. He gave the excuse of a stomach virus, but in reality Jamal hadn't gotten over the night with Claire in the woods. Seeing his girlfriend so manic, so bloody and broken. So close to death.

Max rang the doorbell, flashed a mildly flirtatious greeting at Jamal's mom, and made his way upstairs.

"Jamal Thomas Anderson," Max sang as he entered his best friend's spacious room. "I come bearing Taco Bell." He placed the bag on Jamal's large white bed and began unloading soft tacos, chalupas, and hot sauce packets, "We are going to have the best night ever, dude. I'm talking sports bloopers, bro-talk, Netflix, and, most importantly, nothing involving blind alcoholics or coma kids or robots or any of that shit! Tonight, we are normal teenagers in a normal world. Got it?"

"Um. Dude?"

In all his excitement Max had not yet turned to look at Jamal. When he did he noticed his best friend sitting at his glass and marble desk wearing only a pair of boxer briefs, his laptop open to some sports website. Beside the laptop was a familiar map covered in symbols and illegible notes. And standing above that map was something so unexpected that Max's eyes opened wide and he dropped a taco on the floor.

It was a creature, roughly the size and shape of a full grown man, but his featureless face, like the suit that he wore, was paper white.

PART IV

32

There was an eerie silence to the night. A silence as thick as the tension that lingered over the Valley of Hope. The walls had been built to Pasqual's specification and the Futaran walked the perimeter, blueprints in hand, inspecting every inch. The timeline was the shortest he'd ever worked with, but with Jason literally pulling stone from the earth, conjuring staircases and towers, Pasqual didn't consider the situation completely hopeless.

All around the perimeter, men, women, and other creatures hastily finished their final preparations. The last of the swords and arrowheads were being sharpened. The final scraps of mismatched armor, attached and fitted.

Mindy Sparks stood amidst the bustle of the evening, wearing peasant's clothes and holding her ornate wooden staff. Jason was by her side, wearing jeans and a powder blue hoodie.

"How are you feeling?" he asked.

She paused before answering, lost in the weight of responsibility. Hundreds looked to her for protection. But it was more than that. She couldn't shake the guilt that had she not welcomed so many to the Valley that, perhaps, it wouldn't have been such a target to Nexis.

"I've been better," Mindy replied.

Jason slid his fingers between Mindy's and held her hand. "We will win."

Mindy looked to him with the eyes of a child learning sadness for the first time. Still, she smiled. "How could you say that? There's no way of knowing. And these people. These poor, good people."

"They have you," said Jason with a squeeze to her hand. "You're amazing, Mindy. And you're such an inspiration. To me my whole life and now to all these people."

"That's not enough."

"Well, that's why you've got a kick-ass group of people who love you here." Jason grinned that toothy grin that never failed to pull Mindy out of a funk. "Rumi and Eliza are working on more last minute weapons to shut down the machines. Pasqual is like a freaky super genius. Some of the things we built into those walls, I mean. And I'm here. And Aemon."

Mindy lowered her head. "Yes. I know. You're right. Even some of the refugees are formidable. But Aemon, well, I'm just not sure he really understands how much power he has. He's so timid. He's been practicing, but... And you. You've done so much for us, but eventually you'll wake up and if the machines come then—"

"I'll come back!" Jason shouted and Mindy could easily see the doubt in his words. The overcompensation. "Guilly was teaching me how to meditate my way into Reverie and—"

"You've never done it!"

"Well, I WILL do it!" Jason's cheeks were flushed and he jumped away from Mindy, releasing her hand. "I'll do it because I have to do it because I will never let anything bad happen to you!"

"That's a ridiculous thing to say, Jason."

His eyes burned with fresh tears. "Well, you're a ruler of a nation of dream creatures and my boyfriend is the Greek god of wine. Ridiculous is all we have, Mindy."

She let out a breathy laugh, one void of all humor. She looked into her best friend's brilliant blue eyes and said, "This is life and death."

The conversation was cut short by a young voice shouting, "Jason! Mister Baker!" The two noticed a small velociraptor in awkward battle armor approaching.

Jason nodded. "Hey, Miles. What's up?"

"Pasqual sent me," said the dinosaur through heavy

breaths. "He has some ideas for the west wall and needs your help."

"I'm on it." Jason started off toward the west wall with Miles, but stopped and gave Mindy one last look. "We're survivors, Min. At the end of the day, that's all that matters."

Jason woke up the following morning with a gasp. He had been putting the final touches on one of the walls when he was pulled from Reverie into Cosmos, the physical world.

"Dammit!" He had hoped to remain asleep a little while longer. He'd even turned off his alarm. There was so much he wanted to say to Mindy. So much he wanted to do for her before—

"Jason?" His grandmother's voice from just beyond his bedroom door. "Jason? Are you up? You're gonna be late for school."

"I'm up!" he shouted, a little angrier than he'd have liked.

"Pancakes are getting cold," she said. Then her footsteps disappeared down the hall.

Jason tried his best to drift back to sleep, but it was no use. The stress of not being in Reverie was killing his calm. The irony of that was not lost on him. Even if he could get back to sleep, his grandmother would just wake him up again.

Letting out a raspy grunt, Jason decided that going to school might be the best idea. He showered, dressed, downed a few bites of what were now slimy, cold pancakes, and made his way to his car. At the very least, school had a ton of quiet rooms perfect for hiding.

33

AWWWOOOOOOOOOOOOOOOO!

The war horn erupted from the easternmost wall and sentries every fifty meters echoed the sound around the perimeter. Something was coming.

"Bows at the ready," called Zen, who stood at the top of the walls now, seeing what the horn-blower had. His command was repeated down the line as he readied his first arrow.

A piercing screech sounded from the dark cloud and the winged creatures changed direction, suddenly diving in a hungry spiral toward the Valley.

"Ready," Zen shouted. "Aim…"

As the creatures swiftly descended, their details came into focus. They were demonic things with scaly, midnight blue skin. They looked like babies. Winged infants with orb-like black eyes, sharp teeth, and wings like a dragon's. In unison they screeched a battle cry as they hurdled downward toward their prey, talon-like hands open.

"FIRE!" Zen let loose his arrow. The arrows of twenty other archers along that side of the wall followed after, rocketing toward the enemy.

Zen's arrow caught one of the creatures dead in the chest, killing it instantly. The other archers weren't so lucky. Many had never even held a bow until a few days ago and even the more experienced of the bunch found it difficult to make contact with creatures so small and agile.

When the first of the creatures reached the wall, Zen knew there was nothing they could do. They swooped down and snatched the bow from soldiers' hands. Some spat a thick black liquid that burnt through skin and armor. One poor soldier was covered completely by the little beasts and screamed something terrible as they fed on him and fluttered away, leaving behind only bones and chunks of flesh.

A little ways down the wall five large orbs of mud, paper, and oil burst into flame. Each orb sat in a metallic contraption that was attached to a single lever. A soldier, a woman with powder blue skin and silvery hair, dodged a monster, downed another with her dagger, then pulled the lever. A click and then all five fiery orbs were launched into the sky, orange balls of light against a cloud of small bloodthirsty monsters.

Zen watched as a hundred or so creatures burnt by the fireballs dropped from the sky. Still their best efforts weren't putting a dent in their enemy. The bulk of their preparations were to deter a force of mostly ground-based cyborgs. None of the briefings spoke of a threat like this. The number of soldiers at the wall had dropped to half in seconds. Zen could see no victory, no means of survival here, but he would fight with all he had and make his death a hero's end. A creature swooped past, a blue blur that took a chunk of Zen's skin in its claws. Zen raised his sword and roared, a battle cry that all his comrades could hear.

And then a miracle.

Creatures dropped from the sky by the hundreds. Clean shots to the heart or head, killing them instantly. Zen was confused at first, too busy surviving to take notice of the source of this turn. A second's reprieve allowed him to look beyond the wall. Hundreds of long arrows rose up in beautiful unison. Zen knew of only one creature so skilled with a bow.

"FOR LADY MINDY OF BLACK ROCK!" shouted a voice from below. "Let these creatures know what it means to bring ill to an ally of Pholos!" Hundreds of voices howled in response and yet another wave of arrows was released.

Zen positioned himself nearer to the wall's edge so he could see with his own eyes what he already expected. The centaurs had answered Mindy's call. There were easily three hundred of them, tall and majestic, heavily armored, longbows readied and swords at their backs. The one standing at the lead, a young centaur with near white skin and light gray fur, must have been none other than King Nikkylos. And the bronze-furred hulking brute of a centaur, his uncle Kensen. They were just as Mindy described them.

BEEP-BEEP! BEEP-BEEP!

Zen was startled by the device that sounded, a black rectangle hanging from his belt. Rumi insisted he carry it with him at all times and taught him how to use it. He took the device from his belt and pressed a glowing red button just below a black plastic screen. The screen came to life, displaying Rumi's thin, serious face.

"Zen!" she snapped. "How's the eastern wall holding up? There were reports of a hundred or so flying demon babies in the Valley."

"Down from a thousand," said Zen. "We lost half our force here. But, on the bright side, Nikkylos is here to join us, three-hundred strong. If it wasn't for him, we all would—"

"That's great. That's great. Now shut up and listen." Rumi's frown deepened. "The war horns you just heard, we've got two cyborg forces closing in fast. We need you to drop what you're doing and get yourself and the centaurs to the southwest pronto. Is that clear?" Zen nodded. "Cool. And swing by my post on the way. I've got a new toy for you." Rumi smiled that smile that was a mix of pride and bloodthirstiness that Zen had no idea how to react to. Fortunately, Rumi severed their connection before he had to.

Zen ordered his soldiers to hold the wall as he ran off to catch up with the centaurs.

Hours later Zen stood with Rumi and Eliza in the heart of the Valley, amidst the quiet commotion of people tending to injuries inflicted by the flying creatures that escaped the centaurs' arrows. There were only a handful of casualties inland and Rumi said that fifty or so of the remaining monsters retreated into the sky.

175

"Hey, elf," Rumi called to Zen, "lemme see your sword."

Zen pulled his weapon from its sheath, a beautiful thing etched in strange symbols, a cerulean hilt, a long silvery blade with a slight curve.

Rumi tapped her finger to her chin. "Not bad."

"I—thank you." Zen forced an awkward smile, never quite knowing how to feel about Rumi. "The sword has been handed down eleven generations of the Greggari bloodline, protectors of Fin Argon from the dark forces—"

"That's nice!" Rumi snatched the sword from his hand and hurled it a good ten yards off, into a pile of scrap metal. To Eliza, she said, "Make sure that old relic gets turned into something useful." Eliza nodded with a sly smile. "Oh, and give me that other thing."

Eliza had something long and narrow strapped to her back. She grabbed the item and presented it to Zen. It was a sword, but unlike any he had seen before. The hilt was jet black and metal, crude, adorned with two buttons. The blade was clear crystal and when Eliza pressed one of the buttons it glowed fluorescent blue. She offered the weapon to Zen and he took it. It was lighter than he would have imagined.

"Now this," Rumi explained, "is a real sword. Standard Futaran Model Six, with some mods that will satisfy all your bot-crushing needs. Plasma blade can cut through metal and flesh like butter. Should fry their wiring, too, depending on their bio-electric composition. And see that second button there?" Zen nodded. "That's my favorite part. When you're surrounded and in way over your head and probably going to die, just raise the sword over your head and press it. An electromagnetic pulse will surge out from the hilt and any bot within two hundred feet will collapse, ready for the killing. That'll only work once so use it wisely. Got it, elf?" Another nod. "Cool. Can't have our fearless leader fighting an elite mechanized force with a thousand-year old can-opener."

Zen swallowed. "Well, I will be needing my sword back eventually—"

Rumi took Zen by his shoulders and started pushing him off. "Blah, blah, yeah, yeah, get your ass back to the wall."

"Pardon me." Zen was so distracted he hadn't even noticed they'd been joined by an eight-foot tall dusty gray centaur with messy black hair and gray-green eyes. "I would like to request a word with Lady Mindy," said Nikkylos.

The sight of the massive creature in silver armor silenced even Rumi for a moment.

"The Lady is here, is she not?" Nikkylos asked. "Answer me. War offers no time for dragging one's hooves."

"She is, Nikkylos." Everyone turned in unison as Mindy approached, staff in hand. She wore peasant's clothes fitted with armor that was in parts bronze and parts metallic black—no doubt Futaran. "It is good to see you. Thank you for answering my call."

Nikkylos blushed at the sight of her. "My lady." He dropped down on one knee and took Mindy's hand in his own. Kissed it. "It is my honor and joy to come to your aid. A centaur always fulfills his debt." He added, somewhat more quietly, "And I hope in my heart that the actions of myself and my people will offer me the privilege of you reconsidering our conversation." Rumi, Eliza, and Zen watched and listened quietly. "Even dressed in peasant's clothes, even exhausted by the weight of the coming battle, you are even more beautiful than my memories suggested. I wish for nothing more than your hand in marriage. I wish to be your king. And you, my queen, until the end of our days."

Zen felt his ears tingling and his cheeks going flush. Mindy cleared her throat and gently pulled her hand from the centaur. "Nikkylos, I…"

Suddenly, there was a sound like a puff of smoke followed by a thud against the grass. All eyes turned to the young man who had just landed near them. He pulled the hood from his head, revealing an all too familiar face.

"Jason!" Mindy was at his side in a flash, helping him to his feet. She hugged him, holding him tight against her breastplate. "How are you here? It's daytime!"

"I did it, Min! I did it!" He was on the verge of tears. "I told you I would! I've been trying all morning, but I meditated through to Reverie, just like Guilly said I could! Dion helped calm me down and—"

"Good to have you back," said Rumi. "A Lucid is just the thing we need to—"

KRA-KOOOM!

34

A fiery explosion went off in a distance, destroying a dozen makeshift cottages and killing just as many people in or around them. Jason and the rest felt the heat of the explosion and immediately were on the lookout for the source.

"Look!" Eliza pointed to a faint shape in the sky. It seemed to distort the clouds and every now and again the sunlight would reflect off of its clear surface. "Dammit. It's a hoverbot in stealth mode!"

"Zag this," Rumi growled. "Stealth tech was barely in beta last time I checked. What else has Nexis been working on?"

A small, square-shaped opening appeared on the bottom of the near-invisible flying machine. From it dropped a round gray object.

"It's another bomb!" Rumi warned. "Coming for us."

As most set to scramble, Nikkylos' bow was taut and his arrow ready. "Handled," he said as he let the arrow fly. It made contact with the bomb and it exploded—KRA-KOOOM—at a safe distance.

"Hm." Jason focused on the hoverbot, trying his best to get a lock on its location, on how big it truly was. "Okay, Jason, you can do this." He reached his hands out in front of him, concentrating with all he could on the machine. He pictured its shape, its wings and its hull. Its color and the engines and wires that allowed it to fly. The bombs still nestled inside it ready to drop.

Soon the true form of the ship flickered into existence, its stealth mode being stripped away by the sheer power of Jason's will. In a desperate move, the ship released four bombs. Nikkylos' hands were already reaching for his arrows, but Jason gestured for him to stop with an outreached arm. Jason took in each of the four bombs with his mind. Their shape, size, and weight. He felt the force of gravity that pulled them to the ground. He felt the potential for destruction within each one. Jason inhaled, calm, cool. He drew both hands to his chest, palms outward, and on his exhale extended them in the direction of the bombs. All four changed direction, defying gravity and rapidly returning to the ship.

KRA-KA-KA-KOOM!

The hoverbot was destroyed in a magnificent explosion.

Jason looked to the others and smiled. At once his jeans and hoodie were replaced with black iridescent armor, fitted to his body. With the slightest push from the tips of his toes, he parted ways with the grass and hovered inches above it. "Let's go win a war."

35

In a forest just beyond the southern wall, a griffin was taking a break from her mid-morning hunt to have a drink of water. She was far too full from the elk she'd eaten earlier to notice the eerie silence that had befallen the Black Forest. The griffin lapped up her first slurp of water, sufficiently cooled and refreshed, when a set of long cold metal fingers locked around her muscular form.

The griffin squawked and struggled to break free, but her claws were powerless against the machine; her wings held tight in its clutches. In a moment she was staring into a pair of intense green eyes.

"Ah, such a beautiful creature you are," said her captor. "The talons, that razor sharp beak. Oh, you are a killing machine." The griffin cocked its feathered furry head to the side. "My apologies, how rude of me. You don't even know who I am. I am The Nexis, destroyer of worlds! I am waging a war. And searching for my nephew. And looking darn good doing it, wouldn't you agree?"

The Nexis had indeed gone through a number of transformations in the days leading to war. For starters he had removed that helmet, the one that held his brain in place among other things. It had been replaced with a silver plate. Messy patches of dark gray hair, almost like cables, protruded from his scalp. The world was offered a glimpse of the face of the person he had once been. The creature formerly known as Patrick Ashford, with that crooked smile and mischievous eyes, once green and lively, now red and severe.

The most pronounced change, though, was his suit. It was black and metallic; a massive, complex array of gears and tubes and platinum shells. It was easily twenty feet tall with long powerful mechanical arms and legs, like some monster-fighting power suit from a video game or anime.

The Nexis' actual humanoid body was encased in the chest of the robot suit he had built.

The griffin struggled once more, letting loose a shrieking roar. The sound was cut short when The Nexis' cold metal fingers tightened its grip.

"Calm down," said the Nexis, sweetly. "I'm about to make you better than you ever thought you'd be."
The griffin felt a tingle all over her body. The robotic fingers that held her began to glow, first a faint white, then a brilliant red. The tingle intensified into a searing pain. The griffin cried out, a horrifying sound, until she passed out, no longer able to withstand the agony of what was happening to her.

The Nexis smiled, his eyes riddled with compassion. "There, there, sleep my child. Sleep while millions of microscopic Nexis-bots are transferred into your body, scanning your every cell, figuring out the optimal path of conversion."

The Nexis placed the griffin's limp body on the ground and watched as her tan and brown fur and feathers fell from her pink flesh and that flesh transformed to a light gray.

"Stop wasting your time toying with this creature," hissed that irritating voice in The Nexis' head. "As you dawdle, one of our A-Class hoverbots was destroyed by the enemy."

The Nexis groaned. "First of all, I already know that because I am the Nexis and I see what you see. Second, there are like twenty more hoverbots, so whatever. And third, shut up. Even the most all-powerful and awesome super villains should take some time to sit back and enjoy the miracle of birth."

The Nexis grinned as he gazed upon the griffin. What was once a creature of skin and bones, of fur and feather, was now no longer completely animal. Nor was she completely machine, but something in between. Her smooth skin was gray and pulsed with green light. Her great wings had lost all their feathers but gained flat metal blades of all sizes in their place. A moment passed and the griffin opened her eyes: strange orbs of complex machinery glowing crimson red.

"Rise," The Nexis commanded. And the griffin did as she was told. She let loose another shriek, this one colored with static as if heard through an old radio. "Now fly, fly, my pretty! Join your brothers and sisters and tear that Black Rock DOWN!"

The griffin spread her new metal wings and with a powerful flap, rose up into the sky. Higher and higher she went until the trees were a distant blanket of green below. She soared toward the black rock wall ahead. Beneath her, hundreds of cyborgs marched on in the same direction.

36

"THEY'RE COMING!" called a soldier from the southern tower. He could see the glistening black metal shimmering through the leaves of the thick forest below. Trees trembled as Nexis' army trudged through them, some even falling against their might. "Ready the fireballs!"

Another soldier doused a trio of muddy spheres in oil and set them aflame.

"Wait." Jason Baker descended from above, the sun bouncing off his iridescent armor. "We don't want to burn down the forest." He waved his hand over the flaming spheres and the fire went out. "Let's try something else." Jason concentrated on the spheres and gradually they began to take on a new shape. Incredibly sharp spikes emerged from them, each one over a foot long. "There. That should do." And he flew off to do the same a little farther down the wall.

Zen arrived at the base of the inside wall. He squeezed past a few dozen centaurs and scaled a narrow staircase. Peering over the other side he watched the first cyborgs emerge from the forest. They were gnarled, ugly things. A cyborg gorilla charged forward and began pounding on the wall with its massive fists. Another pair of cyborgs, human by the look of them, drew weapons and began firing beams of red light at a similar spot on the wall. Others joined and attacked as well.

"Shit." Eliza had appeared beside Zen and gazed out over the oncoming forces.

"I know," said Zen. "We have to keep them from getting through the wall."

"Not that." Eliza shook her head, an abnormal tremble in her voice. "Your scouts said there were a couple hundred at this location on the wall." Zen nodded curtly. "Well, they were wrong," she grumbled. "Looks like Nexis is using the same stealth tech he used on that zagging hoverbot."

Zen noticed Eliza's dark eyes. For a short moment he saw a flash of green blinking from behind them. "What are you saying?" he asked.

"Man, I'm saying my optical scanners are picking up at least eight hundred in this spot al—"

Aaaawooooooooooo…

A horn sounded in the distance. Then another closer. And another.

"The east wall." Zen turned eastward, his face rife with concern. "I'm sorry. I didn't."

"That doesn't matter now." Eliza pressed a finger to her temple. "You just ain't tech savvy enough to prepare for—Rumi?" She seemed to be having a conversation with someone that no one else could hear. "I just called to— What? You too? I'm thinkin' a thousand. Wha-— really? Right. Okay. See you on the other side of this, sister." Eliza tapped her temple once again.

Zen's heart was racing. He'd never in his life felt such a loss of control of the situation. Behind and below him centaurs were readying their bows and blades. He spotted Jason disappearing over the edge of the wall into an approaching group of cyborgs. As Eliza made her way for the ladder, pressing buttons into a device on her wrist, Zen called out, "What's the plan?"

"I need to get airborne," she said as she descended out of sight. "We've got an agent behind enemy lines who just might be able to help. In the meantime, your ass needs to keep these fools from breaking through."

Zen took a deep breath and called out beyond the wall. "Jason!" He was far away but close enough to hear his name as he dismembered what could only be a giant robotic scorpion. "I need you inside the wall. We've got a hundred centaurs who need to get high enough to shoot their arrows at these monsters!"

Jason nodded and started toward him after deftly dodging his foe's huge poison-spewing tail.

To the centaurs, Zen commanded, "My centaur friends, directly below me a horde of cyborgs are attempting entrance to our domain. Those of you with swords drawn, ready yourself to destroy them if they make it inside. Archers, you will soon have transport to the top of the wall where you will offer air support."

SCREEEEEEEEEEEEEEEEEEE!

Zen nearly stumbled at the mechanized shriek that preceded the arrival of a frightening gray griffin. He dodged the griffin's razor-like talons just in time to avoid a beheading. The creature landed with a thud down the wall, shoving a soldier to his death as she did so. The griffin repositioned herself so that her red feline eyes bore into Zen.

SCREEEEEEEEEEEEEEEEEEE!

She stalked toward Zen like a lion easing into a kill.

"Need help?" asked Jason as he flew by overhead.

"No." Zen unsheathed his futuristic sword, glowing bright. "You get the centaurs up here. I'll handle this."

Jason nodded and was on his way. Zen and the griffin moved toward each other now, both gaining speed.

A quarter of a mile away, hidden in the thick leaves of an old oak tree, Agalfia Tirk perched, silently watching as the enemy passed by below. Before they sent her out, Rumi and Eliza had made sure Aggie was fitted with the most cutting edge espionage and combat tech. The strong-willed native of Dark Valley was dressed in form-fitting black lined in impact-resistant Futaran Kevlar. She cut off the sleeves with her hunting knife because it impaired her climbing. Her usually untamed blond hair was pulled back into a ponytail and her wild eyes were now housed behind goggles with built-in zoom and anti-stealth modes. Her knives and spears were fitted with futuristic metal blades like Zen's and hugging tightly to her waist was a utility belt heavy with gadgets.

"Aggie. Aggie. Come in, Aggie."

She still wasn't used to the sound of other people's voices in her head. She tapped her finger to her temple and said, "What is the situation, Eliza?"

"Things've gone from bad to worse, Aggz. How many EMPs you got?"

"Five. Why do you ask?"

"Five…five… I guess that'll have to do. I talked with Rumi and we need you to set them off around the wall's perimeter where the cyborgs are most concentrated. And fast."

Aggie clenched her teeth. "And how is that possible? I can only travel so swiftly—"

"I'm hopping in my Acewing as we speak." Aggie could hear the shifting gears of the vehicle through her comms device. "What you're gonna do is turn on your stealth detectors and power down your deflector shields. Any 'bots or 'borgs with advanced sensors will know you're there immediately. Position yourself to take out as many of them as you can and set off the bomb. I'll be there to take you to the next location."

"Understood." Aggie pressed a few buttons on her sleeve and could suddenly see the distorted silhouettes of hundreds more cyborgs coming her way. Without hesitation, she took to the higher branches, leaping and swinging from tree to tree away from the wall. Pleased with her positioning, she deactivated her own stealth tech. Immediately, about a dozen nearby cyborgs turned to her location. No longer hidden, Aggie roared like a wild animal and dropped from the tree, burying her spear into the head of a cyborg below.

They came at her then, practically clawing at each other for the opportunity to take her out. It was the arena all over again. An endless foe. The smell of tainted flesh and oil.

The deafening sound of mechanical moans and shifting gears. Aggie sliced with her hunting knife as she reached into her utility belt, dodging all the while. She felt a strange tingle in her right arm, but thought nothing of it.

Her hand made contact with a small metal sphere in her pocket, no bigger than a baseball. Aggie felt for the button on the bomb and pressed it. There was a deep pop sound, which preceded a wave of cool green energy. Then another. And another. Concentric rings of energy reached out for a mile in either direction.

The cyborgs caught in the waves first lost their stealth capabilities. Their invisible selves flickered into visibility. Next they shut down, some crashing to the ground, others simply standing in place, their eyes gone dark and heads lowered to their chests.

Aggie wiped the sweat from her brow and exhaled, long and hard. She removed that ridiculous band from her hair and let her wild blond locks fly. Aggie returned her knife to its place and made to press her finger to her temple when a cold metallic hand wrapped around her ankle. She looked down to find a cyborg looking up at her with a sadistic smile and unnatural green eyes. In other places she could hear moans rising and machines returning to life.

Aggie produced her knife and sliced herself free of the cyborg's grip. Its hand still dangled around her ankle as she moved around, offering any nearby cyborgs that moved a blade to the skull.

"Aggie!" The voice, Eliza's rang in her head. "I'm here! Climb!"

"But the machines are waking—"

"I know! Just get up here!"

Aggie climbed with impressive speed and poked her head above the canopy to find Eliza's Acewing hovering just overhead. The hatch was lowered and Aggie climbed in just as the ship was struck from above.

Aggie took a seat beside Eliza. The ship shook.

Another hit.

"Looks like some of those bastards were fitted with I-bugs and our Bio-EMPs didn't shut 'em down permanently," Eliza explained. "Only about a fifth, though, according to the readings. That was a major hit. Nice work, Aggz. Lemme take care of this hoverbot on my ass and we'll head to the next drop point."

Aggie nodded, figuring she'd ask what an I-bug was at another time.

37

Along the west wall, Mindy and Rumi held their own against the enemy below, flanked by a handful of soldiers, human, centaur, and otherwise. Nikkylos trotted between the two young women, frowning. "Mindy," he pleaded, "you must not make yourself so easy a target up here. Allow your people to—" He subtly dodged a beam of white-hot light, "——fight for you. Allow me, my cherished—"

"Not now, Nik." Mindy pointed her staff at a particularly brutish cyborg and a torrent of fire burst from it, reducing the cyborg to a smoldering pile of goop. "We are all equals in the Valley of Hope."

"Mindy," said Nikkylos, with a grin, "none are your equal." He sent an arrow that landed precisely in a cyborg's eye.

Rumi sighed. "We interrupt this interspecies teen romance novel for a special report: There's a zagging war going on so shut up and slay some 'borgs!" With that, she beheaded one of the enemy with a clean shot from her absurdly large laser gun.

Jason Baker landed softly beside Mindy. Nik shot him an irritated look, but he ignored it as he had all morning. "Min, the last centaur ramp is up. Catapults are reloaded and spikes are sharp. Time for me to jump into battle?"

Before Mindy could open her mouth, Rumi stepped in. "Negative, pretty-boy. We have no idea how long you're around. Wall maintenance and supply upkeep are your priorities." Jason looked to Mindy who merely shrugged. "An alarm sounded on the east wall not too long ago. I need you to head over there and make sure the defenses are still standing." Rumi smirked. "And, hey, if you've got a spare second, maybe crush a 'bot or two while you're over there." "You got it." Jason nodded and disappeared.

Rumi leaned in close to Mindy. "The fact that he's

gay is the worst thing to happen to womankind since the Futaran Childmaking Edict of 3046. The things I'd do to him…"

Mindy grinned as she melted a trio of enemies. "A hundred girls back home are thinking the same thoughts."

"Ladies," said Nikkylos urgently. He held an arrow, pointed outward toward the forest beyond the wall. "Take notice."

In the distance trees were falling in droves. Something huge was making its way toward the wall. Even now the cyborgs were making way for whatever was coming.

"Centaurs," Nikkylos began, "ready yourselves."

"That goes for the rest of you, too," Rumi added.

Closer and closer it came. Trees toppled over one another and the distinct sound of heavy machinery thumping the ground and the mechanical grinding of gears grew louder and louder. It was moving fast, whatever it was.

A massive machine burst through the forest. A robot in the shape of a giant spider. Like all Futaran robots it was crafted of sleek black metal. Eight bright red eyes peered at the wall from a head the size of an SUV. Its bulbous abdomen would have dwarfed a pickup truck. And then there were the legs. Blocky and strong, all eight were covered in spikes and ended in drill-like claws that dug into the ground.

The centaur wasted no time firing arrows at it, but the projectiles just bounced off of its shell.

"Allow me," said Mindy as another river of fire poured from the orb at the end of her staff. Four of the spider's legs were severed and the machine toppled awkwardly to its side, destroying a handful of cyborgs in the process. Another stream of fire and Mindy melted a hole through the spider's head. Oil dripped and sparks flew as the mechanical beast crumpled to the ground.

The soldiers cheered, hollering Mindy's name. The shouting only grew louder as the cyborgs slowly backed away from the wall.

Nikkylos placed his hand on Mindy's shoulder. "A superb display, milady, truly fit for—"

"Wait." Mindy's face went pale. The cyborgs had moved from the wall, but stood perfectly still, perfectly calm, as if waiting for something else. She could tell Rumi sensed danger as well. "Something's wrong."

The spider's abdomen folded open like a flower and from it crawled thousands of small robotic spiders, each the size of a human hand. Each with a transparent abdomen housing a blinking red light. They moved as one, like water flowing from their destroyed transport, across the grass and toward the wall.

The order was given to destroy them but there were too many. The little robot spiders began their ascent.

Rumi turned to Mindy. "They're going to scale the wall. We can't do anything until they're up here unless—"

"EMP," Mindy suggested.

Rumi nodded. She produced the small sphere from her utility belt and dropped it over the edge of the wall. It landed and exploded, unleashing rings of energy and rendering every robot and cyborg in two miles inert. At last, a moment of calm. Everyone on the wall let out a sigh of relief.

"Guys!" Jason's panicked voice emerged in Mindy's head. "The wall...I was too late...something...something broke through it. Everyone here...dead...What should I—" His voice cut out.

"Jason!" Mindy shouted, her face flushed. "JASON?"

"Eliza." Rumi was pacing, her finger pressed to her temple. "I need you at the east wall, stat. There's been a breach and—"

"Can't talk now." Eliza's voice was breathy, her words coming out quickly. "I've got ten hoverbots on my ass and don't know how much longer I can keep this thing in the air. Aggie? You ready to jump? Okay. Okay. NOW!" The connection was ended.

"Zaggit!" Rumi stomped her hard on the ground. Composing herself, she pressed her finger to her temple again. "Zen? Do you read me? What is your sit-rep?"

"Not great." He sounded as exhausted as everyone else. "Griffin, or something like it, attacked me. It had me on the ground." His voice began to tremble. "One more second and it would've killed me. Milo must've sensed I was in trouble. He saved me. But... he didn't make it. The wall's still up down here, but barely. That evil griffin practically tore my arm off. I'm useless. We got two of those flying things blasting us with bombs. Took three out with the catapults before. All we can do is hide behind the wall until it comes down. A-any word from Jason?"

"My king," cried one of the centaur. "Look below!"

The red lights had flickered on in all the spider's abdomens. Beyond them a handful of cyborgs were powering on and crawling away from the wall. In unison the spiders began to beep, slowly at first, then increasing in frequency.

Rumi's eyes went wide and she disconnected from Zen. "GET OFF THE WALL!" She grabbed Mindy by the wrist and started racing down the ramp. "EVERYONE GET OFF THE WALL RIGHT NOW!"

Rumi and Mindy dashed down the ramp, Mindy shouting, "Back away! Back away!" to those standing close to the wall.

Explosions went off like firecrackers, each one sharp and loud until they all blended into one lingering sound. The portion of wall Rumi and Mindy had been standing on fell in a shower of black rocks. Soldiers unfortunate enough to be caught in the blast were sent flying as well.

The force of the blast knocked Mindy and Rumi to the ground. Both were quick to rise. Mindy found herself lost from all but Rumi in a thick cloud of dust. She could hear things climbing the rubble, shifting and squirming and getting closer. Even beyond the pained cries and moans of their own people they could hear it.

"We need to move NOW," said Rumi through clenched teeth.

Mindy was focused on the wreckage beyond. "But... the fallen..."

"There's nothing we can do for them."

Mindy faced Rumi, her dirt-covered face as stern and regal as ever. "And what of the ones who still live; the ones able to fight? Should we just abandon them, too?"

As Rumi stood silent things emerged from the dust. Humans. Centaurs. Some bleeding, others with limps. Among them was Nikkylos.

"What is your command?" asked the centaur king. Staff raised, Mindy gazed into the thinning cloud. Shapes drew nearer. "We must retreat." Looking to Rumi, she said, "Send a communication to all generals. The walls are coming down. There is no longer a need to defend them. Everyone who is able will join us in the Valley of Hope. There we will stand against the enemy as one united force."

"The lady has spoken." Nikkylos extended an arm to her. "Take my hand and climb upon my back. We must make haste and ensure that when our forces arrive, they are met by their queen."

Nikkylos rode hard through the forest to the Valley of Hope, Mindy and Rumi on his back. Other centaurs offered rides to their allies as well. As they passed through the refugee camp, Mindy shouted, "People of the Valley of Hope! War is approaching! If you wish not to fight, go into my home. There is a secret hatch beneath my table. You will be safe in the passageways below!" She relayed the message over and over until they reached the great clearing at the center of the Valley.

Pasqual was waiting there, cool as always, clutching

his binder to his chest. "Operation: Omega then?"

"Yep." Rumi climbed awkwardly from Nikkylos' back.

Pasqual shrugged. "I had a feeling it would come to this."

With each minute more centaurs would arrive from all ends of the Valley, many carrying other soldiers with them. The incoming injured were taken to Mindy's cottage with the elderly, the children, and those unable or unwilling to fight.

Kensen, that massive bronze centaur, arrived carrying five. "So we are to die today?" He said the words with pride.

"Not today, uncle," said Nikkylos. "Not for some time. We will be heroes by sundown."

"Where's Zen?" Mindy asked Kensen. "You were with him at the south wall."

"Aye," he said. "I was down a ways, but near enough. Said he'd stay behind to hold the enemy back a little longer. Give the rest of us a bit more time to regroup. Made me promise not to stay. Said that getting to you all, getting the soldiers here, was all that mattered. Brave little creature, that one. I'll have a drink in his honor when all is said and done."

The amassed forces were a hundred strong and rising. The sound of an engine whirring sent a wave of fear throughout until Mindy spotted its source: Eliza's Acewing. The vehicle landed at the center of the clearing. It was covered with dents and holes. Smoke snaked from its hull. It was amazing the thing remained airborne at all. The hatch opened with a high-pitched squeal and sparks flew as it lowered to the grass. Eliza stepped out, a small futuristic pistol in each hand. Behind her was Aggie, clothing torn, a fresh diagonal scar across the right side of her face to match the old one.

Rumi pushed past the growing crowd. "Elz, Aggz,

you're alive."

Eliza smirked. "Two badass rebels like us? Girl, we're practically invincible."

"What happened out there? Last time we talked you were—"

Aggie stepped forward and placed a hand on Rumi's shoulder. "We persevered. The metal birds: destroyed. Cyborgs: we reduced their numbers fifty-six percent before they were even able to reach our walls. Business was taken care of, yes?"

Rumi laughed in spite of herself. "Yes, Aggz. Most definitely."

Mindy stood by Pasqual's side. "Any idea what we're dealing with out there?"

Pasqual opened his binder. It was filled with a mess of papers and a screen covered in all sorts of graphs, charts, and numbers moving at incredible speeds. Pasqual only glanced at it and replied, "Yes. And thanks to Aggie disrupting most of the enemy's stealth tech, combined with my advanced surveillance-bots, I believe the numbers are quite reliable. There are roughly seven hundred and fifty-two cyborgs, robots, and other hostile beings moving toward this location. The first wave will be here in no more than ten minutes with two waves following very shortly after. The massacre at the east wall and subsequent breach were committed by a single tyranoid cyborg who is hiding just beyond that stretch of trees." He gestured to a thick row of oaks. "It's awaiting orders from Nexis, no doubt."

"I know that one," Rumi said, grimly. "Almost took out Aggie and me during our escape. Probably the most powerful thing I've ever seen."

"Ten minutes." Mindy processed the timeframe. "I'll be right back."

"Where are you going?" Nikkylos asked. "It might not be safe f—"

"Not now, Nik." Mindy nodded at Pasqual who

offered a curt nod in response. "I've got to check on the final piece of Operation: Omega." Mindy started off, then stopped. She looked to Nikkylos and said, "I hope you can forgive me," before running in the direction of Black Rock.

38

"Dammit! Dammit! Dammit!" Jason punched the wooden door as hard as he could. He had spent most of the morning in the custodian's closet at Addley High. Karl, school janitor and friend, had promised him peace and quiet and as much time as he needed to meditate his way into Reverie.

Jason skipped first period, grabbed Dion for help, and had been in the closet ever since. After a couple tries he was amazed he was actually able to make it to Reverie. But he had been taken by surprise along the east wall and the shock brought him back into the real world. He had been trying ever since to return to Reverie.

Following yet another failed attempt he banged his head against the door. "Come on, Jason, come on! Mindy needs you, you stupid, stupid—"

A loud crash sounded from down the hall. Then screaming. Lots of screaming. The sound of a hundred feet stomping, running, could be heard.

Jason stood up and slowly opened the door. His classmates were running, terror-stricken, from the cafeteria. For a moment he thought he might be dreaming after all (it all seemed quite surreal), but Jason was a skilled enough Lucid to tell the difference between reality and Reverie. He was in Addley.

Jason stepped into the hall as the last kids pushed past him to get away. They were shouting lots of things, but Jason swore he heard one of them utter the word "Dion." Curious, he headed to the cafeteria.

"Stay back. You do not have to do this!"

Jason heard Dion's voice as he made his way down the empty hall.

"I must and I shall," boomed another voice. "You will bring me Jason Baker or I will tear this town apart until he is in my clutches."

Jason shivered at the sound of his name. A very real part of him wanted to run away, but Dion was in danger, so he moved into one of the doorways of the cafeteria.

Dion spotted him immediately. "Jason! Go! Now!"

Standing across the cafeteria was a tall man, alabaster-skinned and thick with muscles. His hair was jet black and cut short. His eyes, a cool blue, almost white. The fitted gray three-piece suit he wore was in great contrast to the giant battle axe he wielded in one hand. And perhaps most peculiar of all, his body seemed to give off a golden glow.

"So you're Jason," the large man said darkly. "You have made my job a lot easier."

"Jason," Dion pleaded, "please, please run. I will hold Baldr back as long as I can."

Jason frowned. "Baldr? Like—"

"The god, yes! And my hunter across the millennia." Dion was frantic. "He was sent here by a very bad creature named Nihilo to kill us."

"Why?"

"Because of your power, Jason. But nevermind that, just go!"

Jason moved to Dion's side. "I'm not leaving you."

"This isn't Reverie!" Dion exclaimed. "You can't stop him."

It was then that Jason took notice of the large human-shaped hole in the wall behind Baldr. Looked like he had made his own entrance without issue.

Jason swallowed his apprehension. "I love you, Dion. I'm not going anywhere."

Baldr raised his axe. "Enough of your disgusting dribble. I will end this crime against nature and affront to the will of Nihilo at once!"

Claire stood in the corner of the small room without windows and doors, gently rocking Anza in her arms. "Are we good?"

"I think so." Victor was seated in the center of the room, rummaging through a canvas duffel bag. "Bottles, water, apples, oranges, some kind of jerky."

"Diapers?" Claire added.

Victor pulled one from the duffel bag as proof. "So many diapers. Bread. Bandages. I think we're set."

"So we're really doing this?"

"We really are." Victor climbed to his feet and walked to Claire and their child. "This is no life for a baby, fate or no fate. All that matters to me is you guys being happy." He planted a kiss on Claire's forehead and another on Anza's.

"Hey, guys!" The voice startled Victor. Muffled and muted, it came through part of the wall that housed a narrow staircase on the other side. "Guys, are you in there?" The voice belonged to Mindy.

"Yep!" Claire replied. "We sure are! Locked in like animals, just like you left us!"

"I'm sorry," said Mindy. She seemed rushed, irritated. "This is just how it's got to be for your own safety. I'll check back with you guys later."

Claire rolled her eyes and turned to Victor. "Let's go."

Victor put his arm around Claire. "Pet!"

The floppy eared creature who had, up until this point, been gnawing at its own thigh, perked up and dashed to Victor, climbing up his skinny frame and perching comfortably on his shoulder.

Victor offered one last look to Claire, then spoke. "Take us back to the road, Pet. The one you brought us to when we arrived from Origin Point." The young family disappeared in a flash of light.

Not far away, at the center of the Valley of Hope, the remaining heroes stood a little under three-hundred strong against Nexis' oncoming forces. They fought with knives and blades, with arrows and beams of light, some with claws and magic. The cyborgs were a formidable foe. Only the most expertly aimed bows penetrated their metallic shells. The machinery that enhanced their fleshy forms made them faster, stronger, allowed them to jump higher, see farther, and attack with such ferocity that a single laser blast or hand-to-hand strike could down an opponent or two…or three.

The first wave had come from all sides and before they even made it to the clearing, the second began to arrive. The battle became a storm of sounds; clanging metal, screams. Crimson blood and jet black oil rose like geysers and crashed into puddles on the earth. In the thick of it all, none noticed what had entered the fray.

BZZZZZZZZZZZZZZZZZT!!!

A blinding beam of light, twelve feet in diameter, ripped through the battlefield, destroying anything in its path. Nexis' forces and the soldiers of the Valley alike lost arms, legs, or were completely disintegrated. The torrent of light persisted for a few seconds only, but its destruction was incredible.

"UNCLE!" Nikkylos pulled his sword from a dead cyborg and trotted to Kensen. The grizzled centaur prince had lost an arm in the blast. Blood poured from the hole. "Uncle, your arm!"

Kensen grinned a toothy grin across his broad face. His teeth were coated in blood. "Just a scratch, my boy." The giant centaur then drew his axe and planted it into the knee joint of a giant three-legged robot.

Rumi's eyes were trained on the source of the attack.

An all-too familiar one. The cyborg tyrannosaurus from the arena stood a safe distance from the action, but the clearing of grass and flesh alike led directly to it. Before Rumi could say the words, Aggie was by her side. "We gotta take that thing out, Aggz, before it charges up another blast."

"Our numbers are down twenty percent!" Pasqual called as he aimed with his laser gun. "Nexis' third wave now approaching."

"Nik!" Rumi shouted to the centaur king, "I need a ride to that dino-bot. In thirty seconds he'll be charged up and—" The centaur grabbed Rumi and hurled her onto his back. Aggie climbed on too as Nikkylos quickened into a gallop.

"Faster!" Rumi held tight to Nikkylos' strong torso, wind whipping her long black hair. Aggie readied her spear.

"Ladies," Nikkylos began, "to your left!"

A pair of human cyborgs charged for the centaur's passengers. Aggie deflected the first to leap at them with a well-timed spear throw. The second pounced on Aggie, knocking her off the centaur. Too disoriented to hear the others call her name, she pushed the cyborg off of her and stuck a hunting knife in its skull. It was in this moment that Aggie spotted the enormous spider robot approaching over the horizon.

Rumi plowed forward atop Nikkylos, the world a blur as they closed the distance between them and the metal tyrannosaurus. "We've got ten seconds!" she hollered. Nikkylos didn't reply. He only charged, hooves pounding faster and faster until it hurt, directly into the hulking pile of lethal weaponry that was the cyborg T-rex.

Its guns were glowing now.

"We're not going to make it!" Rumi shouted. "Abort! Abort! Get out of the—"

BZZZZZZZZZZZZZZZZZZZZT!!!!

First there was a blinding light. The next thing Rumi knew, she was on the ground with a mouthful of grass.

Nikkylos landed beside her. She checked her body. Her arms. Legs. Somehow all there. She looked around and what she saw left her mouth hanging wide open.

The T-rex was floating in the air and judging by its awkward contortions, this was being done against its will. Something had lifted it above the ground, sending its latest beam of light safely overhead.

Other robots and cyborgs were being lifted off the ground as well. Five. Then ten. Then twenty. Then thirty.

"Operation: Omega," Rumi whispered. At those words Nikkylos climbed to his hooves and surveyed the area. Beyond the battleground and the confused floating enemies was Mindy. Beside her, standing tall, arms raised into the sky, was someone that caused Nikkylos' blood to boil and broke his heart at the same time.

"Hey, people!" Eliza stood in the heart of the battle, which had admittedly slowed down when enemies started ascending to the sky. "Don't just stand around staring like a bunch of idiots! Take these fools down while they're incapacitated!" She aimed her double futuristic pistols and shot a floating robot to bits. Soon after everyone once again joined the fight.

Eighty bots and cyborgs were airborne now and more joined them every few seconds.

Mindy approached the battle, destroying any enemy in her path and offering protection to the person beside her as he fulfilled his role in all this...and then some. Aemon exhibited superb focus as he defied the laws of gravity and shifted the tide of battle. He controlled the foes with confidence, seeming more like the Aemon of times gone by than the timid creature he had become. The former lord of Black Rock entered the center of battle in long strides, dressed from head to toe in white Victorian formal wear, adorned at the shoulders, chest, and hands with glistening silver armor.

"Is-is this to your pleasing, dear Mindy?" asked Aemon as a single bead of sweat trickled from his brow.

"It is." Mindy repelled a pair of approaching robots. "It is." She surveyed the area, nothing but death and destruction and the full force of Nexis' army had yet to arrive. Even with Aemon there was little chance of victory. That's when she noticed the giant spider robot. It was closing in fast. "Aemon, do you see that spider-y robot working its way toward us?"

"I do," he said.

"Good. It is filled with thousands of explosives. If it reaches us, we are all dead. Understand?"

"I do, my lady." Aemon carefully moved his focus to the spider. With a flick of his wrist he—

"NO!"

Nikkylos appeared, seemingly out of nowhere, and knocked Aemon to the ground with the force of his sword. At once, all the suspended enemies crashed to the ground, the tyrannosaurus among them, then immediately scrambled to their feet.

"Nik!" cried Mindy. "Stand down!"

The centaur king pushed Mindy aside and loomed over Aemon, who was winded and altogether terrified of the half-human half-horse beast standing over him. Nikkylos extended his sword so that it was pointed at Aemon's exposed neck. "I am sorry, Mindy, but I will not stand down in the face of the man who single-handedly destroyed my kingdom. The murderer of my mother and dear sisters. The mothers and sisters of my proud people."

A handful of nearby centaurs had spotted Aemon on the ground and joined their king in looking down upon him.

"Stop!" Mindy positioned herself between Aemon and the centaurs. "I know you're upset, but this Aemon is not the one that murdered your loved ones! We are engaged in a war and Aemon is our only chance at victory! Killing Aemon is killing us all! Do you understand?"

Nikkylos paused. His light gray skin was turning red with fury and he ground his large white teeth. The sword at Aemon's neck shook under Nikkylos' anger as the sounds of war raged on in the background. "There is only one way this battle can end." Nikkylos raised his sword.

"Move! Move! Move out of the way!" Eliza raced toward Mindy and the others, waving her arms wildly in the air. "It's charged! It's charged! It's about to—"

BZZZZZZZZZZZZZZZZZZZT!

The great beam passed inches in front of Nikkylos' face. Two of his centaurs were caught in it and reduced to nothingness. When the light passed, where once Aemon and Mindy stood, there was nothing but scorched earth. Nikkylos felt his heart stop. He dropped to his knees, tears swelling in his eyes. Eliza, too, began to tremble. Rumi and Aggie had climbed atop the T-rex to disassemble him once and for all.

"Mindy," Nikkylos wept. "My dear, sweet, Mindy."

"Is right here." Nikkylos raised his head to the familiar voice. Floating comfortably above him was the lady Mindy, in the arms of Aemon, her rescuer. "Now why don't you get your act together and fight the true enemy," she commanded. "Aemon, finish this."

Aemon extended his free arm and a hundred of Nexis' soldiers rose up. He turned his attention to the robot spider, now dangerously close, and that too began its ascent. The spider gained more and more altitude until it was directly above Aemon, its long, giant legs grasping desperately at nothing. Then the hundred, now two hundred, three hundred, cyborgs and robots were attracted to it like a magnet, being drawn to it, pulled in ten, twenty, forty at a time, until above Aemon hung a humongous sphere of immobilized machines.

The forces on the ground kept advancing enemies at bay.

Aemon released his grip on Mindy and she floated gently to the ground, into Nikkylos' arms. Aemon raised both of his arms as if lifting a heavy object and the ball of Nexis' soldiers soared even higher into the sky. So high that it seemed as small as a baseball. It changed direction, hurtling away from the Valley, toward the wall and beyond. Aemon inhaled. Then exhaled. He pulled his fingers into two fists and the ball exploded.

Some cheered. Others remained silenced by confusion or fear. Aemon simply turned to set his sights on the next batch of enemies.

"FOUR!" The voice was exceedingly loud and seemed to emanate from every single metallic foe on the battlefield. An instant later a rock struck Aemon in the head and he dropped out of the sky, unconscious. He hit the ground hard.

"UGH," the all-too-human voice continued from three hundred places at once, "NEVER LEAVE A MINION TO DO A MASTER'S WORK, AM I RIGHT?"

First, he wasn't there. And then he was: the Nexis himself. A once-human in a terrifying metal suit, standing high above all those around him. In a flash he grabbed a centaur and tore it in half in his robot hands. A human soldier dumb enough to charge him was crushed into a mess of bone and gore beneath his feet. The Nexis grinned. "LET THE GAMES TRULY BEGIN!"

Baldr came at Dion and Jason with his heavy battle axe. Dion did his best to draw the angry god's attention away from his boyfriend. The previous minutes had been a life-or-death game of keep away, with Jason and Dion climbing, running, and shuffling the cafeteria's tables and chairs to create space between them and their pursuer who tossed the obstacles aside with superhuman ease.

"I'm warning you, Baldr!" said Dion. "Stop this or you'll be sorry!"

Baldr took a moment to laugh at that. "Oh, you disgusting little godling. No matter what form you take, you cannot wash the sins from your soul. Sins worthy of a thousand deaths."

Jason crawled across an overturned chair next to Dion as Baldr marched toward them once again.

"Do you really have a way to stop him?" Jason asked.

"No," Dion snapped. "No, I don't. Which is why you need to get out of here befor—"

"Jump!" Jason shoved Dion away as he dove in the other direction. They only barely evaded a flying table.

Dion stumbled and fell to the ground. Baldr raced toward Jason with all the power and focus of a charging bull. Jason was vulnerable out in the open. There wasn't much he could do but make a break for one of the exits. Unfortunately a felled trash can slowed his escape. Baldr drew nearer, axe raised, filling the cafeteria with his crazed battle cry.

There was no escape. Jason turned away and covered his eyes as Baldr's axe came down.

There was a crunching sound. And a splattering of blood. Then the sound of something falling to the ground with a pronounced thud.

Jason Baker opened his eyes. He could feel the blood on his face and hands. Blood that wasn't his. Then he saw the look on Baldr's blood-speckled face. The satisfaction. Lastly, his eyes settled upon Dion crumpled on the floor between them, motionless and gasping for air, a deep open wound across his chest.

Blood pooled outward, touching Jason's sneakers and Baldr's wing-tipped shoes.

As destruction and violence defined the dream and physical realms, the manifestations of Origin Point simply watched from their empty world of white.

A circular window with a diameter as wide as a bus is long was opened before them, showing them the scene in the Valley of Hope, where an epic battle raged between Nexis' forces and the people of Black Rock.

"Well, this is rather crude," said Vita. She pursed her silvery blue lips and pointed to a human being beheaded. "Though, I can't imagine what else would have happened when the walls came down. The humans of Cosmos beget Reverie ergo Reverie is a den of senseless self-destruction." Initia passed Vita a playful glare. "Oh, sister, your pessimism is as enchanting as ever."

She continued but her voice was joined by Mortem. "But you miss the point. In Reverie, as with Cosmos, destruction is not senseless, but a necessary part of creation. Of life." The pair, intertwined, each placed a hand on Initia's pregnant belly.

"Do you all think the baby's safe?" Somni was antsy, worried. "Can we take another peek?"

Vita brushed her words aside. "Nonsense, child, we looked in on her moments ago. And moments before that. There's only so much entertainment one can get from watching a pair of teenagers, a child, and an admittedly adorable little beast pass the time locked up in a small room."

"The Mindy fluke turned out to be a fortunate one," Mortem added. His eyes glowed like lava through his coal-black dreadlocks. "She has proven a capable leader and protector. The child will be safe."

With Initia, he added, "So long as they win the war."

"They'll win!" Somni had been on edge ever since Rumi and the rest had begun preparing for war. "They have to! They—" Somni fell silent as a rush of anxiety washed over her. Its source was her brother, Timor, manifestation of fear. He loomed over her like a small writhing mountain of darkness. Somni turned to him and saw immediately the thing he had been trying to warn her of.

Nihilo had arrived.

"You!" Somni seethed, her pale sparkling skin becoming red. She floated over to Nihilo. "I know you did this, I just know it! You set these bad robots and things on sweet, little Anza! I don't know how you did it, but I—"

"Of course I did," Nihilo responded. "It is in my very nature to thwart your attempts at peace. At stability. At existence. I have put into motion the forces that will crush this paltry army and lay waste to your chosen one."

Vita rolled her eyes and scoffed. "Oh, darling, darling, Nihilo, you scamp. Honestly, our years of ruling over the spirit realm together have been much more entertaining with your constant attempts at destroying…everything. Cute. Really cute."

Initia and Mortem were focused on the window to the battlefield. "Mindy and her army are fighting valiantly, Nihilo," they said. "Where there is life, there is hope, and your victory is by no means secured."

Nihilo laughed; a low, grumbling sound. "You think this is all I have planned? You think I have not learned from my past failures? Trust me when I say, this battle is only beginning. And my schemes run deeper and farther than this war. And farther, especially, than some useless baby, the impulsive whim of ignorant would-be gods."

"This is crazy, dude." Max walked beside Jamal, down a short cracked sidewalk and onto the porch of an old yellow house. Both were a little tired, a little off their game. Jamal offered Max a side glance as they stood before the door. "Just be cool, man." He knocked lightly.

Max ran his hand through his red messy red hair. "Cool? Really? Look, I'm a fan of doing stupid stuff. Like, a big fan. Like, it's why I was put on this earth. But, when some paper white man…thing without a face appears in your room and tells you to—"

The doorknob turned and the door opened just enough for a pair of large brown eyes to peek through. Vic's mother Ornella examined the boys on her porch, recognizing them enough to ask, "How can I help you?" in her thick Argentinian accent.

"Ma'am," Jamal took a step forward, placing a hand on Max's chest, a gesture to keep his friend quiet. "Ma'am, I don't know if you remember me, but I'm Robbie and this is my friend Greg." Jamal hadn't intended to give false names, but the impulse made sense considering what he was about to do. "We were very close friends of your son and happened to be in the neighborhood and wanted to see how you were doing."

Ornella scrunched her stubby nose. "Shouldn't you be in school?"

"It's a free period," Max blurted out. They had actually taken the day off.

"We've been meaning to drop by for the last few days," Jamal explained. "But we had some pretty important tests."

"English," Max added. "Algebra. So much honors stuff. We're geniuses. Like Vic. Super smart."

"Anyway," Jamal shot Max a nasty look, "how are you doing? Do you need anything? Do you want to talk? I mean, when my Uncle Jon died last year I spent every day with my cousins just, like, being there with them, you know?" Jamal smiled his warmest, most compassionate smile. "Oh! One more thing." He nudged Max, who immediately dug into his large mostly empty backpack. Max produced a journal and presented it to Ornella.

"It's Vic's," Max said. "We came across it in the lost

and found. At the library. Where we hung out. Because we're so smart."

Vic's mother took the journal in her hand. She opened it, saw the handwriting, the images, and she began to tremble. Tears filled her eyes.

Ten minutes later the three were sitting in the cozy, cluttered kitchen of the Soto residence, eating chocotorta, an Argentine dessert. Ornella cycled through some of the fondest memories of her son. The times she'd been the most proud of his accomplishments. How he finally applied himself and went to Harvard. Jamal and Max were in no place to tell her that her son had been swapped out with his dream self a year ago and her memories were actually about two separate people.

Jamal kicked Max under the table. Max downed his half-full glass of milk and said, "Mrs. Soto, can I use your bathroom?"

"Of course. It's just around the corner. Down the hall. Across from the washer and dryer."

"Got it. Thanks." Max rose to his feet and started down the hall. Before disappearing around the corner, he poked his head back into the kitchen. "I may take a while. I've been feeling sick. And, like, ate too many beans. So, like, enjoy yourselves." And he was gone.

Jamal shrugged. "He's...strange."

Ornella grinned. "Geniuses always are a little eccentric."

Jamal continued to listen to Ornella's stories until Max returned a while later. Jamal could tell by the girth of Max's backpack that he'd gotten what they came for.

Soon after, Jamal announced that the boys had to get back to school. They thanked her for the dessert. Ornella thanked them for stopping by and said they were welcome anytime. She waved as they hopped in Max's car and drove off.

"I hope you got the right thing," said Jamal. He

pulled Max's backpack onto his lap and tugged at the zipper. Max sighed. "Of course, I did, bro. It was pretty unmistakable."

Jamal opened the backpack and found an object decorated with painted vines of gold and royal blue. He had actually never seen an urn in real life before, but after screwing off the top and finding the ashes inside, he was convinced this was it.

The Nexis sowed joyful destruction across the Valley of Hope, having gruesomely killed fifty of Mindy and Nikkylos' soldiers in minutes; slipping into stealth mode and becoming visible again at will. The last of the EMPs had been used out in the field and weapons barely seemed to penetrate his armor. He was quick, despite his bulk, deftly avoiding Mindy's rivers of fire. Three hundred of Nexis' forces remained against no more than eighty fighting on behalf of the Valley.

"Okay," said the Nexis, feigning fatigue. He now spoke from his own mouth and not the mouths of his army. "I think it's time to wrap things up, don't you?" He shot a hole straight through a nearby centaur. "I've been biding my time, but I think I've reached that point in my life where I take out the big guns. Starting with…" The Nexis made a production of searching the area and then pointing his long metal finger at Aggie and Rumi. "Oh yes. You two. The swanky, sleazy bitches who totally killed my buzz back at the arena. Don't think I forgot, ladies. You're the reason why I'm here. You're the reason why all your weak, fleshy friends are dead and their blood and guts are literally all over my big robot body. Well…you and my heir." The Nexis began moving toward Aggie and Rumi. Laser beams bounced off of him. He skipped over an attack from Mindy's staff. A dozen or so hulking cyborgs kept centaurs at bay. "Speaking of, where is that bouncing baby girl? I'm sure you've all met Claire, right? Skinny? Blonde? Dull? An unfit parent if I ever saw one! I mean, who locks their brother in a basement? Granted she did free me, but that goes against the narrative I'm trying to m— AHHH!" The glowing crystal blade of a small hunting knife lodged itself in the Nexis' right eye. The wound bled black. "OW! THAT HURT! THAT WAS, LIKE, SUPER MEAN!" With his remaining eye he spotted Aggie preparing to throw another knife. "How DARE you take advantage of my pro-level super villain monologuing to take a cheap shot? I'm gonna take care of you first."

Dozens of cyborgs disengaged their various targets and moved in on Rumi and Aggie. One, a familiar cyborg yeti, struck Aggie with his massive hand, separating her from her friend.

The Nexis used the opportunity to go invisible.

Mindy was too busy keeping Nexis' forces from reaching Aemon, who still lay unmoving in the grass, to go to the women's aid. And Nikkylos, despite his conflicting emotions, remained nearby to protect Mindy.

Eliza, Pasqual, and all the rest were desperately fighting to stay alive and didn't even notice what was going on outside of their immediate threats.

Aggie shook off the blow and ran toward Rumi. She was hit hard by something huge and rolled back to the ground, bruised and bloodied, her right arm and a handful of ribs broken.

The Nexis became visible once again, standing over Aggie. "Ah, how does it feel?" he asked, wearing that joyful, child-like expression that made him all the more frightening. "How does it feel to stand helpless before a god? Ha. Awful, I bet." He stopped himself, sniffed the air. "What's that I sense? Ah, yes. A work of art, incomplete." He offered Aggie an intense stare and immediately she felt that tingling feeling in her right arm stronger than ever. "You escaped my conversion then, but the Nexis-bots still live inside you, yearning to join with their brethren and transform you completely." Nexis leaned over Aggie, his great form casting a shadow over her. "I don't know about you, but I am super-psyched."

Aggie tried to move, but couldn't. She struggled as the vice grip of the Nexis' metal fingers closed around her. She was lifted from the ground.

"It's all been leading up to this," he said.

The Nexis' fingers glowed white and then red. Aggie howled in pain as microscopic Nexis-bots infiltrated her system.

"Let...go..." were the only words she managed to get out before she started to grow weary, delirious from the pain.

"No..." Rumi's faint cry was lost in the sounds of battle. No longer able to hold her own against the enemy surrounding her. Rumi fell.

Not far away the skin on Aggie's arm began to turn gray. The Nexis had almost finished the transfer.

Then the mechanical arm holding Aggie was torn from the Nexis' body. The Nexis gasped, dumbfounded. The fall and the feeling of the cool grass against her skin brought Aggie back from the brink of unconsciousness. Her vision was blurry at best, but she caught sight of a figure moving toward her. Human. Muscular. Dressed in black.

The figure leaned close to her and said, "Are you okay?"

Aggie's eyes went wide. She looked into the man's eyes. Purple as amethyst. "J-Jack? Is it really you?"

"I'm sorry I couldn't find my way to you earlier. I tried, but this time...this time I felt your pain and—"

"It doesn't matter," she said. "Just kill that bastard."

Jason's heart was thumping in his chest. Tears poured from his eyes. He felt like he was suffocating. Unable to stand he dropped to his knees, shaking all over, sitting in the pool of blood that had poured from Dion's body.

Baldr spoke, but Jason could barely hear his words. "This is the pain and suffering he brought upon himself."

None of it seemed real. None of it.

"Jason…" Dion said weakly, his words drowned in the blood pooling in his mouth. "…run…"

"I can't leave you!" Jason was hysterical. "I-I don't know how. Okay? I can't. Please don't…don't make me—"

"Pathetic whimpering human." Baldr tightened the grip around his axe and raised it high above his head. "You will join this filth in Hell."

"I love you, Jason Baker." Dion coughed blood before losing consciousness. Before dying.

Jason cried, heaving, as Baldr smiled and readied his final blow.

"I'm afraid I must step in." Suddenly, everything was dark; pitch black as if night had fallen in an instant. It was a thick, impenetrable darkness that Jason could actually feel against his skin.

"What!" Baldr barked. "What is the meaning of this? What—" He shouted, surprised. "Unhand me! Show yourself and fight like a m—" Baldr made a sound as if being struck. "When I find you, I'll—" Another series of sounds followed, then the sharp clang of his axe hitting the ground.

As quickly as it had come, the darkness retreated to the center of the cafeteria and took the shape of a beautiful woman. Olokun stood tall and proud, wearing a glistening gown of deepest blue. Beside her was Baldr hanging like a marionette from a dozen writhing black tendrils.

Baldr's eyes opened wide at the sight of his captor. "O-Olokun?"

"It has been a while, Norseman," she said, her tone as cool and deadly as the sea. The harsh light of the cafeteria reflected from her bald head and gold hoop earrings. "You seem to have caused quite the commotion here."

"This doesn't concern you," Baldr said. The fear in his voice was palpable.

"I'd beg to differ." Olokun looked to Dion's lifeless body and Jason hunched over it, trembling. "You see, you've gone and killed one of my dearest, oldest friends. And, had I not intervened when I did, you would have killed a boy my friend was quite fond of. A boy of great power and interest to me. Do you see now how this concerns me?"

The tendrils that bound Baldr began to rotate, turning his body upside down. "What are you going to do to me?" he asked.

"An excellent question." Olokun leaned into Baldr, as close as she could without touching him, and whispered, "I could kill you. We both know that. But, no. That would fulfill nothing in the long term. And I am a long term sort of goddess." She backed away and folded her arms. "Here is how this will go: I will release you. First, you must denounce your allegiance to Nihilo and promise it to me. Then, at some point in the future, near or far, I will need something from you. And you, Baldr, like the good god of truth and justice that you are, will appease me. Are we at an understanding?" Baldr nodded. "Excellent."

The black tendrils disappeared and Baldr crashed, head-first against the linoleum floor.

Before he had even crawled to his knees, she said, "Leave this place immediately."

Baldr lifted his axe from the floor and walked away, toward the hole in the wall he had made.

Olokun turned her attention to Jason and Dion. She walked to them without sound, so quietly that Jason hadn't noticed her until she reached down to pick up Dion's limp body. He seemed so frail in her arms. Nothing like the energetic, witty, confident boy Jason had come to love.

"I'm sorry for your loss," she said to Jason and turned away. She began to walk.

"Can you save him?" Jason rose from his knees, his

jeans saturated with blood.

Olokun stopped. A single salty tear trickled down her cheek. "Darling," she said, "he's dead." Jason's crying began anew. "I'm sure he told you how this goes. He will return in fifteen years as a fifteen year old god. Reborn. Renewed. That is simply the way of things." Olokun paused. "If it is any consolation, even in your short time together, I had never seen him love someone they way he did you. In thousands of years. No one." She lowered her head and began to walk away again.

"Wait!" Jason ran ahead of Olokun and turned to face her. He felt so small in her presence. "You were the one who cast the spell. You're the one who made the rules." Olokun said nothing. "Dion always said you were the most powerful god he knew. And... and if you need him for your plans or whatever then why wait fifteen years when you can do it now? And...and..." Jason wiped his eyes and looked at Olokun with more sadness, more genuineness, than she had seen in quite some time. "...and I honestly don't know what to do without him..."

Olokun inhaled. The weight of Dion in her arms seemed heavier now. "Jason. While I do possess great power, my abilities over life and death are limited—"

"Then find someone who can do it!" he shouted. His fists were clenched. The blue of his eyes seemed to flare.

"Jason Baker." Olokun smiled warmly. "I see what he loved about you. And I see now why your love grew so quickly. There is power in you, Jason. Power beyond Reverie." She winked and Jason felt a wave of warmth go through him. She then looked upon Dion and frowned. She offered Jason a curt smile. "I will see what I can do."

With that, Olokun and Dion vanished in a cloud of darkness, leaving Jason alone in the cafeteria, the sound of police sirens rising in the background.

In the Valley of Hope, Jack faced the Nexis. His hands were outspread as if welcoming the Nexis to attack.

"Gaah!" The Nexis pulled the hunting knife from his eye, leaving only an empty socket in his gray head. Reddish black oil bled from the wound. He looked at the severed arm of his giant mechanical suit on the grass below and groaned. Then his attention turned to Jack. "It's you…" The Nexis sighed. "Oh well. Killing you the first time was so freakin' satisfying I'm actually kind of psyched I get to do it again."

Jack bristled. "Patrick?"

The Nexis shook his head. "I am the Nexis, now. Patrick Ashford is long dead. Just like you'll be. But for keeps this time."

"I doubt it." Jack glanced toward Rumi who was becoming overwhelmed by the cyborgs. He did little more than twitch his pointer finger and all of the cyborgs around her crumpled like paper into a ball and fell to the ground leaking wires and oil and guts. Rumi collapsed, too tired to do much else.

The Nexis' remaining eye brightened to neon green. "Destroy him."

The dozen cyborgs at the Nexis' side were joined by thirty more and they all marched toward Jack. Those equipped with weaponry fired shot after shot of scorching light.

Jack remained still, unperturbed, as the beams bounced off of an invisible shield around him. "You can't defeat me. I spent the past two years in Reverie, learning to fight, honing my skills as a Lucid." Cyborgs were closing in on Jack from all sides. The ones that got close enough were instantly disintegrated by his shield, falling in clouds of shimmering dust around him. "So here I am. Watch." Jack made a plucking gesture and the right leg of Nexis' suit tore from its torso and rolled away, causing the Nexis to lose balance and fall to the ground.

Another cyborg disintegrated against Jack's shield.

The Nexis climbed out of his suit and tried to run for it. Unfortunately for him he was so focused on Jack that the fist to the face he received took him by surprise and landed him in the grass. Aggie looked down on him, clutching her strange gray metallic fist in her fleshy one. Jack disappeared and reappeared beside Aggie.

"You die today," Aggie growled.

The Nexis smiled that smile. "Oh, Jacky boy," he said, playfully. "Your showmanship is B-plus, totally. Respect." The Nexis winked with his one eye.

Ten hoverbots became visible above. Each let loose their entire loads of bombs. On the ground, every single cyborg and robot, well over two hundred at this point, froze, stood completely upright, and exploded. The Nexis and Jack locked eyes as the entire Valley of Hope went up in flame. The explosions were deafening, shooting sharp metal shrapnel in all directions. The bombs hit, there had to have been a hundred, and the great blue sky was blotted out by fire.

The entire occurrence lasted no more than a minute, but it left most of the Valley destroyed. Robot parts were strewn across miles of scorched earth. Houses were ruined, torn apart and engulfed in flames. And the corpses. So many who had fought valiantly for the Valley were dead, in pieces, anywhere you looked. Cries of pain sounded all around. As the smoke cleared, Jack could see more of the results of the massacre.

"Oh, oh god." Jack dropped to his knees. "Oh god." He had been shielding himself and Aggie in case the Nexis tried anything, but he didn't expect something like this.

Aggie didn't speak. She didn't move. The carnage was too much to take in. The only respite was the very much destroyed corpse of the Nexis at her feet. He lay there, dead, still holding that twisted smile on his burnt face.

"Hello?" The voice was faint, but came from the far side of the battlefield, still mostly concealed by a wall of thinning smoke. It was Mindy. Her staff had sensed the danger a split second before the first explosion and put up a shield around her, Nikkylos, Kensen, and a handful of other soldiers. Nine in total. Aemon was protected as well, the sound and vibration of the blast finally drawing him back to consciousness.

"Is anyone else alive?" Mindy asked, shouting. "Are there any other survivors?"

"Yes." The voice sounded strange, distorted. From the smoke something was approaching. It was Eliza, but she had changed. While most of her left side looked like the Eliza everyone had known, her right side was a silvery machine. As if her humanity was just a skin wrapped around the robot inside. She was carrying someone slumped over her shoulder, unconscious, bruised, and bleeding. "I tried to shield him, but Pasqual was hit hard. He's got burns over most of his body. If he doesn't get medical attention soon, he'll die." Eliza added, "I did a scan. The hoverbots left as soon as they dropped the bombs."

Five more of Mindy's soldiers approached, having survived with luck or special abilities of their own.

"We are alive." Aggie approached Mindy and the rest. Jack was there, too, but lagging behind.

"By the gods." Nikkylos shook his head. So many of his centaurs fallen. He turned his attention to Kensen, who was barely able to stand. He had lost too much blood. "Uncle, we must get you aid and fast."

"I'm fine, my boy," said the old centaur. He stumbled a little to the side.

"Jack can heal," said Aggie. She turned to find him, but he was gone. "Strange. He was right behind me."

Mindy addressed one of her few remaining soldiers, a native of Black Rock. He was mourning the loss of his brother on the battlefield. "Bolek, go to my cottage, or what is left of it, and instruct all who are hiding in the room below to join me out here. I have an announcement to make." Bolek did as he was told.

Jack appeared in the middle of everyone. He tried to speak, but couldn't. Tears were streaming from his eyes. He turned to Mindy first. Then to Aggie, his bottom lip quivering.

"What happened?" Aggie asked. "What did you see?"

"I-it's my fault." Jack's breathing was erratic. It was clear he was trying very hard to stay upright. "I-if I could have come earlier or…or if I wouldn't have talked so much and just came in and…and fought…"

Aggie placed a loving hand on his shoulder. "One cannot think this way—"

"Rumi's dead," said Jack. The words fell like a bomb on already rattled ears. Mindy gasped. Eliza shook her head in denial. Aggie only watched and listened with sad eyes.

Later, when the smoke had cleared and all the survivors were collected near the ruins of the cottage, Mindy placed herself atop a rock and spoke. To her left stood Aemon. To her right, Nikkylos.

"I will keep this short because there is work to be done. There are tears to be shed. People of the Valley of Hope, I allowed you to think this place was a place of safety. And for that I'm sorry. We live in a world of monsters, of flying demons and evil robots and much more. There is no safe place. There is no sanctuary. But despite odds stacked against us, we persevered today. We survived. We lost many, many wonderful friends and companions. Zen. Del. Rumi Inyonara. Hundreds of brave souls sacrificed themselves so that I am able to speak with you right now. They will be missed, and they will be mourned. But right now we must talk of what happens next." She paused, took a deep breath.

"The Black Rock, this great mountain, is a symbol

of pain and suffering and loss for every one of us. It is a target as well. As long as we remain here we, too, are targets. That is why, by dusk today, we will leave this place and never return." Worried rumblings arose from the crowd. "I will lead you and protect you along the journey. Well, myself and my two lieutenants: Lord Aemon and King Nikkylos. Before you protest, know that he is not the Aemon from times gone past. I will tolerate no harsh will toward him." Nikkylos lowered his head. "Those of you who are injured, go to Jack and he will heal you to the best of his abilities. Those nearest to death will be served first, please. The rest of you, rummage the ruins of this awful place and gather supplies. Peeps?" The goblin stepped forward. She could not take her eyes off of Aemon. "Manage the process. Thank you." Mindy took another deep breath and addressed the crowd once again, stone-faced. "There will be no exceptions. The time for talking is over for now."

Nikkylos stamped his front hoof. "Queen Mindy has spoken!"

"Nik," she leaned to the centaur and whispered, "you know you don't have to do this. You have a kingdom awaiting you. This is not your problem."

"Mindy." Nikkylos took her hand in his. "Have I not made myself clear? You are the only woman I could possibly love. I belong to you and you will learn to love me. I am yours, as is my kingdom. We will follow you to the ends of this great, strange, land. Always."

"Lady—er…sorry…Queen Mindy," interrupted Aemon. "Do you have any idea where we're going?"

"There is one possibility," she said. "If I want to protect these people, my people, then what better place than my own dream world?"

"Mindy!" A middle-aged man still in armor approached her. He quickly added, "My queen," in response to a look Nikkylos had given him. "We've tried multiple times to contact Victor and Claire. They didn't respond from behind the wall—"

"It's fine." Mindy nearly smiled. "They escaped with that teleporting pet of theirs. Probably didn't want to risk endangering their baby. Smart move. I wish them all the best. And, on the bright side, four fewer mouths for us to feed."

Claire, Victor, Anza, and Pet moved through the misty forest they had arrived in over a year ago.

"Any idea where we're going?" asked Claire.

"Not really," said Victor. A heavy duffel bag hung from his shoulder and in his hand he held the large sword he had stolen from Mindy's cottage. "I think the important thing is that we distance ourselves from that path. And stay low in the fog."

They walked for nearly an hour when Pet came to an abrupt stop. His ears perked up.

Claire immediately began to look around. "What is it?"

Victor squinted. In the distance fog was being kicked up into the air. "Something's coming. Hide!"

They crouched as low as they could, squeezing behind the nearest tree. Claire held a hand over Anza's mouth.

Something passed by in a blur. It was black and hovered off the ground. Victor noticed someone riding on top of it. As soon as it had arrived it was gone.

"We're still too close to Black Rock," Victor said. "There could be more robots—or whatever that was— nearby."

Claire bit her lip. She looked back and forth, keeping keen watch around them now. "You heard the refugees. There are robots everywhere. Just about everywhere Pet could possibly take us is full of things that want to kill—" Claire's face lit up like she was just struck with an idea.

"What if we teleport to Guillelmina's old world? That was cool, right? Just a bunch of mermaids and mushrooms and fairies and stuff."

Victor shrugged. "It's worth a try. Pet?"

Pet yelped and hopped into Victor's arms. Victor took Claire's hand and they all disappeared in a flash of light.

The gang reappeared in a world far from what they'd expected. Instead of beautiful flowers as tall as buildings, giggling nymphs and babbling brooks, there was only ruin. The land was brown and empty. Hints of a once-vibrant world remained, but they were in a state of collapse or decay. The sky was thick with the scent of rot.

"Looks like the robots got here first," said Victor, stating the obvious.

"Dammit." Claire lowered her head. Anza was getting restless so she rocked her in her arms. "What else is there to do? Just wander aimlessly until we starve to death? At least our prison at Black Rock had food."

"Uh, Claire?"

Claire turned toward Victor to find him staring at the man in white, who had appeared out of nowhere. He was gesturing for them to join him.

Claire reached for Pet. "Hey, boy, get us out of—"

Victor raised a hand. "Wait." To the man in white, he asked, "You want us to follow you?"

The man in white nodded enthusiastically.

Claire held Anza tightly and took one step back. And another. "Victor, you're not seriously considering—"

"If it wasn't for this guy," Victor said, "Anza would be dead. I think we can trust him."

Claire sighed. "What happened to us going off on our own?"

Victor's lips drew into a frown. "I'm just a dumb kid trying to figure this all out as I go. The video games back home had tutorials. I just—this is—I dunno. This guy is the reason Anza is alive. He knows stuff we don't. I trust him.

That's all I've got right now."

Claire handed the baby to Victor and marched up to the man in white. "Can we trust you?" The man in white offered two thumbs up in response. Since he had no discernible facial features his expression was impossible to read. The man puffed up his chest and, again, gestured for the others to follow him. "Ugh." Claire gestured for him to lead the way.

They followed the man in white through the tattered world. They left the flat lands for rolling hills, equally charred and destroyed, to an area littered with machine debris of all shapes and sizes. There were corpses as well. A battle had taken place here. The man in white teleported forward to what, from a distance, seemed to be yet another hunk of metal scrap. When they arrived, Victor noticed it was something quite different. He reached down and pressed his finger to a black screen. Instantly the control panel to the hoverbike lit up.

"It's just like Jack's," he said. He grabbed one of the handles and attempted to pull the vehicle right side up. Claire helped and they eventually got it. As soon as the hover-bike was properly positioned a low hum emanated from underneath it along with a pale green light. The bike rose a foot off the ground. To the man in white, Victor asked, "Should we—do you want us to ride it?" The man in white nodded. "Cool." Victor started to hand Anza to Claire. Claire refused to take her.

"Victor, do you even have your learner's permit?"

"Uh." Vic's cheeks reddened a little bit. "I was gonna get it, like, the week after we came to Reverie."

"Uh huh." Claire climbed onto the bike. "I drive." She took hold of both handles. She squeezed the lever on the right handle and immediately the vehicle lurched forward. She squeezed the one on the left and the vehicle slowed to a stop, then, after a clicking sound, moved into reverse. Claire spent the next fifteen minutes acquainting herself with the controls before inviting Victor, Anza, and

Pet to join her. Victor held on tightly around Claire's waist with Anza comfortably wedged between them. Pet sat on Claire's lap.

The man in white nodded and then took off at an incredible speed. Not missing a beat, Claire squeezed the right handle and followed.

The journey lasted for hours, speeding through worlds strange and new; worlds that had not been touched by flood or by Nexis. Maze-like forests, lush jungles, bustling marketplaces, a shopping mall the size of a small city, an underwater amusement park, an enormous ball pit, the surface of the moon, a vast desert, and many more. Some worlds had residents more hostile than others, but the man in white guided them away from any real trouble. They only stopped once so Claire could feed Anza.

Their trek came to an end at a very unassuming place: a hilltop covered in bluish grass. Trees with narrow white trunks and orange rustling leaves grew here and there. A blanket of clouds covered the sky, like the sort that precede a snowstorm.

Claire stopped the bike and everyone climbed off. "What now?" she asked.

The man in white simply sat down. He gestured for the others to sit, then placed his hands together as if in prayer and gestured for them to join once again.

Victor cocked his head to the side. "I think he wants us to wait?"

The man in white nodded. And then disappeared.

"Whelp, this seems pointless," Claire said for the twentieth time in the hour that followed.

"He wouldn't've just brought us here for nothing," Victor hoped.

Anza finally fell asleep. Victor pulled out a piece of jerky and chewed on it to pass the time. Claire began pulling grass from the ground out of sheer boredom.

Time droned on. The sky grew darker and darker.

Fwip!

Pet was cleaning his fur when something hit him so hard he flipped over backwards.

Claire jumped to her feet.

Victor leaned forward and noticed Pet had been hit in the chest with some sort of tar-like liquid. Pet whimpered and clawed at it to no avail as it burned through his flesh.

"My babiesss!" She landed with a crash, twenty pairs of legs trying to gain footing on the hill. Mother Bug arrived, her massive wings melted into her dark scaly body. Victor stumbled backwards to his feet, Anza in his arms, wakened by the sudden movement. "Ssso many of my babiesss dead! Dead!" Mother Bug scuttled closer to Victor and Claire. Four pairs of arms reached out to Anza. "I sssensssed her. Oncssse Mother Bug touchesss one of her babiesss ssshe can find them anywhere. I will take my baby now and ssshe will be fully transssformed."

Victor gave Anza to Claire and, fumbling, lifted his sword from the ground. He positioned himself between his family and Mother Bug.

"You wisssh to ssstop me with that pathetic weapon?" Mother Bug hissed.

Victor could feel his entire body trembling. The monster was nearly eight feet taller than he was and forty feet long. With sharp teeth. Covered in hard scales and plates. Still, Victor stood his ground. "You will not hurt my family," he said.

Mother Bug grabbed Victor with one of her long, spidery arms and tossed him aside. "Sssilence, fool." She advanced on Claire and the baby.

"No!" Victor leapt to his feet and planted his sword in the side of Mother Bug's long torso. She howled in pain. He removed the sword and stabbed her again. And again.

Mother Bug spun around and backhanded Victor, sending him flying to the ground. He felt the sting of three deep claw marks across his left cheek.

In an instant Mother Bug was above him. With one of her many arms she pulled the sword from her body and held it over Victor's chest. "Thisss isss what happensss when you keep from me what isss rightfully mine."

Anza screamed and reached out for her father. Victor looked away from Mother Bug to see his distraught daughter crying out for him. He noticed a faint light around her.

His attention snapped backed to Mother Bug as she rammed the sword downward. Victor closed his eyes and braced himself. A second later and he opened his eyes, puzzled. There was indeed a sword through his chest, but he felt no pain. There was no blood. No wound. It was as if the sword had literally gone through him as if he were a ghost.

Victor rolled out of the way, the sword staying put, lodged in the ground. A shocked and enraged Mother Bug released the sword and moved to grab Victor. Her hands passed through him.

Victor tried to pull the sword from the earth. To his surprise, his hand made contact with the hilt and he was once again armed. Mother Bug went in with another flurry of scratches, this time taking a chunk out of Victor's shoulder.

"Ssso, you can bleed." Mother Bug grinned and spat a thick black liquid onto Victor's left thigh. Overcome by the pain of it, he dropped to his knees. His head hung low. Mother Bug made her final approach.

"Victor!" Claire screamed. "Victor, get up!"

Mother Bug leaned close. "Thissss issss how it endssssss." She raised one long clawed hand.

Victor faced her, the intensity of his glare disarming. "Screw you." He rammed the sword through her throat. Mother Bug jerked backwards. She flailed as she reached for the weapon lodged in her neck. When she was finally able to remove it, blood sprayed from the hole. She tried to speak, tried to scream, but there was only blood pouring from her mouth. Mother Bug died while crawling toward Victor, trying to draw blood one last time. Her yellow eyes went dark and a few of her legs twitched for one final moment.

Victor hobbled over to Claire and Anza. "Are you two okay?"

"Yeah." Claire examined Victor's face. The claw marks. His shoulder. His thigh. "You're bleeding. You can hardly walk, I—"

"I'm fine," he said, trying his hardest to swallow the pain. "If you're fine, I'm fine."

"We have to get out of here." Claire was already reaching for the duffel bag. "The man in white set us up!"

Victor shook his head. "That doesn't make any sense. Why would he bring us all the way out here? There are a million things that could kill us."

"How am I supposed to know why any of these psychopaths do the things they do?"

A whimper drew their attention to Pet. He lay on the ground, weak. Fading. Mother Bug's black spit had burned a hole in his small cream-colored chest. Skin, bone, and organs had been burned away by the acidic liquid. His entire body was stained with blood.

Victor knelt by Pet's side. "Oh God, Pet." The creature couldn't respond. He only watched Victor with big, scared eyes. Victor could feel the tears swelling. He looked away. Until the whimpering stopped.

Pet was dead.

"We have to bury him," Victor said. Claire was about to object, but he went on. "We'd all be dead if it wasn't for him. He saved us from that monster in the school. He saved us from Patrick. He…We're burying him. And then we can go away to wherever you want."

Claire only said, "Okay."

It was late afternoon, but seemed much darker under the thick canopy of the woods. Max and Jamal left the car at the side of the narrow dirt road a few minutes ago and were walking deeper into the forest. Max was carrying the backpack.

"Are you sure this is a good idea?" Max asked. "You haven't said anything for, like, the past hour. Your hands are shaking, dude."

Jamal groaned. "I'm fine."

"Right. Right. I'm just saying, the last time you were here you kind of had a breakdown."

Jamal stomped ahead, increasing the distance between himself and Max. "The white man-thing said this is where we need to be. He said it would help make Claire better. She hasn't talked to me for days."

"I get that, dude." Max jogged a little to catch up. "I do. I mean, I don't, because that white creature doesn't talk, so how could it tell you anything?"

"It just does, okay?" Jamal said, briefly losing his temper. "Like, you watch what it does and you feel what it's feeling and you just get it."

"Ah. So it used some sort of telepathy-charades to tell you to steal the ashes of a dead teenager and travel to the spot where your girlfriend almost killed herself?"

Jamal ignored that comment and picked up his pace.

Max caught up again and took hold of Jamal's shoulder. "I'm just trying to understand."

"Well, stop it!" Jamal forced Max's hand off of him. "If you don't want to do this with me, then don't, okay? Just go back to the car! Or drive away, leave me here, for God's sake. Go, if that's what you want!"

Max sighed and looked at his friend, at the desperation, the anger, and truly understood how important this was to him. "We're bros. Okay? I'm with you to the end."

Jamal offered Max a friendly punch to the shoulder.

"Thanks."

"It's just that you hate all this weird, magic sh—" A hard glare from Jamal and Max fell silent.

It was a short walk to the spot Reverie's Claire Ashford nearly met her demise.

"Here we are," Jamal announced.

"Ugh." Max looked around. "How could I forget this place? That night. What now?"

"Not sure."

"Alrighty."

Moments later, something began to take form. It was tall. Easily five feet taller than Jamal or Max and eight feet wide. Under the shadow of the canopy it was barely visible, a thin wall that rippled like water and reflected slivers of gold and cerulean light.

"Whoa." Max's mouth hung open. The wall had begun to glow and what had been transparent became opaque, fuzzy variations of dark blues and oranges and grays distorted by the ripples.

"It's the door," said Jamal. "It's real."

Another shape entered the frame of the door. It was blurry, a mix of pink and yellow, green and white. It moved closer and the shape became a silhouette. And the silhouette seemed human. Shortly after another shape appeared, this one all tans and blacks, beiges and browns. Like the one before it, this one moved in a way that was human. Albeit, much more awkward. Lopsided, almost.

"Who or what is that?" asked Max.

Jamal shrugged. "No idea. Too blurry."

One of the figures, the first to appear, placed its hand against the door, its fingers spreading against it as if it were a flat surface. The figure tapped on it a few times, then turned to its companion and shook its head.

Max gasped when the man in white appeared. The ghostly man pointed to the door and gave a slow nod.

Jamal took a deep breath. He turned to his friend.

"Are you ready for this?"

Max wasn't. He wasn't at all. But he grabbed the straps of his backpack and planted himself confidently at Jamal's side. "To the end, bro. To the end."

The two walked, side by side, to the door. They felt a soothing warmth wash over them as they passed through it.

The world they entered was certainly not the one they'd left. They were on top of a hill. The sky above was cloudy and a cool breeze chilled them. Max's heart raced when he spotted the long, giant monster on the ground. It looked like an alien. Or a centipede. As far as he could tell, it was dead, but he chose to step away from it regardless.

"Agh!" A small explosion sounded and Max flew forward, tripping and falling face-first into the bluish grass.

A hole had been torn into his backpack. There were broken ceramic pieces inside and not much else.

A shuffling sound from behind startled them.

In front of the backdrop of a door that faded away to nothingness before their eyes, stood Vic, alive and well. And naked. He checked himself. His short-cropped black hair. His angular face. His lean, muscular body. Satisfied, Vic looked to Max and Jamal. With a sly smile, he said, "Well, boys, I don't know how we got here. I'm sure you can fill me in along the way. But I assume we're in Reverie?" They were too surprised, too wrought with disbelief, to offer anything. Vic looked around. "Dead giant monster. Unusual flora. I think I'm right." Vic walked between Jamal and Max, patting them both on the shoulder as he passed. He examined a duffel bag on the ground then hoisted it onto his back. "Come on, boys. I've got a lot of hypotheses to test out. Who's up for bringing a little order to this chaotic place?"

Victor and Claire watched nervously as the door—the

portal—closed behind them. They found themselves in the thick, dark forest.

"We shouldn't've done that," said Claire. "Now, we've got no food, no vehicle, no—"

"Claire." Victor took in the environment. The smell of the air and the biting chill of it. The sounds of the forest, birds chirping and cicada songs. "Do you feel it? Everything seems a little more raw. A little more normal." He almost couldn't say what he was about to say. His heart raced, his breathing intensified, but in his heart he knew it was true. "I think we're home."

Epilogue

Karen Ashford sipped whiskey from a crystal goblet. She had grown tired of refilling her smaller glasses. Before her was an untouched plate of canned peas and dry chicken. "Claire, do me a favor and flush this garbage down the toilet, will you? Honestly, girl, you've got the looks of a supermodel and everything else of a bumbling idiot."

Claire sat at the other end of Karen's long mahogany table. She played with her food which, admittedly, she had done a terrible job preparing. She ignored Karen's offensive jabs. She wasn't in the mood to talk back to the woman who wasn't technically her mother. Claire was preoccupied with something that she couldn't quite put into words. For the past—what was it now?—hour she felt…different. Like something had changed. Something important. Like she was being pulled in a direction against her will. And the pull only grew stronger as time passed.

"Claire!" sung Karen. "Refill! You don't want your quasi-mommy to get all sober and depressed, do you?"

"Karen." Claire plucked a pea across the table. "Do you see anything?"

Karen let out a nasty laugh. "Oh, you sick bitch. Blind jokes? How low-brow."

"No." Claire rose from her seat. "I mean, like, the future? Like last time. Do you feel anything?"

"Aside from thirsty? No." Karen snapped her fingers to drive the point home.

Claire sighed and walked down the hall, into the kitchen. She grabbed the biggest bottle of whiskey and, after a little thought, grabbed a glass for herself.

"Claire."

The voice that whispered in her head almost caused her to drop the bottle. It felt like so long since she last heard it. "Go away."

"No, Claire. Not this time. Not ever again."

"Who are you?" she asked, looking around as if she'd ever been able to see its source before.

"There were rules, Claire. Rules that made it so I couldn't reveal my name to you. Among other things. I thought you'd figure it out but now that the rules…wait a second. You're not Claire."

Claire's brow furrowed. "I am Claire."

"No. Well, maybe, but…I can see it now. Something has changed. Someone has bent the rules and now the order is falling apart. Something that should never happen…"

"What's taking you so long?" Karen asked from the other room. "If you're slitting your wrists or some other desperate cry for attention, do it in the neighbor's lawn!"

"You're not my Claire," said the voice, somehow more real now. Claire could feel the breath of the other against her face when he spoke and the surprise of it caused her to drop the whiskey.

Inches before the bottle would have shattered against the floor it stopped. It rose and as it did the person who caught it, who was lifting it, became visible.

He was in his late teens, from the look of him. Translucent like a ghost. His head was a mess of dusty brown hair. His eyes, mischievous green. He wore an old brown jacket lined in wool. His jeans were torn and a pair of worn flip-flops were on his feet. He was handsome in a strange way. Especially his trickster's smile, crooked and big.

"Do you know who I am now?" he asked. Claire was leaning against the island, trying not to fall. She nodded nervously. "Yes, I do. I saw you in the pictures. You-you're dead."

The young man raised an eyebrow. "It's been years, I think. Three? It's hard up there. Time, I mean. Keeping track of it. But the rules have changed. I'm here now.

Somehow." He eased closer to Claire. "Say my name. Please."

Claire pressed herself against the island. She opened her mouth, lips trembling, and uttered the word, "Patrick."

Tears swelled in his ghostly eyes. "That's right." He smiled. "That's me. Ha. That's really me."

Suddenly, a crash from down the hall.

"CLAIRE!" Karen yelled. "Claire! No! No! Please, come here!"

Patrick mouthed the word "Mom" as Claire raced away from the translucent young man and down the hall. She slid into the dining room to find Karen Ashford on the floor, kicking and failing.

"What is it, Karen?" she asked. "What's happening?"

Karen shrieked, her arm batting at something Claire could not see. A moment later it stopped. Karen lay in the fetal position, rocking back and forth, mumbling to herself.

Claire gathered the courage to go to her side. "Karen, you're fine. You're in the dining room. You're—" She noticed Patrick's ghost hovering over his mother, concerned, holding the bottle of whiskey. "You're fine, Karen."

Karen Ashford wiped the sweat from her brow. "No," she said, "I'm not fine. None of us are." She climbed to her chair. "It was a vision."

"Of what?" Claire asked as Patrick filled her goblet.

"Something's happened," she said, urgency in her tone. "I'm beginning to understand it now. Three realms. Three separate worlds. Colliding. This world. Reverie. And the third. Winged warriors in search of freedom. A red-haired monster. Unspeakable. The ocean depths. A crystal palace falling. A dark puppet master behind it all. Guilly. I can almost feel her. The dam has been broken, Claire. We're all doomed unless…unless…" Karen's black eyes opened wide. "Anza."

Author's note.

Hello again.

Thank you SO much for continuing on this wild adventure with me. Having set the groundwork and general rules of this world in book one, I was beyond excited to really play with Victor and Claire, Mindy and Jason, and the rest in this book, letting their personalities shine as they took more control over their journey now that they all have a better understanding of how Reverie works.

And now that the big villain has been revealed, just about all the pieces are in play to set us up for the big finale in **Book 3: *Eternia***. Trust me when I say all the craziest twists and turns are yet to come as Nihilo's master plan comes to fruition.

If you enjoyed the ride (so far), I would be beyond grateful if you:

- Follow me on Instagram and/or Twitter **@trystinbailey**
- Subscribe for exclusive content at **trystinbailey.com**
- Leave a review on **Amazon** and **Goodreads**

Until *Eternia*! The spirit realm awaits you...